MENACE

Also by L.R. Wright

MENACE

An Edwina Henderson Mystery

L.R. Wright

Seal Books

Seal Books and colophon are trademarks of
Random House of Canada Limited.

MENACE
Seal Books/published by arrangement with Doubleday Canada
Doubleday Canada hardcover edition published 2001
Seal Books edition published October 2002

ISBN 0-7704-2798-7

Cover image by Gerry Johansson/Photonica

Seal Books are published by
Random House of Canada Limited.
"Seal Books" and the portrayal of a seal are the property
of Random House of Canada Limited.

Visit Random House of Canada Limited's website:
www.randomhouse.ca

PRINTED AND BOUND IN THE USA

OPM   10 9 8 7 6 5 4 3 2 1

This book is for John,
without whom
it wouldn't be

ACKNOWLEDGEMENTS

The author wishes to acknowledge the information, advice, suggestions and support provided by Brian Appleby, Virginia Barber, Aaron Bushkowsky, Elaine Ferbey, Nancy Hardy-Banting, Martha Kanya-Forstner, Maggie Nevin, Del Surjik, Johnna Wright, several members of the Royal Canadian Mounted Police, Katey Wright; and to offer affectionate thanks to the Sunshine Coast Festival of the Written Arts for their kind support.

PROLOGUE

It had been a cold, wet spring and then all of a sudden, the sun came out and all hell broke loose. Soon the whole community was in a state of panic — half the population were scared for their lives, the other half scared of becoming suspects.

The cops talked to him, of course, along with everybody else. And there was this one cop in particular, an arrogant young bastard who strutted around like he owned the place while the pages of his notebook fluttered in the breeze — he was the boss, and, oh, did he love ordering his flunkeys around.

He couldn't help but admire this cop. And so he started following the guy.

He was fascinated. Enthralled and excited by this astonishing situation, by the transformation of ordinary life into a goddamn movie, and by the fact that he had a role to play, however small, just because he was there. The world seemed folded in on itself. Even though the horizon was as broad as ever, it felt to him like nothing existed except this small, green patch on the planet.

And so he trailed after the cop — at a distance, but watching his every move, checking out who he talked to, trying to imagine what he might be scribbling in his notebook. And finally, the cop began to notice him. He'd glance at him, casually at first, then irritably, and he'd frown and shake his head. And one morning, the cop saw him and whirled around fast, his arm outstretched, his hand made into a gun that was aimed right at him.

He pointed with his thumb at his chest: "Who, me?" And the cop nodded, looking grim. So he went up to him, feeling sheepish, but defiant, too.

"Explain yourself," the cop said.

And so he did. He bought the guy a coffee and explained himself.

At first, the cop was skeptical, but then he looked amused. He sort of shrugged, blew a big mouthful of air at him, and said, "Okay. But stay out of the way."

And later that day . . .

. . . hurrying across a wide sweep of lawn, feeling puffed up and cocky, he turned a corner really fast and almost collided with a long-haired girl carrying an armful of books — who screamed out loud at the sight of him.

"Shhh," he said.

And she stopped screaming. But she shrank even farther away from him. Her eyes had become so huge he could see the whites all the way around the irises, and she gave off a powerful scent of fear that was stronger than the smell of the lilac trees that grew all around them.

The place was crowded with people, as usual. But for just a couple of moments, in the tree-green alcove between grey stone buildings, they were alone.

And when he thought of it later, he saw them in explicit attitudes. He loomed tall and broad above her, his strong right arm raised threateningly; she was crouched, small and cowering, her head averted and her hands raised, and the spring breeze caught the skirt of her pink dress and pulled it above her knees, and her bright, fair hair spilled around her shoulders.

This wasn't the way it had looked in real life. He was quite sure of that. But the memory-picture was vivid and unambiguous. And it carried with it the thrill he'd felt. Like electricity. The shocking buzz that her helplessness had delivered.

ONE

"You're there," he typed. "Good."

"Yeah. Can't sleep, Harry. You know how it is sometimes."

"Yeah. Tough. But I like it when we catch each other in real time. I wanted to tell you — I saw a ghost today," he tapped, the computer keys softly clicking. The window was open, and the front door, too. It was a hot night, the Saturday of the Labour Day weekend, and he was sprawled on the sofa wearing only his underwear. "My mom. Good old Mom." He didn't know why he called himself Harry in the chat room. Unless maybe he thought of himself as a prince.

"Ouch," said Jemima. And he pitched her silent reply to reflect compassion.

"Just for a minute, yeah, I really thought it was her."

It would have spoiled his day — except for the miracle that followed.

"Made me shiver," he typed, "made me shudder, made my fucking skin crawl."

He lifted the laptop from his thighs, which were sticky with sweat, and pushed a section of the day's newspaper under it. He heard the waves washing up on the sand only fifty yards away. From the pub down the beach, laughter splashed onto the breeze and drifted into his small house.

"What a bummer."

"I was feeling good, too. Real good. Spiked," he typed, "and ready to rock and roll."

He moved smoothly down the street with his fingers slid flat into the back pockets of his jeans, feeling lithe and lean and strong and sexy, like the car he drove, like the silvery Lexus LS 400 he'd got, used, only 50,000 K on it, for 35,000 bucks earlier in the summer. He was in big debt now, but it was worth it. He was gonna drive the Lexus all the way down the coast to California someday, maybe next spring.

He was heading for the grocery store, with the Lexus slogan for some reason echoing in his head like a mantra, calming him even as it inspired: "The relentless pursuit of perfection."

He held the glass door open for an elderly man and followed him into the store.

He was a cavalier consumer, shopping without a list, relying upon his excellent memory. As he prowled through the grocery store, he was as relaxed as he ever got. He enjoyed stocking his kitchen — he always thought of groceries as provisions, as if he were planning a back-country hike. Sometimes he bought things on impulse, but not often. His tastes were commonplace; he liked basic things, like red meat and potatoes — and canned spaghetti, he thought, tossing three tins into his buggy. In restaurants, though, he made a point of ordering dishes that to him were extraordinary, because he didn't like the idea of living entirely in a rut.

Jesus. It was true. He lived in a goddamn rut. His job. His meals. His clothes. A goddamn rut. Except for the Lexus.

He rounded the end of an aisle too quickly and almost collided with a buggy pushed by an attractive young woman wearing shorts and a halter top.

"Whoops. Sorry," he said, smiling.

She didn't respond: she was too busy trying to deal with an irritated toddler sitting in the baby seat. She took a soother from the shoulder bag that was slung across her chest and thrust it into the child's mouth, but the child spat it onto the floor and continued to bounce fretfully up and down, her face screwed up. She was crying and screaming, "Home! Home! I wanna go home now!"

No wonder people smack their kids, he thought grimly. He was tempted to haul the child from the buggy and give her a smart slap on her little butt. Instead he wheeled quickly away, down the cereal aisle and around another corner into canned vegetables.

He manoeuvered past two middle-aged women who had stopped to chat and past a young guy carrying one of the small red baskets provided by the store for shoppers with not much to buy. He noticed as he passed that this guy was studying the various brands of canned corn with an absorption usually accorded more urgent matters.

Ahead of him now was a couple in their twenties. The young man was pushing the buggy and his girlfriend was leaning into him, her head on his shoulder. His head was tipped sideways, toward her, and their closeness spoke to the man who was following them of an intimacy so profound that he experienced a spasm of envy. He stayed close behind them, feigning an interest in beans and asparagus and artichoke hearts, imagining their murmured conversation, eventually convincing himself that he could hear whispered endearments, seductive allusions to what they had done last night and what they would do tonight.

He followed them until they took their places in a cashier's lineup.

He left them there, reluctantly.

He glanced into his buggy. By now he had coffee in there, and a loaf of bread, and the spaghetti, half a dozen bagels, some cream cheese, a litre of milk, three apples, several tomatoes, a couple of baking potatoes, a box of cereal.

He headed for the meat department, and tossed into the buggy packages of ground beef, pork chops, and chicken legs, looked again, and added a T-bone steak. Music played from somewhere, unobtrusively. It wasn't real music. It was a long, drawn-out drone; it was instrumental wheel-spinning. If it had been any louder, it would've been irritating.

As he spun his buggy over the red tiles of the meat department he noticed a woman in her sixties with curly grey hair who was wearing orange cotton pants and a white sleeveless top. Her handbag sat in the top part of her buggy, and it was this that first got his attention. These damn women — she had her back to it, for godsake, while she was bent over, peering into the refrigerated case in which were displayed various cuts of meat. She picked up a package of chicken breasts and brought it close to her face to read the label — she probably had a pair of glasses in that purse, he thought. She was probably too vain to wear the damn things. He watched, increasingly exasperated, while she picked up, studied, and hesitatingly replaced a large number of items. Eventually she sensed his attention, and turned.

Jesus, he thought, shaken. No wonder she irritated him so much. She looked just like his goddamn mother.

He gestured to her buggy. "You shouldn't leave your purse unattended," he said brusquely.

The woman's face flushed. She glanced at the buggy and pulled it closer to her. "Yes," she said. "Thank you."

He nodded, and moved off quickly. He was chagrined to realize that she could still get to him, even though she was long dead. It had been something in that woman's bearing as she leaned over the meat counter, a phony diffidence that set his teeth grinding. Plus she was the general size and shape his mother would have been if she had lived to sixty-two, appropriated the shape of a senior citizen, and not bothered to dye her honey-coloured hair when it got to be mostly grey.

But what really did it for him was her eyes. Wide-apart brown eyes. A steady gaze that had but two expressions he could remember: boredom and anger. And then there was that one time she'd laughed with joy, and all because of him.

But that had happened only the once.

He had never seen this old woman before. He hoped never to see her again, although that would be difficult in a town as small as Gibsons. He wondered if she had just recently moved here. He wondered if he would have to do his shopping somewhere else from now on.

Unloading the buggy, he couldn't think about anything else. He felt her presence behind him, somewhere in the store, and it was as if his real mother was there, searching for him.

As a child he'd trusted her, oh yeah. It killed him to think how many fucking years she'd taken him in — taken them *both* in — with her lying double-talk. There was nothing, absolutely nothing, as horrible as a discredited mother.

He was unloading his groceries so rapidly that the cashier couldn't keep up with him.

"Hey, slow down," she said sharply.

The conveyor belt was piled high, and some of his items tumbled to the floor — the coffee, a package of pork chops, the loaf of bread.

"Sorry," he mumbled.

He picked them up and took a couple of deep breaths, trying to calm down. That woman was not his mother. And he was no longer a child.

He managed to get out of the store without seeing her again.

"Really shook you up, huh?"

"Yeah," he typed, and he felt a shudder ripple through his body.

"But she can't get at you anymore, right?"

"Right. She got buried. I saw it with my own fucking eyes. So what's going on here? What the fuck's the matter with me?"

The cursor throbbed in place for a while. "Jemima?"

"Yeah. Well, Harry, I guess you've got some kind of fixation, right?"

This irritated him, although he knew it was true. He didn't want to talk to her (him? who the hell could know?) any longer.

"Gotta go, J," he typed. He wouldn't tell her about the second part of his morning, about the event that had transformed this day into a miracle.

He'd been rattled as he walked home from the store, carrying his grocery bags. He remembered to nod politely to people he knew despite the frown of distraction he knew was scrawled upon his face. He was struggling to push his mother out of his head, and this was never easy. He was trying to think instead about Jemima, and how much of what she told him about herself he could actually believe; about the Lexus, how he felt driving the Lexus, like he was riding, bareback, a big old tiger; about the occasional hit of satisfaction he got at work, *anything*. . . .

Suddenly, ahead of him, a young woman hurried out of the bookstore and down the sidewalk toward him.

She burst into his vision, into his life, like a comet.

He stopped moving. It was as if he had forgotten how to use his legs.

She was coming closer and closer. He had to think of something to say, something that would make her stop and talk to him. All he could think of was "Hey."

He got ready to say it. He hoped his voice would work. He hoped desperately that it wouldn't come out like a croak.

She was carrying a bag from the bookstore. With her other hand she was rummaging in her shoulder bag. She stopped walking and propped the bag against her bent knee to make it easier to look inside, and eventually she pulled out a set of keys.

She glanced up and met his eyes — and his breath was sucked from his lungs. No way could he speak. No way could he squirt "Hey" out of himself. He couldn't even breathe.

She turned away and stepped off the sidewalk and as she did so, she tripped and fell, grabbing at the front fender of what he assumed to be her car, a dusty blue Accord that had seen better days. Her shoulder bag went flying, scattering its contents into the street. Swiftly, he set his grocery bags down and went to her aid, stooping to scoop her into his arms.

"Are you alright?" It seemed that he could still speak after all.

His entire body sizzled from the touch of her. He stood, depositing her gently on the sidewalk. His hands rested lightly on her shoulders as he looked down into her face; he thought it the most beautiful face he had ever seen. He laughed, full of delight.

"Yes, I'm sure it was a very amusing sight," she said stiffly, and she pulled away from him, brushing at her shorts, at her T-shirt. Her skin was slightly tanned. He loved the contrast between her golden arms and his darker ones. Her cheeks were flushed and her grey-green eyes snapped with embarrassment. She reached up and removed a large clip from her ash-blonde hair and shook her head vigorously, then grasped the hair in one hand and clipped it fast again.

"I'm sorry," he said, as humbly as possible. "I wasn't laughing at you. Really." He stooped again, and gathered the scattered contents of her bag: a Daytimer, a pocket-size packet of tissues, a small hairbrush, a compact, several pens and pencils, a paperback novel — and then she was next to him, taking the bag from him, hastily collecting the rest of her belongings from the pavement.

"Let me drive you home," he said a minute later, and offered his hand, introducing himself with a warm smile.

She hesitated before taking his hand, firmly, giving it one shake, then letting go. "I'm Rebecca Wilson. I don't need a ride home, thank you. I'm perfectly fine." She went around to the driver's side of the Accord. "Thank you. For helping me."

"You're welcome." He watched her start the car, attach her seatbelt, and pull out into the street before he picked up his grocery bags and resumed walking.

He was still finding it difficult to breathe. It was obvious that something momentous had happened. Maybe he'd just met his soulmate — but he quickly smothered the thought. He knew from experience that it was best not to fan this particular flame too soon. If he blew on the damn thing and it wasn't there, all he'd get was dirt up his nose.

The Accord — he thought that was probably somebody else's idea. A father, maybe a brother, knowing shit-all about cars, figuring to set her up in something basic, wanting her to have transportation but no fun.

He walked on passed Molly's Reach, once a set for a television series, now a restaurant; past the pub on the corner; past the Chinese guy's café; and down the ramp to the beach.

He knew her name. He would find out where she

worked, where she hung out. He would cultivate her acquaintance, and wait, and observe, and make certain that the connection he had experienced was real. It had certainly *felt* real. Oh yes.

He walked more quickly, aware of his physical strength and proud of it.

The smell of her. The caress of her swinging hair against his face as he picked her up, gently, from the pavement.

And then, later, their hands clasped, she had given him her name, in the softest possible voice, a voice as soft as cotton wool, or the purring of a kitten.

And the squeeze of her hand, pressing palm and fingers against his. It had been deliberate, provocative and inviting.

And then she had moved away, quickly, so as not to appear forward.

He smiled as he approached his house, and his heart was crammed with excitement.

Three days later he was riffling through the new announcements at work, which he did regularly, when he spotted what could only be called a sign; a portent.

Some of the information provided was important, like who was working when. Then there was a lot of material that in his opinion simply stated the obvious, over and over again. Sometimes he came across information about positions open elsewhere, and he had once been interested in these, but not any longer. He was more than happy now not only to stick with his job, but to continue doing it right here in Gibsons. And this was because of the girl he'd met, who he'd found out was a social worker.

And in this day's announcements it caught his eye. A list of committees. And there was her name: Rebecca Wilson.

It zoomed from that list and hit him square in the eye, rocketed to him through the air trailing pennants of fire. And he grinned and went off to volunteer.

Just north of Vancouver, there is a blue crack in the continent called Howe Sound, ten miles wide. Across it, the province of British Columbia juts abruptly west and then extends northward for almost a thousand miles. Its intricate coastline is fissured by innumerable inlets and channels, cluttered by countless small islands, and is at first sheltered from the open Pacific by Vancouver Island, 285 miles long.

Highway 1, the Trans-Canada, comes to a halt on the shores of Howe Sound, at Horseshoe Bay. Ferries leaving from here provide the only access from the mainland to the Sechelt Peninsula, otherwise known as the Sunshine Coast. This is the southernmost forty-five miles of that long, long coastline. Along its seaside are towns and villages called Langdale, Granthams Landing, Gibsons, Roberts Creek, Wilson Creek, Selma Park, Sechelt, Halfmoon Bay, Secret Cove, Madeira Park, Garden Bay, Irvines Landing, Earl's Cove, Powell River.

Gibsons, near the southern end, has a population of 3,800 and was named for the first white settler there.

This part of British Columbia gets more hours of sunshine every year than most places in Canada — five hundred more hours, on the average, than Vancouver. Because its winters are also very mild, things grow here that will not grow anywhere else in the country.

There is only one major road, a mostly two-lane highway that follows the coastline for eighty miles and then ends, in the northern reaches of the Strait of Georgia.

In the summer, the area is clogged with tourists, even though it is not a quickly accessible place. Getting there depends upon ferry schedules, and once you've arrived, traversing the coastline takes time, because the narrow highway is winding and hilly.

The tempo of life on the Sunshine Coast is markedly slower than that of Vancouver, and its people, for the most part strung out along the shoreline, have a more direct and personal interest in the sea.

The coastal forests are tall and thick with undergrowth, but they come gently down to the water and are sometimes met there by wide, curving beaches. The land cleared for gardens is fertile, and the things growing there tempt wild creatures from the woods. In the sea there are salmon, and oysters, and clams, and crabs; there are also otters, and thousands of gulls, and cormorants. There are Indian legends, and tales of smugglers, and the stories of the pioneers.

The resident police force is the Royal Canadian Mounted Police, with detachments in Gibsons, Sechelt, and Powell River. They have their fair share of crime to deal with, but in comparison with most urban areas, the Sunshine Coast is a gratifyingly law-abiding part of the world.

There are traffic accidents, and drunk and disorderlies, and theft, and wife battering, and some vandalism, and recently, drugs have become a presence.

But there is not much very serious crime.

There is seldom, for example, a murder.

TWO

"I'm looking forward to working with you," said Edwina Henderson on Tuesday to her new second-in-command, shaking his hand.

Corporal Brian "Buster" Sheffield said, "Me too, Sergeant. Welcome aboard."

"Thanks," said Eddie, sitting down behind her very large desk, with a smile she hoped was wide and fearless. "Have a seat." She wished she could have brought the black leather chair from Alberg's office in Sechelt with her; she needed something familiar in here.

Sheffield sat in a chair that looked like it belonged in a diner. It was made of aluminum and red vinyl, and there was a gaping gash in the seat.

The corporal looked older than his years — he was only thirty, five years younger than Eddie.

"How long have you been in Gibsons?" Eddie asked, although she knew. She was nervous. This was the first of fourteen interviews she would be holding over the next weeks with members of her new detachment.

"Four years," said Sheffield, glancing at the closed file folder sitting on her desk. "Came here from northern Alberta."

The file had already told her this. She also knew that he was married, that his wife's name was Irene, and that they had one son, two-year-old Ian.

She had first met Buster Sheffield three weeks earlier,

on a hot day in August when Eddie had driven down
from Sechelt to introduce herself to the outgoing
sergeant. She parked her old green Mercedes on the
street, switched off the motor, and examined the front
of the detachment curiously. She wasn't in uniform; she
was on holiday, taking two weeks off between postings.
She'd dressed up for the occasion, though, wearing a
pair of linen pants and a tailored short-sleeved shirt.
When she looked at herself in the mirror before leaving
home, she realized that she'd only exchanged one uniform for another; it was even the same colour, she'd
thought glumly, a military beige. She was wearing her
thick yellow hair in a braid, as usual, and had considered
crowning her high forehead with a wide-brimmed sun
hat but decided this might appear frivolous. She had
applied a small amount of makeup — mascara and a
pale shade of lipstick — and she wore tiny gold studs in
her ears and a businesslike watch, a gift from her father,
on her wrist.

She climbed out of the Mercedes, feeling sweaty even
though it was only a half-hour drive from Sechelt to
Gibsons, less if there wasn't much traffic. And her
trousers were well and truly creased. Shit. She slung her
bag over her shoulder and marched up the walk to the
public entrance to the detachment.

Inside the small reception area, a citizen was express-
ing agitation to a large, craggy-faced corporal Eddie later
discovered was Buster Sheffield. "It's harassment is what
it damn is," said the citizen, an extremely thin man in his
fifties with stringy grey hair that hung to his shoulders.
He was shaking, perhaps in rage, perhaps as the result of
substance withdrawal.

Beyond the glass partition, a black-haired, elderly
woman sat stiff and goggle-eyed at what Eddie assumed
was the reception desk, her eyes fixed on the citizen.

"I live in the fucking house, Sheffield," the man

shouted. "I wasn't lurking there, I was hanging around
my own fucking house, goddamn it."

"Hey, Mickey," said the corporal, "watch the lan-
guage, okay? There's a couple of ladies here."

Mickey glared at the receptionist. "I do not call that
person a lady no sir no sirree, not the way she talked to
me." He glanced at Eddie. "And as for this one who
knows, she's not automatically a damn lady just because
she's female. I want to know," he said, poking the corporal in the chest with his finger, "what you're gonna do
about this harassment I'm talking about and I want to
make a report out of it too that'll go straight to the damn
guy in charge around here."

"Can I help you?" said the receptionist to Eddie. It
came out as a sorry bleat.

"Mickey, let's sit down here for a minute," said the
corporal, his open hand hovering just behind the citizen's shoulder. "Here on this bench."

Mickey sat.

"Uh, I'm here to see Sergeant Jablonski," said Eddie.

"That's right," said the corporal soothingly, sitting
down next to the citizen.

"Is he expecting you?" asked the receptionist.

"I take your point," said the corporal seriously. "I'll
speak to the officer myself, explain the situation to him."

"Yes, he is," said Eddie.

"You gotta understand, though, Mickey, there was a
grow-op going on right next door to you, and it's not
surprising, right? That an honest mistake happened.
What with your background and all."

"Name?" asked the receptionist.

"Now, I'm not saying it was right," said the corporal
quickly, anticipating a protest from the citizen. "I know
all that's in the past now. But —"

"Henderson," said Eddie, and the receptionist picked
up her phone.

The corporal hesitated. His eyes remained fixed in Mickey's face, and his posture didn't change: he was bending earnestly toward the citizen, one hand on the back of the bench, the other in the air, gesturing. For a moment he was immobile, processing information. Then, smoothly, he continued. "I know it," he said, standing, helping Mickey to his feet. "And you know it," he said, ushering him to the door. "And in a couple of minutes the other officer will know it, too." He opened the door. "Okay, Mickey? Good." He closed the door and turned to Eddie.

"The sergeant will be right out," said the receptionist.

They were about the same height, Eddie and the corporal. He was thick through the torso. The bony ridges above his eyes were unusually pronounced, and the brows that grew there were shaggy. Eddie couldn't make out the colour of his eyes.

His expression was a familiar one. Eddie had one herself. It reminded her of a faceplate in a suit of armour, a shield that could be raised and lowered according to the requirements of the situation. He'd been looking at her that day through the shield, making a dispassionate, impersonal appraisal. Then he extended his hand.

"Sheffield," he had said. "I guess we're going to be working together."

No shield was up today, Eddie was relieved to notice. "Tell me about the place," she said. "Gibsons." He seemed perfectly at ease, settled comfortably in the diner chair, which Eddie envied. She had always found it difficult to be the new kid on the block. It was especially hard now that she was the new *boss* on the block. But it was just a matter of time, she told herself. She'd feel at home here, too, eventually. Even though that was hard to imagine at the moment.

"No different from Sechelt, probably," said Sheffield. "We're just a bit smaller. You've got your grow-ops. Your log thefts." He ticked them off on his fingers. "Your reckless drivers. Your drunks."

"What about the personnel?" asked Eddie.

"Well, you'll make up your own mind about them, I'm sure," he said prudently. He hesitated, studying her. "Tell you what. You got questions, concerns, as you go along, we'll talk about them, if you like."

Eddie nodded. "Okay. Fair enough. Meanwhile, is there anything you think I ought to know about?"

He looked up into a corner of the ceiling. "Let's see. We've got these — I don't know what you'd call them. Citizen groups? Advisory panels?"

"You mean Neighbourhood Watch, Court Watch, Traffic Watch — like that? Yeah, we've got them in Sechelt, too. And bike patrols?"

He shook his head. "No bike patrols down here. Good idea, though." He looked thoughtfully at the single small window that sat rather high in Eddie's office wall. It looked out into the detachment parking lot, which was sheltered by rows of mature cedars. "The civilians. Beatrice and Willy. William. You talked to them yet?"

"I thought I'd start with you," said Eddie.

"They've been here since long before me. I think they've been here since before the Flood."

"Okay. I get it," said Eddie.

"Excellent idea to get on their good side," he said earnestly.

"I get it," she said wearily.

He looked at her curiously. "You gonna move down here?"

"Don't know yet."

"Okay," said Sheffield amiably. He looked at his watch. "Are we about done?"

"Yes," said Eddie. "Done. Thanks."

He stood up and they shook hands again. "People call me Buster, by the way."

"Thanks, Buster. And I'm Eddie."

"Eddie. Good."

She watched him amble to the door and out into the hall, then pulled her journal from the bottom drawer of her desk. She smoothed its dark green cover with the palm of her hand and opened it at the ribbon that marked the first empty page. She got to her feet and went to the window, which was wide open, and peered out through the security bars. The sun glinted from the windshield of the Mercedes. She should have left the windows open. She returned to her desk and picked up a pen.

"Brian 'Buster' Sheffield," she wrote. "It doesn't seem to bother him that his new boss is a woman. I think he's shrewd. I think he's politically aware. I hope he'll be supportive." She read it to herself. "Shit," she muttered, and scratched out the last sentence.

"We're probably going to lose you, I'm told, in a few months."

Constable Nick Orsato arranged his face in an expression of regret. "Sorry."

"Yeah, sure you're sorry," said Eddie dryly. "You did good on the exam. Congratulations."

"Thanks. I *am* sorry, you know. Sort of. I've liked it here. And I've never worked for a woman before."

"Well, you've got plenty of time to decide if it's any different from working for a man," said Eddie briskly. "You're not leaving for another few months, after all." He was sitting slightly forward in the red vinyl chair, his right ankle resting on his left knee. "Tell me why you joined the Force."

Nick Orsato groaned. "What kind of a damn question is that?"

"I'm curious," said Eddie.

He stared at her for a moment, his forehead creased.

He was an attractive man of thirty-two, dark-haired, slim but wiry, a couple of inches short of six feet. "I want to help keep order," he said finally.

She waited.

He shrugged. "That's it. You can laugh if you want."

When he'd left, Eddie wrote in her journal, "Very good record. I'm guessing this guy won't ever want to be far from the street. I think he's got principles. I also think he's gay."

Later that morning, a social worker with the Ministry of Children and Families called the RCMP detachment requesting assistance. She was about to take a child into care and wanted police standing by in case of trouble. Eddie took the call herself, accompanied by Nick Orsato.

It was almost noon when they arrived at the house and pulled up behind a somewhat grimy Honda. The driver climbed out and walked toward the patrol car. "Hi," she said, as Eddie rolled down her window. "You're new, aren't you?"

"That I am," said Eddie. "Eddie Henderson. And this is Constable Orsato."

"Yeah, I know," said the young woman. "Hi, Nick." She pushed her fingers through her hair. "I'm Rebecca Wilson. Thanks for coming out. I don't think I'll need you, but you never know." She stepped back to allow Eddie to get out of the patrol car.

"What's the story?" said Eddie, folding her arms, examining the front of the small, dilapidated, single-storey house.

"We did an investigation based on a report from the child's school," said Rebecca, who was in her early thirties, with light brown hair falling loose to her shoulders, and hazel eyes. "She's eight years old, in Grade 3, comes to school with unwashed hair and shabby clothes, then the teacher sees cuts and bruises, and the principal calls us. The family's been here only a few months. She's the only child. The parents don't seem to give a shit, pardon my French. I've got the paperwork in the car, if you want to have a look before we go in."

"No, that's okay," said Eddie. "As long as you've got copies for me."

"Sure do." Rebecca Wilson took a big breath and turned to face the house. "Okay. Here goes."

"Wait a minute," Nick Orsato protested. "Give us some background on the parents. What're we likely to contend with in there?"

"They're drinkers, so who knows?" she said, exasperated. "Don't worry about it, Constable, they don't seem to know where they are half the time, and I'm sure the kid's the only person they beat on. Can we go in now, please?" she asked Eddie.

"Let's go." Eddie led the way but stood back when they reached the steps that led to the front door, she and Nick flanking Rebecca as she marched onto the small ramshackle porch and began knocking.

No response.

"Mrs. Perkins?" Rebecca called out. "Mr. Perkins? Is anybody home?" She continued knocking.

Finally the door opened a crack and a small face appeared.

"Elizabeth," said Rebecca. "Hi. Do you remember me?"

The child nodded.

"Are your mom and dad at home?"

The child nodded again.

"Can you ask one of them to come to the door, please?"

The child hesitated. "I think they're asleep." She spoke so softly that Eddie barely heard her.

"You *think* they're asleep?" said Rebecca. "But you don't know for sure?"

Elizabeth closed the door, slowly, then opened it again. "The door's shut."

"What door?"

"Their door. I'm not supposed to go in there if the door's shut."

"Ah." Rebecca glanced back at Eddie. "Well, *we* can go in there. I think we have to come inside and wake them up. Okay? It's important that I talk to them."

The child backed away from the door and Rebecca pushed it fully open. Eddie and Nick Orsato followed her into the house.

The hall floor was littered with dust balls and refuse. The small bedroom that the child said was hers smelled of urine.

Rebecca Wilson pounded on the closed door of the parents' room, calling out to them, while Elizabeth hovered in a shadowy corner of the hallway. Finally, the social worker opened the door and looked inside, then stood back so Eddie and Nick Orsato could do the same.

The room stank of booze and vomit. Ashtrays overflowed with cigarette butts. Empty beer cans vied for space on the tops of the two dressers with several mickeys that had once contained scotch. The unmade bed reeked.

Rebecca turned to Elizabeth, crouching so as not to loom over the child. "Your mom and dad aren't here, sweetie. Do you know where they might be?"

Elizabeth stuffed her fist into her mouth and shook her head. Her short black hair was greasy; her pale face was dirty; but her blue eyes, long-lashed and bottomless, gazed at Rebecca, then at Eddie, with apparent equanimity. She was wearing mismatched pajamas. Eddie figured she had changed the bottoms when she woke to find that she'd wet the bed.

Rebecca sighed. "Okay." She took Elizabeth's hand.

"You and I are going to collect some of your stuff now, and then we're going to go to another house, where a very nice lady will take care of you."

The child pulled away. She shook her head again. Eddie thought she saw the glimmering of tears.

"Sweetie," said Rebecca, "we don't know when your mom and dad will be home. And meanwhile, you're hungry." She touched the child's cheek with her fingertips. "This house is out in the country a ways. There's a big tree in the front yard with a tire hanging from one of the branches, on a long rope. Have you ever swung on a tire?"

Elizabeth shrugged.

"And in the backyard there's rows of raspberry bushes. I think they'll still have some berries on them." She looked up inquiringly at Eddie, who shook her head helplessly. "Well if the raspberries are all gone I know the blackberries aren't. Have you ever picked blackberries?"

Another shrug.

"And this lady who lives there, she has two cats, one dog, and a goat. Have you ever met a goat?"

"No."

"And she makes the best waffles I have ever eaten. Do you like waffles?"

A reluctant nod.

"Okay." Rebecca stood up. "Let's go get the stuff you'll need from your room." She turned to Eddie. "Thank you very much, Officer, and Nick. Elizabeth and I will be fine on our own now. There's a folder on the front seat of my car with your copy of the paperwork."

Eddie nodded. "Okay. Good luck. Goodbye, Elizabeth."

Elizabeth said, "Will you look for my mom and dad?"

"You can count on it," said Nick.

"How will they know where I am?" said the child.

"We'll tell them," said Eddie. "Just as soon as we find them."

Eddie and Nick left the house, and Nick grabbed the file from the Accord's passenger seat.

"Jesus Christ," said Nick in disgust, as they drove out of the Perkins' neighbourhood. "Some people shouldn't be allowed to have kids."

"I don't know how they do it," said Eddie, merging onto the highway. "Social workers. I mean, when we deal with a kid in trouble, it's mostly temporary. You can stay detached when it's temporary. But social workers — I don't know how they do it."

"So how are you liking it down here?" said Nick, turning to her.

"Fine," said Eddie quickly. Then she laughed. "Well, it's okay. I'm liking it okay. I don't feel at home yet, that's all."

"You've only been here a couple of weeks. Give it time," said Nick comfortably. "Are you going to move, eventually?"

"I don't know," Eddie told him, turning off the highway onto the street that led to the detachment and, eventually, to the centre of the village. "I love my house. And Sechelt's only a twenty-five minute drive from here." She hadn't yet decided whether the geographical separation of home and work was a good or a bad thing. She enjoyed her neighbours and had close friends in Sechelt, where she used to work, first as second-in-command to Staff Sergeant Karl Alberg, then, when he retired, as his temporary replacement.

"So what do you think's gonna happen there?" she asked Nick. "Will the parents end up getting the kid back?"

"Christ, I don't know. The sad thing is, they probably don't even want her back."

"Maybe she'll get herself adopted," said Eddie wistfully. "By people who'll care about her."

"You never know," said Nick, as Eddie, slowing, wheeled into the parking lot, crunching over gravel.

Inside, she checked in with Beatrice Fitzgerald, the civilian employee who manned the reception desk.

"Only two phone calls," said Beatrice. "And I think they're both personal," she added reproachfully.

She was a small, thin woman of seventy, with short straight hair that was dyed black and square, black-rimmed spectacles. Her pale blue eyes were large and surprisingly soft, in contrast with the brittle, lecturing tone of her voice.

Eddie took the messages and headed across the reception area, greeting the officers on duty as she encountered them: Glen Hammond, with the lazy grin; Beverly Brooks, who glanced at her warily with bright green eyes; Johnny Grieg, affable and exuberant.

She entered her office with a sigh of relief. Newcomer stress. New boss stress.

But she looked around her with pleasure. The office pleased her greatly — except for the red vinyl chair. The moment she had first stepped inside the office, she had found herself itching to do things to it: paint the walls, replace the horizontal blind with a vertical one, shift the junk on the long table beneath the window and put a plant at either end, sand the enormous wooden desk and refinish it. So far, she'd shifted the junk and done the desk.

"Wow," she had said, the day she'd arrived at the Gibsons detachment to introduce herself to the outgoing sergeant. She had gazed hungrily at the desk. "I guess that goes with you, huh?" It certainly wasn't standard issue.

But Sergeant Jablonski had laughed and shaken his head. "It was a gift," he said. "To the detachment. We found this guy's Jaguar for him. In the ferry lineup, believe it or not."

Eddie liked Sergeant Jablonski, liked his easy manner and the light in his eyes.

"He comes in here to tell me it's gone missing," Jablonski had continued. "I had this metal desk then — you know the kind. And mine, you could never see the top of it — always covered with the damn paperwork. So the guy, he leans toward me so he can get closer, stare right in my face, persuade me how important it is that we find his car. Which is red, by the way. Tomato red. Don't think I'd ever seen a Jag that colour before." A frown briefly creased his forehead, then he went on.

"And in his right hand, there's a photo of the vehicle which he's reaching out to give me, and he goes to put his left hand on the desk — except the paperwork extends out beyond the edge, you know? And so he misses, and it was gonna be a heavy lean, I guess, because his chin damn near hits the desktop. 'Whoa, whoa,' I say, and I'm standing up now, I'm gonna grab hold of him or something, I don't know. But he ignores the whole thing. Hands me the photo, and on we go. But I guess he decided I needed a bigger desk." He had grinned complacently at Eddie then. "Not any more, though. I plan never to sit behind another desk in my entire life. It's all yours, Sergeant."

Eddie stroked the surface of the desk, smiling to herself. Sergeant Jablonski had retired to Pender Harbour, which was less than an hour's drive up the Sunshine Coast from Gibsons, but she doubted she'd ever see him again.

She had sanded, oiled, and Verathaned the desk herself. A pot of ivy sat in one corner, opposite plastic trays that were labeled IN and OUT. Paperwork sat in neat stacks between the edge of the desk and the blotter.

There was a knock on her door, and Buster Sheffield stuck his head in. "How was the apprehension?"

"No parents. The place stunk. The child's been moved into foster care."

"Good. I'm off to talk to the Chamber."

"Enjoy."

"Oh, sure." He grinned. "See you later."

The telephone messages were from her father and her friend Cindi, a newspaper reporter in Sechelt. Her father could wait. She called Cindi, and they agreed to meet for a late dinner at a Sechelt pub.

Then she sighed and buzzed the reception desk.

"When I'm not here," Beatrice said, her eyes fixed on the front of Eddie's desk, "either the duty officer takes over, if it's at night or on the weekend; or it's William, if I'm out for lunch on one of his days; or it's just whoever happens to be around." She twisted the fingers of her right hand in the skirt of her lemon-coloured cotton dress. Over her shoulders, she had draped a cardigan that was a slightly deeper yellow. She wore stockings and white sandals with a low heel. Like William Kirkpatrick, she needed bifocals.

"I see," said Eddie. "Good. Well, we're lucky to have you, I'm told."

Beatrice considered this. "You probably are." For the first time in the interview, she met Eddie's gaze directly. "But then I'm lucky, too, of course. Not many places would hire an — an aging woman and keep her on for eight years."

"And I hope you'll be here for another eight," said Eddie.

"I'm hard to get along with sometimes," Beatrice barreled on, both hands clenched in her lap now. "I don't deny it."

Eddie nodded.

Beatrice leveled at her a look of great intensity. "What have you heard about me?"

"Uh . . . let me think. . . . You're efficient. Punctual. Dependable. Loyal." She grinned. "And sometimes hard to get along with."

Beatrice brooded for a moment. Then, "That's fair," she said sturdily.

Eddie's journal entry, written later that day, read, "Impatient. Mistrustful. Tends to believe the worst of people, at first. But I think she's open-minded enough to change her opinion. And, so far, she is indeed efficient, punctual, dependable. Whether her loyalty will eventually extend to me, god only knows."

She thanked Beatrice and asked her to send in William Kirkpatrick.

"I know you've been with the detachment for a long time, Mr. Kirkpatrick."

"Eleven years," he said. "Ever since I retired."

"You were a teacher, weren't you?"

"I was." He slid his hands under his suspenders and flattened them across his chest. "High school. History."

"Are you married, Mr. Kirkpatrick?"

"Call me William." He was a tall, thin man, slightly stooped, with thinning white hair and bushy white eyebrows. "Yes, I am. Been married fifty-six years." His eyes crinkled behind his glasses. "You can't imagine such a thing, can you, young lady? I can see it in your face. So, what happened in your life — did your parents get divorced?"

"My mother died," said Eddie.

He was instantly compassionate. "I'm sorry."

"We didn't get along," Eddie confessed.

"Still," he said gently.

She nodded. "Still."

"Is your father alive?"

"Yes. You reminded me of him, when I first met you."

"Is that a good thing?"

"Nope," she said grimly.

He looked at her in astonishment and laughed. "Do you at least have a brother or a sister you're close to?"

"I'm an only child." Eddie pronounced this with a certain solemnity. "Do you have kids?"

"Two," said William. "And I've always believed we got along pretty well, the four of us. Listening to you, now I'm not so sure."

"Oh, I think you can be sure," said Eddie. "My father is quite aware of the distance between us."

William Kirkpatrick studied her curiously.

Eddie picked up a stack of files and moved them from one side of her desk to the other. "How on earth did we get on to this?" she said uneasily.

"We're just talking," said William soothingly. "Getting to know each other." Comfortably, he crossed his legs.

And Eddie was suddenly wary. "You're right, William." She put the stack of files back where it belonged. "Now. Tell me what you do for us here." She picked up a pencil, sat back, and smiled at him.

"General office work, I guess you'd call it," he said. "I keep the paper files in order. I keep track of the supplies, let Beatrice know when we need something. I make sure the cells are clean. Don't do the cleaning myself, of course, we get somebody in to do that." His hands clasped one knee. His gaze wandered from time to time from Eddie's face, to her desktop, around the office.

"You aren't full-time, are you?"

He shook his head. "I work twelve hours a week. I see you're already making this office your own." He nodded at the pot of ivy.

She smiled at him, and stood up. "Thank you very much, William, for coming in to see me. I'm sure we'll work well together."

When he had left, she wrote in her journal, "Intelligent. Curious. Probably efficient. I'll either like

him a great deal — or I won't trust him as far as I could
throw him."

His first reaction was astonishment. He squinted at her
in disbelief and shook his head a little, as if to clear it. He
glanced quickly at the other people huddled around the
table that warm and sultry late September evening. They
seemed completely unaware that she had insulted him.
Or maybe they just didn't care. There wasn't a hell of a
lot of enthusiasm among this group, he had noticed.
Which was one reason he'd made his perfectly reasonable suggestion. In fact, he had considered it more than
reasonable, he had thought it might even have been brilliant. He had expected it to generate some lively discus-
sion. What he hadn't expected was that it would excite
Rebecca into dissing him.

"I'm afraid you don't fully understand these situations," she'd said impatiently, not even waiting for him to
finish. And he'd watched her, open-mouthed, as she'd
then gone ahead to tell everyone what *she* thought
ought to be done when incorrigible brats acted like
hooligans with their foster parents.

He sat back with dignity, crossing his legs, crossing his
arms, levelling looks at her that he hoped she would
interpret as reserved yet reproachful.

When the meeting was over, he left the room right
behind her and walked with her to her car. Even the
wind was warm that night. They'd make things up, then
maybe they'd go to the bar, he thought, and sit outside
looking at the sea, imagining themselves in Greece.

Suddenly she turned, and gave a little shriek. "Christ.
I didn't know you were there."

"Sorry." He had a lot more to say, but she interrupt-
ed before he could go on.

"That was a really dumb idea, you know." She strode
on, car keys jingling in her hand. "I get so sick of all this

'spare the rod and spoil the child' shit." She unlocked the Accord and looked at him over the roof. "You guys are all the same."

He didn't particularly want to stand there watching her drive away, but he couldn't help it, he was at first humiliated, then paralyzed with pain.

He heard car doors slam and engines start up; soon his would be the only one left in the lot.

"Jesus bloody Christ," he muttered furiously to himself. "That fucking bloody woman."

THREE

Jim Partridge, twenty-eight, was what some less-than-kind officers called a "mini-Mountie," a man who fell below what had once been the minimum required height. He was sensitive about his stature and had made up for it with a passionate dedication to working out. He was by far the strongest person in the detachment and was often kidded about his size; he had to have his uniforms altered to accommodate his inflated muscles.

He was also a computer whiz. Eddie, who knew only as much about computers as she had to, had been relieved and delighted to learn that there was such a person among her troops.

"Sit down, Constable. Make yourself comfortable." He sat. Eddie continued to stand, hands on her hips, looking down at him speculatively. "Have you been training anybody else to do what you do?"

"What do you mean?"

"I mean, if you get hit by a truck, what're we going to do without you?"

He blinked.

"I'm pointing out to you the extent of your importance around here," said Eddie.

He blinked again.

"Actually," she said with a sigh, "that was kind of a joke." She sat down behind her desk. "But I do want you to teach somebody else what you know. Not everything you know — just enough so that when you're not here, we can still cope." Buster Sheffield had told her about some kind of computer emergency they'd had the last time Jim was on leave. Eddie hadn't fully understood the situation as he had described it, but she had gleaned enough to know that she sure didn't want it to happen on her watch.

Jim Partridge screwed his face into a frown that reflected deep thought. "I could do that," he said finally. "Is the new girl computer literate, do you know?"

"The 'new girl'?" said Eddie, incredulous. "Did you say, 'the new girl'? I don't believe I heard you right."

"Yeah," he said, confused. "The new one. I only ask because —"

"Do you mean our new constable, Constable Marlise Beyer, by any chance?"

"Yeah, that's the one."

Eddie watched him closely, and saw the penny finally drop.

"Oh jeez," he muttered. "Sorry. That's not very p.c., is it?"

"It's not very professional, is what it's not."

"Sorry. The thing is, nobody else seems interested, so I hoped . . ."

"Ask her," said Eddie. "And if she isn't interested, immediately go elsewhere."

"Sure." He was crouched low in the red diner chair, as if she had just beaten him about the shoulders — a thing she would never dare to do, given the size of him.

"Now, Jim. Tell me something about yourself that isn't in your file." She was repeating herself, and suspected that the interviewees would compare notes and talk about this, but so what, she had to do something to get these conversations started.

"What kind of stuff do you want to know?"

"Your choice."

He looked at her helplessly.

"Why did you decide to become a cop?"

"Jeez. I can't even remember, it was so long ago."

Eddie was becoming exasperated. "Okay, why do you think the Force is an important part of Canadian society?"

No response.

"Or *is* it?"

Still nothing. He was looking desperate.

"Okay, try this. What are your personal and/or professional ambitions?" She stared at him. He stared back. "What do you *want* out of life, Jim?"

Obviously bewildered, he replied, "I've *got* everything I want, Sarge." He shrugged, apologetically.

"Good," said Eddie, her head bobbing up and down. She felt like a damn woodpecker. "Good, Jim. Good."

Later, she wrote in her journal, "He might be a tad thick. Maybe all that working out has popped a blood vessel in his brain. He's a genius at the damn computer, though. And good-hearted, as far as I can tell."

She'd first met Jim at a Labour Day barbecue she had felt obliged to attend, even though (or perhaps because) she had just barely arrived at the detachment and didn't feel like socializing with a bunch of people who were still strangers.

She arrived late, which she figured was okay. It was a good idea, in fact, to let everybody else get there first. They could gossip about her in her absence, maybe get it out of their systems.

Jim Partridge lived in a small, brown-shingled house with an enormous backyard, which was where the party had gathered. A gas barbecue and a picnic table occupied a concrete patio. People were sitting at the table or standing nearby, holding glasses. They greeted her warmly, but cautiously.

"Buster's the chef," said Jim, "and Bev's getting everything else organized."

Eddie offered to help but Bev said no, it was all under control.

Eddie's gaze had wandered to the flower beds that flanked the lawn. "Is this your handiwork?" she asked Jim. "The garden?"

"It sure is. Would you like to see it?" He took her on a tour, identifying dahlias, chrysanthemums, marigolds, and, in a raised bed, adolescent seedlings that he said would eventually produce broccoli and brussels sprouts. Eddie noticed Bev Brooks watching him with a smile on her face that spoke volumes. She wondered if she'd ever look at anybody that way.

There was nobody interesting present in the chat room that night, and the messages he scrolled through were long and boring. He hunted for Jemima but she was totally absent, hadn't even posted him a few words in absentia. He went to bed with a pounding headache and burning eyes and still lay sleepless throughout most of what remained of the night, trying not to go over it again and again, the exchange that had ruined his evening, cut him to the goddamn quick.

When he finally slept, he dreamed of her. In his dream she was standing on the sloping lawn outside an office building. He was inside, pounding on the window glass, but she didn't hear him. Something was threatening her. It wasn't yet visible; it was approaching along the road beyond the lawn — he could hear it coming, a huge mother of a truck, maybe, that he knew intended to run her down. But she couldn't hear it. He watched as she crossed the lawn to stand, unsuspecting, in the middle of the road and he was torn, in his dream, between being desperate to save her and wanting to see her killed. Smashed into pulp.

The sound of the advancing machine was deafening, sinister; it must be enormous, much bigger than even the biggest truck — it must be a tank, he thought, in the dream. Whatever it was, it was huge, big enough to pulverize her.

He wakened in shock. He didn't want her dead. He *knew* this was true, and was horrified by his dream, hated having been betrayed by that part of him that dreamed.

It was dark in his bedroom, and still dark outside. He got out of bed and went to the window, where he pulled back the curtain and looked out on the pensive sea, rippling quietly in the moonlight. Across the channel a few lights burned on Keats Island. To the left, in the dark eastern sky that was imprinted with the darker presence of close-by mountains, there was a suggestion of impending day.

He turned from the window, dressed, picked up his wallet and car keys from the top of his dresser, took a jacket from a hook near the kitchen door and left the house. He climbed a long set of crumbling cement steps to the village's main street and crossed it. He pressed the door opener on his key ring and his neighbour's garage door rumbled quietly upward, revealing the Lexus, gleaming where the streetlight caught it. He would drive and drive. Today was not a work day.

He unlocked the car and got in, closing the door, enjoying the solid *thunk* that echoed in the hollow silence. He started the motor and while waiting for it to warm up he caressed the steering wheel, breathing the smell of leather, letting the Lexus calm him like it always did. Then he backed out of the garage, pressed the button that closed the door, and drove quietly away.

He covered the length of the peninsula, all the way from Gibsons to Earl's Cove, relishing the power beneath the hood of the Lexus, occasionally letting it loose on the highway . . . yeah, it was like a tiger, he thought. His car, with him behind the wheel — a goddamn tiger.

At Earl's Cove, where ferries crossed Jervis Inlet at regular intervals to Saltery Bay, which was a short distance from the town of Powell River, he parked, locked up, and entered the restaurant that was the only building at the terminal. There were two other patrons in the place, a pair of worried-looking young guys wearing jeans and denim jackets. He took a table next to one of the large windows through which customers could watch for the ferry and wondered absently what the two guys had to be worried about.

He ordered toast and scrambled eggs and a coffee. The ferry arrived and the other two customers left, hurrying to their vehicle, which was a mud-spattered Ford pickup with Alberta plates. The ferry docked, unloaded, loaded, and departed. He watched, dully. His mind felt uninhabited, except for a throbbing sensation that wasn't pain, but dismay.

He finished his breakfast, checked the time, got a second cup of coffee — this one to go — paid the bill, and left.

It was full daylight now, a clear, cool day. Puddles gleamed from the side of the road, corroboration of the rain that had fallen over the last week. The deciduous trees in the woods clothing the mountainsides were still green, even though it was autumn now, no more summer in the air. He climbed into the Lexus, turned around in a driveway, and headed back toward Gibsons.

The highway wound through thick woods, past an occasional lake. There was little traffic. He'd been up here before, of course. Many times. During the years he'd worked in Gibsons he'd become familiar with every road, track and trail on the Sunshine Coast, because before he got the Lexus he'd had a primo Blazer that had taken him anyplace he'd wanted to go. But he wasn't interested in exploring any longer. He was getting bored with the place. Bored with evergreen forests, with cold blue lakes, with small towns — and especially bored with the concept of "village."

As he travelled, drawing closer and closer to Gibsons, to home, his mind began to work again. He felt it stir, stretch, and start to function. He was relieved. He wanted to consider this thing coolly, logically, with no bullshit dumbing up the works.

He was approaching Sechelt, which was halfway between Earl's Cove and Gibsons, and slowed down, following the road that circled the town. He caught a glimpse of the ocean as he neared the main intersection; straight ahead was Porpoise Bay. He turned right, drove down the hill, and pulled off the road at Davis Bay.

Across the highway several cars were parked near a take-out hamburger place. He got out of the car and walked the gravel beach, looking out at the broad stretch of blue sea and beyond, on the other side of Georgia Strait, to the far-off sprawl of land that was Vancouver Island. The ocean brushed languidly upon the beach. Seagulls sailed, squawking. A tugboat made its steady, muscular way along an invisible watery highway, pulling an enormous barge piled with logs. There were a few other people walking by the water: a middle-aged couple holding hands, a young woman carrying a plastic shopping bag, two teenage girls engrossed in conversation. At that moment he would have traded places with any one of them, regardless of gender or occupation, knowing absolutely nothing about their lives, their characters, or their circumstances.

Soon he got back into the Lexus and sat there for a while, flexing his hands on the wheel, looking out at the sea, at the tugboat, which was almost out of sight now, and at the barge that trailed behind it.

When he left Davis Bay, he drove more quickly. She had no bloody right to treat him that way. And he had to decide what he was going to do about it.

Abruptly, she filled his mind. He saw her frowning, chewing on the end of a pencil. He saw her laughing, her head thrown back. He saw her at her front door, holding a bathrobe tightly around her, leaning down to pick up the morning paper. He saw her face to face, wearing an expression that was at first thoughtful, then distant, and finally dismissive. He pounded the steering wheel to banish her image.

He was nearing Gibsons. He would soon be on the strip of highway north of the village that was lined with motels and service stations and fast-food outlets, a shabby, shoddy piece of road that he hated.

He'd ignore her from now on. Act as if she didn't exist. Stop seeking her out. Deal with her only when the meetings required it, and then he'd treat her like a stranger, like an alien person.

Or he could confront her, demand that she explain herself. He flinched, though: what if she didn't know what he was talking about? What if she *had* hurt him purely by accident? What if the stupid bitch was totally oblivious to his feelings for her?

He could see the look of astonishment on her face as clearly as if she were actually there in the car with him. He blinked several times to clear his vision. He made himself lift his foot slightly from the accelerator — he was ripping along the goddamn highway far too quickly.

What had been the damn point of this drive, of this quiet time, of leaving his house in the darkness, watching the dark sky lighten as he guided the Lexus along the highway, experiencing the peacefulness of dawn, of the coming of the day? It was gone, now, all gone. The serenity. The calmness. The conviction that he was right, that his cause was just, that his complaints were irreproachable — honourable, in fact. He was appalled to realize that he was near tears, that sobbing aloud had become a distinct possibility.

As he approached the corner where he'd leave the highway, a gravel truck roared rapidly toward him. One of its wheels caught a stone and hurtled it into the windshield of the Lexus, creating a stunningly loud cracking noise and a small star almost exactly in the centre of the passenger side of the glass. "You fucking asshole!" he shouted into the rearview mirror at the gravel truck disappearing into the distance. "You sonofa-bitching asshole!"

He was trembling as he made the turn. He passed the RCMP detachment and continued on, down the long steep hill into the village and off to the left, heading for home, attempting — without success — to keep his speed down, fighting the urge to throw caution to the winds and let the Lexus have its head.

FOUR

That same morning, Beverly Brooks leaned across Eddie's enormous desk and confided, "I hate wearing the damn hat. I hate wearing the whole damn uniform."

"You can probably be chucked off the Force for that attitude," said Eddie.

"Probably."

"And fined."

"Huh."

"Possibly incarcerated."

Beverly laughed. "I retract the statement."

The uniform didn't suit her. Or maybe it didn't look good on her because she *thought* it didn't suit her.

"I don't know if this is in my file or not," said Beverly Brooks, "but you ought to know, I sometimes jump to conclusions. And this sometimes gets in the way of the work." She scratched her scalp furiously with both hands and immediately smoothed her auburn hair, which was short and wavy. She was of medium height, stocky, with an olive complexion and bright eyes the colour of spring leaves. "A belated welcome to Gibsons, by the way," she said. "I am, I've gotta tell you, dead pleased that you're a woman."

"Well, you know," said Eddie, "I am, too."

Her journal entry on Beverly Brooks read, "Smart. Capable. Self-aware."

———

Olive Parfit was close to tears when she set off early that
morning, walking quickly along the edge of the road,
and she tried to fight them off by concentrating on the
world around her. The sun was shining, which ought to
make a difference. And maybe it did, she thought.
Maybe she would be feeling even more abandoned,
more desolate, if it had still been raining. The forest on
either side of the road was washed and gleaming, and in
the yards of the occasional houses she passed, chrysanthemums and dahlias bloomed. Olive noted this and
admired the gardens, what she could see of them, with
determination.

She wouldn't have minded walking into the village
under ordinary circumstances, and in fact she often did
so. She enjoyed striding down the road, swinging her
arms and feeling fit despite the fact that she was now
sixty-three. But not today. Not today. Today she badly
needed her car, a 1990 Chevrolet Malibu, blue, with four
doors and air conditioning.

There were puddles by the side of the road. She had
been automatically stepping around them, small pools
of still water mirroring the sky above, blue with puffs of
white. She approached an especially large one and
couldn't avoid treading in it, which caused small waves
to shudder across its surface, destroying the serene
reflection.

Olive had never felt as lonely as she did today. She
wanted to slump against the nearest tree and let herself
weep.

But she didn't do this. She pushed her shoulders back
and resumed walking, listening for traffic, half expecting
someone she knew to pull up in front of her and offer
her a ride. But it was early in the day. Few cars passed,
and those that did carried only strangers.

Olive was wearing her orange pants, a T-shirt with a
brown flannel shirt over it like a jacket, running shoes,

and a fanny pack. She tried to imagine as she walked
that she wasn't herself — at least that she wasn't in
familiar territory, but in a strange exotic land to which
she had come as a traveller, strong and inquisitive and
tolerant of eccentric foreign sights and customs. She was
ashamed of how little travelling she'd done in her life.
Seeing the world had never been one of her dreams. But
lately, lately . . . She had recently seen a television documentary about winemaking and couldn't wrest from
her mind the golden light she had seen falling upon the
Italian landscape. So here she was, trudging along, lifting
her feet, swinging her arms, walking in grief toward a
service station, imagining herself on a highway outside
Florence, heading toward the statue of David.

When she had awakened, the morning after watching
the documentary, she had seen a monotonous grey sky
through her bedroom window and had realized that she
would be seeing a lot of grey skies and falling rain during the next months. And then she had thought, *Maybe
I'll go to Italy.* This was definitely a new idea.

Olive had been instantly fully awake. She lay in bed
gazing at the grey sky and at first didn't recognize the fluttering sensation in her stomach, which was excitement.

Was that the day of Danny's first call about his father's
illness? She thought it was. And of course she had put all
plans aside then, travel, everything.

Olive was on a comparatively straight stretch of the
road now. She would soon be in the village proper. Her
destination lay on the other side of town, over the hill,
on the highway that led to Sechelt and beyond.

A car was approaching. It was only the fourth or fifth
vehicle to have appeared that morning. She hadn't seen
anybody at all on foot. It suddenly felt to Olive that she
truly was in a strange country, that when she finally did
see another human being he would speak to her in an
incomprehensible tongue.

The car was advancing toward her quite rapidly, Olive observed, worried. She knew that the road behind her became much narrower, the hills more steep, the curves more sharp: if the driver didn't slow down the car was going to career into a tree, or somebody's yard. As she thought about this, attempting to telegraph her concern, knowing that dismay must be written all over her face, the car actually speeded up, and — although she could hardly believe this — aimed itself directly at her.

Olive was frozen in place as the vehicle rushed toward her. Its hood was colossal, the most terrifying thing she had ever seen. Behind the windshield rode only a silhouette. It was as if a shadow, or a ghost, was driving the car. At the last possible moment it swerved, and flew past her. The wind it created blew her hair wildly. The right front tire smashed through a puddle, soaking her pant legs. The roar of the car's engine faded as the vehicle disappeared around a bend in the road.

Olive stood loose and limp by the roadside, shaking, panting. There was still nobody in sight, not a soul. There was only silence in the world, except for Olive's ragged breathing. "Oh my god," she was whispering. She said it again and again. "Oh my god."

She turned around, flapping her arms like a scarecrow, and finally stumbled across the ditch, waded through knee-high weeds to the nearest tree and leaned against it, letting her body slide down the trunk until she was sitting on the damp ground, clutching her knees. I will stay here, she thought, until I stop shaking.

She should have memorized the licence number. She couldn't even be sure that it had been a British Columbia plate. Had the driver been alone in the car? Had it been a man? She wasn't sure.

It couldn't have been what it seemed, it couldn't have been that this person had actually tried, deliberately, to run her down. Olive wrapped her arms around her body, huddling into herself. He must have been distracted, she thought. Maybe he'd been using one of those damn cell phones. Yes. That was it — that had to be it.

But why hadn't he stopped, then, pulled off the road and rushed back to apologize for almost killing her? It was possible, she thought, that he hadn't even seen her. But more likely he'd been horrified, and then too ashamed of himself to stop. And besides, he'd been going so fast that his own momentum would have kept him going.

She realized that she was making excuses for him, for this person who had damn near killed her.

Was she certain that he was a he? Yes, she thought, concentrating, trying to remember. Yes, the driver was a man. But that was all she knew of him.

Eventually, she struggled to her feet, slapping dirt and grass from her clothing. She took a deep breath and walked firmly back to the road, and followed it into the village, and through it.

Olive trudged up the hairpin hill and along the highway, listening for traffic, and every time a vehicle approached, she moved quickly off the road. Finally, she arrived at the service station that looked after her car.

Well, it was Vincent, who owned the place, who looked after her car.

Vincent was a very large man — tall, yes, but also very big around. He was a human column. Olive found this comforting, even more so today than usual. He wore a soiled blue jumpsuit and a billed cap that used to be green. It was now so badly worn and faded that the writing on it, which spelled JOHN DEERE, could barely be read.

Vincent was filling somebody's gas tank when Olive arrived. She waited while he took the driver's credit card and ran it through the machine inside, then returned it, giving the car a friendly slap on the roof as it pulled away.

"Vincent," she said, "my car won't start."

"God, woman, what happened to you?"

Olive looked down at her mud-spattered pants. "Somebody almost ran me down." She lifted her hands to her hair and tried to tidy it.

"Report the bastard." He was wiping his hands on an oily rag.

"Yes, but Vincent, I really need my car today, and it won't start." She made her hands into fists and dug her nails into her flesh, distracting herself with pain. But it wasn't enough pain, not nearly enough. She knew she was going to start crying. God damn it, she thought, furious.

Vincent sighed and headed inside, and Olive followed. He tossed the rag on the counter, which was littered with tools. A cardboard box sat on the counter. Inside were some screws and a pack of cigarettes and a big, square, chrome lighter with a maple leaf engraved on either side. Vincent perched on a stool and lit a cigarette. He shifted his weight, planting himself more firmly in the middle of the stool, whose four legs, Olive imagined, staring at them intently, might have begun to bend. A stool with four bowed legs, she thought, now that would be a sight.

She wondered how long it would take to learn conversational Italian.

"What kind of a sound did it make when you tried to start it?" Vincent asked.

Olive grappled with the question. "Whu-whu-whu," she said after a minute. "Like that."

"Probably the battery," said Vincent. He held the cigarette almost daintily between his wide, fleshy fingers. "I don't remember if we've ever replaced your battery."

"I don't think we ever have," said Olive.

"Then that'll be it." He squinted at her, through the smoke from his cigarette. "Are you okay? You look kinda shook up."

Olive opened her mouth to assure him that she was fine. "No," she said. "I'm not. My brother died." Tears trickled from her eyes, spilled down her cheeks. "Oh dear. Last night."

Vincent dropped his cigarette onto the concrete floor, crushing it under his foot. He stood up and came to Olive awkwardly, his huge arms outstretched. "Olive. I'm sorry, girl." He put his arms around her.

"I have to get to Vancouver," she sobbed, pressed against his overalls, which smelled of gasoline and perspiration. "I have to get over there today."

"Don't worry about it, girl," said Vincent. "I'll get you there, never fear." He patted her shoulder, oblivious to the car that had pulled up at the pump outside. "There, there. There, there."

Johnny Grieg, thirty-four, was relaxed, affable and charming. But today, as he sat across from her, Eddie was also acutely aware of the intensity of his concentration. He had been asking her questions — what was it like being a female Member, what were her professional ambitions — until finally she protested. "Hey, you're in here to talk about yourself, not to get me to talk about me."

"Sorry, boss. Do you mind if I call you 'boss'?"

"I do, yes," said Eddie.

He laughed. "Okay." He leaned forward, hands on his knees. "I'm married, my wife and I have four kids, she runs a corner store, and we live in the rooms in behind. But you know all this, Sergeant, it's in my file."

One recent Sunday afternoon Eddie had taken herself off to the snack bar at Davis Bay and ordered a burger and fries, which she ate in the Mercedes. A teenage couple was huddled together at one of the outdoor tables. The two tables indoors were empty, but the proprietor was a chatty fellow and Eddie craved solitude that day.

She'd winced when Johnny Grieg appeared in her rearview mirror, followed by his wife, each of them holding hands with two of their children. She was in a mood to brood and didn't want to be distracted. But she needn't have worried. Johnny and his family remained unaware of her. Eddie had thought the Mercedes would catch anybody's attention, and in fact, one of Johnny's two sons gave it a curious glance as the family swept past and entered the snack bar. But he said nothing to his father and soon lost interest.

"I know it's in your file. Sure. But go on."

"Oh boy." He sat back in the red vinyl chair and folded his arms. "I find that other people are a lot more interesting than I am. That's one of the things I like about being a police officer. You get to meet so many people."

"What else do you like about it?"

He thought for a minute. "Well that's it, I guess." He cocked his head at her. "The Job isn't the only thing in my life, after all. I've got my wife and kids, the store. Plus I paint." He said this with a little smile, watching for her reaction.

Eddie's mind instantly flashed back a few months, to the days she had spent painting her house. But she knew that wasn't what he'd meant.

"Watercolours," he said. "Oils. I'm gonna get into sculpture as well, I think. And I fish, too. Though there aren't many fish left around here. Salmon," he offered, as if she'd asked.

She'd watched them through the greasy window. He looked much different, Johnny did, out of uniform. He looked like someone who'd be completely at home driving a dump truck, or prowling the aisles of Home Depot, or playing Scrabble with his kids.

The family had looked neither happy nor unhappy. They were just absorbed in their food, the parents keeping a watchful eye on the younger kids, making sure

nothing got spilled, and occasionally adjudicating argu-
ments. Eddie had felt very peaceful, watching them.

"Easygoing," she wrote in her journal. "Generous.
Quick to laugh. Not particularly ambitious. He probably
assumes the best in people — a nice contrast to
Beatrice."

As she closed the journal and put it away in her desk
drawer, she considered the fact that there were some
sexy guys among her troops. Howard Peck owned the
reputation, but she personally admired Matt Tomlinson's
easy grace, and Johnny was attractive too though married and therefore unavailable, and Glen Hammond had
stunning bedroom eyes, and Buster wasn't bad either, and
then, oh god, there was Bert Chapman. . . . Eddie
slammed the drawer shut and leaned back in her chair,
linking her hands behind her head. She couldn't get
involved with any of them, of course. She'd have to look
elsewhere.

She hadn't had a lover since Alan McCurdy. They had
had a passionate affair while they were both working out
of the Burnaby detachment. She'd been so preoccupied
with lust she thought it must be physically obvious, that
people must be able to see it, smell it.

It was obsessive, while it lasted. She couldn't remember anything about those months except the sex. She
must have done her work, lived the other parts of her
life, but she couldn't remember doing it. She couldn't
even remember what she and Alan had talked about
when they weren't having sex. Maybe they hadn't talked
about anything. Maybe the only thing they had done
together was fuck.

And that was the right word for it, too. It was harsh,
almost violent sex, certainly not lovemaking, and Eddie
knew it, always, for what it was. Her passion burned itself
out, flared high and hot and was soon extinguished. In
fact, it lasted longer than she had expected. But when it

was gone, it was completely gone. She told him in a coffee shop.

"It's over, Alan. We're history." She said it cheerfully, which she soon regretted.

"What are you talking about?" he said with a slow smile. He reached across the table and took her hand and breathed sexy words at her. A day earlier, a mere twenty-four hours earlier, this would have made her shudder. She would have had to pull away so as not to have an orgasm just from his touch, his whispers.

She squeezed his hand affectionately. "Come on, Alan. You heard me."

His face became very still. He stared directly into her eyes. "It's not over, Eddie. Not until I say so."

Eddie disengaged her hand from his and sat back. "I'm sorry, Alan."

"It's not over."

She picked up her handbag from the floor. "I'm sorry." She left the coffee shop, half expecting him to shout something after her, but he didn't.

She had thought that would be the end of it. But it wasn't. For a while, he tried persuasion. Then he tried bullying her. Once he got violent, in the lobby of her apartment building. She threatened to report him, and he backed off.

And then she got transferred to Sechelt and breathed easily again.

Until the phone calls began.

She still looked with apprehension at the blinking light on her answering machine, even though he hadn't called since she'd screamed at him over the telephone one night several months ago.

Eddie shivered, and reached for the pile of paperwork that seemed never to shrink in size.

FIVE

It was Sunday afternoon. Olive was leaning on the roof of her car in the ferry lineup at Horseshoe Bay. She had been staying in Vancouver since Friday with her nephew, Danny, the son of her dead brother Horace — her younger brother, whose wife had predeceased him. What an odd word, she thought. It seem to imply deliberateness, as if Wendy had long ago decided to die first.

In her mind Olive saw Danny's face, wide and unlined, ingenuous. He had the patience of a saint, Danny did, and the smile of a cherub.

During the weekend he had touched every object in his father's house, it seemed to Olive, as if he had never seen them before, picking things up and turning them in his big hands, wonderingly examining them, with his head bent and his shoulders hunched. Olive had repeatedly restrained herself from patting him on the back and stroking his thinning blond hair, afraid that if she did so he would begin to weep, brokenly, and not be able to stop.

Too many things had been removed from him: his mother, his wife, and now his father. He was a good man, and perhaps he was strong. But she didn't know how strong. His company had given him compassionate leave, but he had decided to go back to work early, and Olive thought this was a good thing.

They had finished that morning, loading boxes into her car and more into Danny's. Then he had locked up the house and they had driven away, in their separate cars.

Olive leaned on the roof of her car and considered the fact that she was truly alone in the world: orphaned, bereft of her only sibling. There was Danny, yes, and she was glad of that, but how very hollow she felt just now, watching the ferry manoeuver into position at the dock beyond the blue waters of the bay, which was embraced by the slopes of Mount Black to the east and Madrona Ridge to the west. Soon cars and trucks and recreational vehicles began streaming from the car decks, and Olive got back behind the wheel of her Chevy, whose engine started right away, thanks to its brand new battery.

About noon that day, he'd backed the Lexus out of the neighbour's garage into her driveway to wash it. He paid the neighbour fifty bucks a month for the use of the garage. She was an older woman with a Volkswagen Golf that she didn't mind parking out on the street. He figured she didn't have a pot to piss in, only this house of hers, a small blue bungalow set back from the road with a single-car garage next to it. He knew the fifty came in handy, helped pay for her cigarettes — she was one of those people who just couldn't manage to quit, or didn't want to, anyway. She was watching him, now, from her dining-room window, peeking out through the curtains — he could see her big orange hair moving around behind the lace. Suddenly he looked up and grinned and waved at her. She waved back, then disappeared.

He had vacuumed the interior of the Lexus with the battery-powered Black & Decker, polished up the dash, cleaned the interior windows until they squeaked, and now he was flooding the exterior of the vehicle with streams of clear water, washing away the suds. Next he would dry it, and it needed a wax job today, too.

The star in the windshield irritated the hell out of him.

His gut squirmed every time he thought about how he'd nearly run that old woman down. But two days had passed; if she was going to report it, she would have done it by now. Sure.

He turned off the hose, looped it neatly over the receptacle attached to the wall of his neighbour's house, and bent over to reach into a blue plastic pail that was stuffed with soft, clean rags.

The water drained away down the driveway, making a faint gurgling sound. The October sunshine caressed his back. The muscles in his thighs strained against the denim of his jeans. He was strong, goddamn it. Young, and strong, and in fucking control of his life.

He finished waxing the Lexus at about four o'clock, just as the sun was going down. He tucked the car back inside the garage and locked it up, closed the garage door, and gave the dining-room window another wave in case his neighbour was looking out again.

He went home and put away the Black & Decker, the pail, and the rest of his supplies, and dropped the damp rags into his laundry hamper. He rolled up his sleeves and switched on the computer — and immediately switched it off again. It was too easy, too fucking easy; he needed something real.

He went outside, onto the sandy beach that stretched off toward the marina on his right and around a long slow curve to the left. It was a gentle beach. A thoughtful beach. Pretty. But he craved the granite sea-coast he knew better than this one — long, smooth attenuated fingers of granite stretching into the sea. It was where he had gone when something puzzled him, when he needed comfort. When the world just got too fucking hard.

This beach didn't do it for him. Never had.

He sat down anyway, on a big log that sat so perfectly horizontal to the water it might have been arranged there.

The woman he'd nearly run over, she was the same old broad he'd encountered in the grocery store. Dead ringer for his mom, if she'd been allowed to age.

He swore his mom had him under some kind of fucking spell until she died, which had happened when he was in his late twenties. He had been perpetually distracted by peripheral, inchoate but disturbing thoughts of her throughout his adolescence. He was unable to give a girl, or his tumultuous feelings about her, his full attention.

His mother's focus on him had been unpredictable, shifting. Sometimes she seemed hardly aware of him for days, even weeks at a time, eventually turning to him with her eyebrows raised (like the wings of a just-awakened bird, fluttering, making sure the reassuring air was still in place), looking at him as if to say, "You're still here, then?" in mild, unworried astonishment. He would feel then as if he had roared across the continent and back on a train, his face out the window half the time, first pounding away from her, then rushing home, only to find that his absence hadn't even been remarked.

He tried hard to fall in love, because that was what was supposed to happen now that he was a teenager. But in the years during which his mother lived, this turned out not to be possible. He had sex, and at first he believed that this would do, this would save him (from what, he couldn't have said), but the sex event had no far-reaching consequences. Sex, he ruefully decided, was the ultimate instant gratification, and although it was immensely pleasing, and he found in the act from the very beginning something tantalizingly empowering, it didn't last. He knew it was unrealistic to expect the physical sensations to last — a person couldn't function in such a state. But he had hoped for something, *something* sturdy and authentic to be winkled out of the experience that would provide at least some information about love, about the bonds that held together, for example, such unlikely persons as his parents.

He preferred, as an adolescent, to hold up as examples to himself people like — oh, Wayne Gretzky and his wife, the blonde American, or passionate couples from the worlds of music and entertainment. He didn't like to think about what sexual relationship his parents might have experienced over the years. He was interested only in their mutual loyalty.

He stood up from the log and dusted off the seat of his jeans and headed back to his house. He remembered one night — he was what, twelve? thirteen? — he'd been lying in bed, eyes trained on the window, watching the front-yard tree branches shudder restlessly in a silent breeze, and suddenly he'd wondered about his mother's loyalties. And the more he wondered, the more mysterious and menacing she loomed.

He'd thought about her plump bare shoulder, glimpsed that evening through the partially open bathroom door. No guile there. He figured he was old enough to look for it and smart enough not to see it where it didn't exist.

She'd finished her shower. The bathroom was full of steam. She'd opened the door to come out into the hall and had dropped something and was bending over to retrieve it. When she stood upright, the bathrobe slipped from her shoulder. That was all. There was nothing remotely sexual about her gaze upon him or about his perception of her. Her gleaming face was dispassionate. Her hair, brushed severely back, had already begun to reinstate its inevitable curl. She glanced at him, half bemused, half irritated, and started down the hall toward the room she shared with his dad. Then suddenly she wheeled around and returned to plant a loud, smacking kiss on his father's cheek.

Inside his beachfront house, he sprawled in the big leather chair that had been his father's, which he'd lugged (at his dad's insistence) across the country, a big brown leather chair that was badly worn on the arms and the headrest; but it enveloped him like shelter.

He'd take the Lexus out after all, he decided. He'd power up the highway to a place he knew where the waves struck hard against rock, breaking high and white and spraying his face.

The point was that her existence — her very existence — in some way had skewed the way he'd grown; this he had worked out later. For when she was gone, everything had changed.

He realized that his feelings about Rebecca had undergone a change. Maybe his mom showing up in the guise of that old lady had been a sign, he thought. A message. Or more likely it had been only a small, inconsequential event, something that could happen in anybody's day, except that it had ended up fueling his conviction and strengthening his resolve.

For he had decided that he couldn't possibly be wrong about her. Rebecca. That unpleasant thing that had happened between them — he had to put it aside, he had to concentrate on mending the relationship, repairing the small rent she'd created without meaning to.

He sprang from the chair, feeling positively exuberant. He'd drive up to that rough-water shore, yeah, and think things through. Plan his next move.

By the time the ferry docked at Langdale, the sun had begun to set. It was the end of another clear, bright day in what had been a long, languid autumn, with mild, sunny days and golden leaves that clung stubbornly to the trees.

Olive drove slowly along the crooked road from the ferry terminal to Gibsons, with a steep hillside climbing upward to her right and another descending downward to her left, ending abruptly in the sea. She imagined the car that had almost run her down rocketing at high speed along this narrow, winding road; she hoped it had scared the hell out of him; she hoped he had damn near run himself into a tree. She had to report him. It was her civic duty. But could she do it now, days after the fact? Wouldn't the police wonder why she hadn't gone to see them immediately?

Just before she reached the town's main street she pulled into a side road, rounded a corner and parked in front of her house, which was hidden from its neighbours by trees and underbrush and hedges. By now the sun was even lower in the sky, and the temperature had dropped, and the wind had come up; when she climbed out of her car, Olive heard it rustling in the crisp, dry fallen leaves, noodling them aimlessly, like a snuffling dog. She looked up into the branches of the poplar trees that clustered along the western edge of her property. They looked flaxen and crinkly, as if the leaves were made of golden aluminum foil. Olive, studying them, estimated that fewer than half the leaves had so far fallen. There wasn't much point in raking the lawn yet. Although, she considered, if it should start to rain — which of course it would, eventually — raking would be a much more onerous task.

Olive did all of her own yardwork. She took pride in this and enjoyed it, too, and if she were to start hiring someone else to do it, as Danny had several times suggested, what would she do for exercise? She had never been enthusiastic about exercise for its own sake, preferring activities with some point to them, like walking into town, or cleaning the house — or raking the lawn. She'd better not put it off, she thought. Better rake up the damn leaves tomorrow, before the rains came.

Standing by her car, contemplating the trees and the lawn, she was aware of the new coldness of the dying day, and the crackling of the fallen leaves as the inconstant wind poked around in them, pushing them up against tree trunks and Olive's fence. She heard bird sounds, too, and recalled a column in the local paper in which a birdwatcher had reported spotting twenty species during a forty-five minute walk in the woods. Olive knew a Stellar's jay when she saw one, and could identify robins and herons and crows and maybe sparrows, but that was about it.

She didn't know why she was dallying, shivering now that the sunlight had retreated and the sky had begun to darken. Why on earth do we insist on getting rid of daylight saving time? she wondered crossly.

There wasn't another person in sight up or down the road, except for a teenager gliding on a skateboard, a ghostly sight, tall and thin, a pale spectre vanishing into the distance. But she saw no bundled-up senior citizens hiking off to town. No cars, ambling slowly because of the curves in the narrow street. Not even a dog or a cat.

Olive finally turned from the car and went up the walk to the front door of her house, a small, two-storey A-frame which she had had built when she moved to the Sunshine Coast from West Vancouver a year earlier. She inserted the key in the lock and turned it, and attempted to open the door. But it wouldn't open. She fumbled again with the key, turned it — this time it worked.

Olive wasn't sure what had happened. Had she forgotten to lock the door when she left last Friday? So that when she thought she was unlocking it, she had actually locked it? Or had she just not turned the key the whole way, or the right way, the first time? Flustered and uneasy, she stepped inside and closed the door behind her.

She was standing in a shadowy hall that ran the length of the house, from the front door past the staircase on the left, past the living room and the powder room and the dining room on the right, all the way to the sliding doors that led outside onto the wide concrete deck.

She turned on the hall light and put her handbag and the keys on the small table that sat against the wall and hugged herself, shivering. She walked a few steps down the hall to turn up the thermostat. And as she did so she heard a sound from upstairs. Or thought she did.

Her heart took a mighty leap and her hands began tingling unpleasantly. She glanced quickly into the living room, which was undisturbed: the TV was still there, and the VCR, and the CD player. Olive stood very still, straining to hear over the roaring in her ears. How can people be expected to react well in crisis situations, she thought, with all this interior noise going on? She couldn't decide whether to run to her car and drive rapidly away, call the police, or attribute whatever she'd heard to the workings of her imagination.

She found herself tiptoeing down the hall and into the kitchen, where she took a cleaver from the knife block on the counter. She went upstairs, the cleaver tight in her right hand, but my god could she actually strike someone with this thing? There would be blood all over the place, and maybe he'd die. She should have brought the wooden mallet used for tenderizing meat. It had metal on one side of its head. That would have been a much better weapon, thought Olive, creeping up the steps, holding the cleaver high.

Upstairs there was a bedroom on either side of a narrow hallway, with a bathroom next to the smaller bedroom. All three doors were slightly open. Olive couldn't remember whether she had left them that way. She stood at the top of the stairs, waiting for someone to hurl himself out of hiding straight at her, wondering if she could

maybe step aside quickly and cause him to fall down the
stairs. Then she would run into her room and jump from
the window and pray not to break anything significant
when she landed.

But nobody emerged. Everything was still. Olive
couldn't hear a sound, not a single sound. She nervously shifted her weight, causing the floor to creak, and her
heart vaulted again, beating wildly in her throat, roaring
in her ears. She rushed forward and threw the guestroom door fully open and marched inside. The skin on
her back blenched, pulling her entire body swiftly
around as she recoiled from an attacker emerging from
the closet — but there wasn't one. Olive wrenched open
the closet door and flailed among the out-of-season
clothes that hung there: nobody.

She found no one in her own room, or her closet; no
one in her bathroom.

She slumped onto the toilet, the cleaver dangling
from her hand. Her heart had quieted and she could
hear properly again. She found that there were all sorts
of noises to be heard: outside, the rising wind; inside, the
small sighs and murmurings of the house itself, familiar
and comforting.

Olive sighed. Her knees hurt as she stood: it was
going to rain. Maybe she should rake those leaves now,
before it was completely dark outside.

And then she remembered the boxes in her car.

She went downstairs — chagrined to notice that her
legs were shaky, hanging on to the banister all the way
down — and returned the cleaver to its wide slot in the
knife block. She grabbed her keys from the hall table and
opened the front door wide.

The fallen leaves were rising in the blustering wind,
dancing in the air, falling to the ground, rising again. The
rustling of the swaying poplar trees was vociferous and
disquieting. And the wind made a noise of its own, a low,

mournful howl that sounded to Olive like a distressed animal.

The car was too close to the fence for her to open the doors on the right side, so Olive went around the vehicle and began wrestling the first carton from the back seat. But she suddenly felt something brush against the backs of her legs, and she lurched backwards in shock, knocking her head against the top of the door opening. She turned and lifted a hand to her head, touching the site of the injury, and looked at her fingertips, expecting to see blood, but in the fading daylight she saw none. Another gust of the mocking wind threw another cluster of leaves in her direction. She brushed them away and leaned again into the car. She lifted out the first of three boxes and carried it into the house, placing it on the kitchen counter.

The remaining boxes were smaller but heavier, containing mostly books. Olive turned on the porch light before going outside for the next one, which she deposited on the living-room floor. She stayed there for a moment, squatting, resting.

The window that looked out into the front yard rattled suddenly in its frame, and the front door blew shut with a tremendous bang. Olive pushed herself upright, wincing at the pain in her knees, and went to the front door. She opened it and hurried through the wind, through the crazily blowing leaves back to her car, and reached inside for the third and last box.

But the back seat was empty.

Olive looked in the front seat. Nothing. She looked again in the back, felt around on the floor, but the box was not there. She climbed inside and flailed a hand about in the shadows on the floor behind the passenger seat. Nothing. She got out, went inside the house for her keys, came back, and opened the trunk. Empty. As she had known it would be.

Olive slammed the trunk door shut and stood, bewildered, in the wind, the back of her head throbbing, one hand holding her wildly blowing hair. She looked up and down the street. She looked across the street into the woods, which were full of shadows and restless undergrowth.

"I'll be damned," said Olive. "I've been robbed."

SIX

As she gazed across the desk at Howard Peck, Eddie realized gloomily that she still knew her troops not at all well. Howard Peck's eyes, meeting hers, revealed nothing. And as Eddie thought back to the others she had interviewed so far — Buster Sheffield, William Kirkpatrick, Beatrice Fitzgerald, Nick Orsato, Beverly Brooks, Johnny Greig — she knew that however frankly they might have regarded her, however openly they might have seemed to talk to her, they had quite successfully, for the most part, kept themselves to themselves.

Howard Peck was twenty-nine. "I want to stay here as long as possible," he told Eddie. "I like the Sunshine Coast." His smile transformed his face. It was sweet and dazzling, bringing genuine warmth into his eyes.

Eddie's eyes wandered to his mouth. "Huh," she said. "You've got a lot of friends here, have you?"

"Right," he said.

She busied herself with his file for a moment. It was a record of satisfactory service, but so far he hadn't sought out or created for himself many opportunities for excellence.

"Actually — no," he said.

She looked up at him. His expression was once again impenetrable.

"It's not exactly accurate that I've got a lot of friends. I know a lot of people, that's all."

"What do you like to do when you're off duty, Howard?"

"I like to socialize," he said promptly. "Nothing serious." He smiled again. His smile was a potent thing, and he knew it.

"What about the Job? What do you see yourself doing five years from now?"

"Well . . ." He sat up straight, stretching his back. "What do you see yourself doing five years from now, Sarge? It might have a bearing."

Eddie closed his file folder and leaned back in her chair. "Do you have a problem with me, Constable?"

His eyes widened and he lifted his hands, as if in surrender. "Absolutely not. I only meant — if you plan to move on from here, maybe by the time you're ready to go, I'll be in a position to apply for your job."

Her journal entry about Howard Peck read, in part, "Buster says he's got a big rep with women. His record is clean but unimpressive. Can't tell if he's got career goals or he's just stringing me along. This is a frustrating guy."

The seasons were turning. Fall was becoming winter. It was a subtle thing, on B.C.'s coast, the changing of the seasons. Not a dramatic event. Just an insinuation of change. The breeze acquired a new bite.

Eddie got home from work around seven on this early November evening. She immediately unbraided her thick, blonde hair and brushed it until it popped and snapped, then showered and changed into a pair of jeans and a flannel shirt. Half an hour later she was sitting on a barstool, drinking red wine and waiting for Cindi Webster.

"I'd better eat something," she said to the bartender, whose name was Ted.

"Just what I was thinking," he said. "How about a roast beef sandwich?" He held up a hand. "Wait a minute. Let me guess. You're gonna want mayo on that. And mustard. And lettuce. And some nice, thick tomato slices."

"Hold the tomato," said Eddie.

"Done." Ted retreated to the window into the kitchen and called out the order.

A dugout canoe and an enormous chainsaw, among other things, hung from the bar's high ceiling. A ship's figurehead, battered and bruised — a naked woman with her hands behind her head — was suspended in one corner. There was a fireplace in the centre of the far wall, and a dartboard hung next to it.

"And a coffee, please," said Eddie when Ted returned.

"What're you doing New Year's Eve?" he asked, pouring coffee from a round glass pot into a white mug.

"Don't know yet. There's plenty of time."

"You should come here." Ted delivered the coffee and leaned against the bar, looking down at her. He was a bit shorter than Eddie, and balding, but he had a body that reminded her of Alan, and his cheek dimpled when he smiled. Eddie had always been a sucker for a dimple.

"Oh yeah?" she said, amused. "Why?"

Cindi slid onto the stool next to her. "Why what?"

"I was telling her, the Sergeant, here, she should come here for New Year's Eve. There's gonna be live music, lots of food." He flushed, and started to laugh. "Shit, I don't know — balloons? Fireworks? It'll be fun, that I know for sure."

"We'll think about it," said Cindi. She pointed imperiously at Ted. "A vodka martini. Straight up. With a twist. Please."

He turned away to prepare the drink.

"Let's get a table," said Cindi, picking up Eddie's coffee.

"You're awfully bossy tonight," Eddie grumbled, but she grabbed her purse and her wine glass and followed

Cindi to a table next to the window.

"It might not be a bad idea," said Cindi, tossing her hair back. It rippled across her shoulders like a fawn-coloured cloud. "New Year's Eve in this place." She dropped her oversize shoulder bag on the floor and unzipped her red Gore-Tex jacket. "What do you think?" She shrugged. "We've gotta do something."

"No we don't," said Eddie.

Ted approached with Cindi's drink in one hand and Eddie's sandwich in the other. The plate was garnished with a sprig of parsley, a slice of dill pickle, a scoop of coleslaw and a heap of potato chips.

"Ooh. I'll have one of those, please," said Cindi.

"Think about it," said Ted, looking from one of them to the other. "It's gonna be a blast. Another roast beef sandwich coming up," he said to Cindi.

"Of course we have to do something," said Cindi irritably. "It's the millennium, for godsake."

Eddie had at first been cautious in her friendship with Cindi Webster, who was a reporter with the Sechelt newspaper. She'd become more relaxed in the last months, though, since her job had been moved to Gibsons.

"I might get me a dog," said Eddie, picking up a sandwich.

Cindi stared at her. "What's that got to do with anything?"

"Nothing," said Eddie. She took a bite, thinking that tomorrow she would confer with Matt Tomlinson, whose twelve-year-old daughter had a German shepherd. The child lived in Vancouver, with Matt's ex-wife. "I might get a dog," she said, chewing. "That's all."

The chalky shadow of frost was sprawled upon the grass when Eddie hurried down the walk from her small yellow house to her car the next morning. She wondered if there would be any snow this winter. She loved the sight of snow falling upon the beach. She could do without it on the highway, though. People forgot between one year and the next how to do winter driving. Eddie didn't understand this. All they had to do for pete's sake was slow down, but oh no, they'd panic or some damn thing, and it would end up pedal to the floor, car crumpled against a telephone pole or against another car being propelled along by another equally inept civilian.

She climbed into her car and drove off toward Gibsons.

It was a gloomy day, the first of many to come over the next four months. By March there would at least be some warmth in the air, and lots of blooming going on. Four months wasn't so bad, she thought, tooling along the highway, which cut through thick forest and passed a closed-up restaurant here, an empty, mournful golf course there. Narrow roads and lanes led away from it into the woods, or toward the sea.

Eddie reminded herself to call her father when she got to work, to try to smooth things over.

"I've got to work, Dad. I'm sorry," she had told him the day before on the phone.

"Work? On Christmas Day? I thought you were in charge over there."

"I am."

"Then delegate, Edwina. Delegate."

"I'm working on Christmas, Dad," she said doggedly. "And I'm on call over New Year's," she added quickly. "I just got here for pete's sake," she said loudly, talking over him. "Easter. I'll take Easter off."

"And what am I supposed to do? Have Christmas alone, I suppose. You expect me to ring in the New Year alone, I suppose."

Eddie had stared wearily at the leaden patch of sky

framed by her office window. He's got lots of friends, she had told herself.

"Lots of them," she said aloud, pulling into the parking lot behind the detachment. Although she didn't actually know whether he did or didn't.

Inside, Matt Tomlinson was waiting for her.

"I need to talk to you," she blurted. "About dogs."

He lifted his eyebrows. "Sure," he said. "But first, there's a lady here to see you." He was a tall, muscular man with thick, dark hair and eyes that were full of humour. "She asked who was in charge. Won't settle for anybody else. I tried," he said, spreading his hands. "Offered my services in the politest possible way."

"I'm sure you did," said Eddie. "So where is she?"

"On the bench by the front door."

"What's her problem?"

"Don't have a clue," said Matt, with a sunny smile.

A slim, grey-haired woman stood up as Eddie approached her. "Good morning, I'm Sergeant Henderson," said Eddie, offering her hand. "Let's go into my office."

"Thank you, Sergeant. I'm Olive Parfit. Ms. Olive Parfit."

"How do you do, Ms. Parfit," said Eddie, smiling at her, thinking about her father, imagining him in the rocking chair he'd had since Eddie was a toddler, sitting there looking through his apartment window at the freighters in English Bay, feeling sorry for himself and reproachful of his only child.

"It was such an odd thing, I simply could not believe it had happened, at first," said Olive Parfit when they were seated in Eddie's office. She was wearing a quilted jacket over a track suit, holding on to a box-shaped handbag that sat in her lap.

"Tell me about it." Eddie pulled her notebook from a desk drawer and took a pen from a mug that held several, plus pencils, a glue stick, a letter opener, and a pair of scissors.

Olive hesitated. Shook her head. Squeezed her cheeks up toward her eyes and wrinkled her forehead. It was on the tip of her tongue to begin by telling the sergeant about the car that had tried to run her over. But she had nothing to report, other than the event itself. No details, except that it had been a big car, light in colour. She hadn't managed to get the licence plate. She could offer no description of the driver. It was better not to muddy the waters, she decided.

"I am occasionally forgetful," she confessed, with an awkward little laugh. "Which is why I didn't report this right away. I wasn't entirely sure . . .

"It actually happened almost a month ago, you see. At first I thought that maybe I'd . . . and so I telephoned my nephew, to be sure I'd taken them with me, that I really had *had* them."

"Had what, Ms. Parfit?" asked the sergeant patiently. "What happened?"

"A box of books." She looked directly at Eddie. "It was stolen from my car."

It wasn't a serious crime. Olive knew that. She also knew there was little chance that the police would catch the thief. It was the principle of the thing that had brought her here. That, and the fear the experience had instilled in her, like a virus, causing her skin to grow cold and clammy, creating that sickening, clangorous noise in her ears.

The sergeant flipped open her notebook. "Okay. Let's get the details down here."

Marlise Beyer, twenty-seven, was almost as tall as Eddie. She had black hair and blue eyes and a slim, athletic build.

"I confess it's a relief to me that somebody here is even newer than I am," said Eddie, smiling at her.

Marlise Beyer sank into the red chair as serenely as a dancer. Eddie had decided that this physical confidence was the foundation of her courage, that she clung to it like a wounded bird to a tree branch. She had no good reason to consider Marlise Beyer anything but what she seemed, a hard-working young police officer, a person with enormous grace and considerable beauty. But she thought she saw serious strain behind the constable's eyes, and knew from the flush that frequently suffused her throat that she struggled with shyness.

This was a battle Eddie waged herself. She had learned how to convince herself when she blushed that it was anger, not embarrassment, that was the cause. Marlise Beyer would come up with a trick of her own, eventually.

"Are you settling in okay?" Eddie asked her.

"Oh yes. Thank you."

"Tell me about yourself," said Eddie. "Stuff that's not in your file."

Marlise pulled her shoulders back and placed her hands in her lap. "Let's see." She riveted her gaze on the African violet that had joined the ivy on Eddie's desktop. Its flower petals were bright purple on the edges and pure white in the middle. "I find it difficult to get to know people."

"Me, too," said Eddie. "Well, that's not precisely true. I find it difficult to get to know them quickly."

"I guess that's what I mean."

"What else?"

She glanced at Eddie. "I like to work with kids. Adolescents. Is that in there? In my file?"

"Don't think so. That's interesting. You mean, talking to kids in school? About drugs, fast driving — that sort of thing?"

"Yes, but it ought to go beyond that, don't you think? This is a real small town. How much is there around here for kids to do? Probably not a lot."

"Why don't you look into it?" said Eddie.

"I could do that."

"Tell you what," said Eddie. "Do some research. Ask around in here, then out in the community. Find out what's available. Then talk to the other Members and give me a report on what you figure we might be able to offer."

Marlise was nodding. "Okay. I will."

Eddie's journal entry read, "This is only her second posting. There's not much in her file, but what's there is very encouraging."

Later that day, Eddie got a call from an old friend. Marjorie Gillam was a colleague with whom she had worked in Burnaby. Distance had grown between them when Eddie embarked upon her steamy, ill-fated affair with Alan McCurdy. By the time Eddie had told Alan to take a hike, Marjorie had been transferred to the Surrey detachment, and they had never really re-established their relationship.

"I think we should talk," said Marjorie once they had exchanged pleasantries. "Are you off over Christmas, or New Year's?"

"I'm working Christmas," said Eddie. "Off but on call New Year's Eve and New Year's Day, back at work January fourth."

"I've got two weeks. Taking holidays. But I'm going to my folks' in Calgary. How about if I come over there to Gibsons right after New Year's?"

"Sure. Great. But what's this all about?"

"Are you getting on Alan's case? Officially, I mean?"

Eddie's stomach plummeted, as if she were in an out-of-control elevator. "Why?" she managed to say.

"It'll keep until I see you," said Marjorie. "Don't worry. It's not urgent. But I think we ought to talk."

———

He never did figure out what to do next. He mulled it over for weeks, avoiding the meetings, unable to come up with a plan. He was frustrated and fed up with himself when one day he saw her on the street, hurrying through the rain to her goddamn Honda, no umbrella, rain flattening her hair and pissing into her briefcase — and just like that, he felt that she was in his life again.

And now it came back to him, all of it, every minute: the day they met; their friendly exchanges at the meetings; the gradual deepening of their relationship; her snapping at him that time . . . it was hard to believe he'd taken that so seriously. Friends disagreed, it was one of the things that happened between them. Moments like those could be forgotten, set aside.

Certainly, at the very least, she deserved a chance to apologize. She took her work seriously, just like he did, and he decided he could overlook the way she'd insulted him, if — if — she had the grace to say she was sorry.

Yeah, she was sorry, alright. Had to be. In fact — he couldn't believe he hadn't thought of this before — she'd probably been stewing about their little dust-up for all these intervening weeks. Worrying about having offended him. Afraid that she might have thrown a spanner into the works here, destroying what had been slowly, surely developing between them.

And so, with no plan in mind, he prepared himself carefully for the next meeting, selecting a tight pair of jeans, a shirt that set off his eyes, and his favourite jacket, made of soft black leather. It was a cold, drizzly evening, but his spirits rode high and hopeful.

He was the first arrival, which conferred upon him the responsibility for turning on the lights and making the coffee. She got there soon after. The door opened and she stepped into the room and the light fell upon her like summer sunshine; she was for a moment outlined in gold, her fair hair incandescent. She closed the door, put her shoulder bag on the table, and joined him at the coffee machine.

"Welcome back," she said. "Need any help?" She gave him a shy little smile and ducked her head, linking her hands behind her.

His heart literally melted. He felt it dissolve and flow away into veins and arteries and capillaries and he kept his eyes on her face; if he was going to die because his heart had liquefied, he wanted Rebecca Wilson's eyes to be the last thing he saw.

"Are you alright?" She placed her hand on his arm, and at her touch, his heart plunged back into his chest and reconstituted itself. He wanted to laugh out loud. She was a magician.

He put his hand over hers, where it rested on his black leather sleeve, and gave it a quick squeeze. "Yeah. Fine. Somebody walked across my grave, that's all."

She chattered on for a few moments about graves, and how many of them must have been trodden upon by Canada geese, and he watched and listened, baffled but charmed. Finally she clasped her hands and said, "So let's do it. You make the coffee and I'll put the stuff out. Okay?"

He smiled back at her and allowed her to put out mugs, spoons, bowls of sugar and sugar substitute, and the tiny tubs of cream that were kept in the meeting hall's refrigerator. He sighed to himself, watching her, imagining her in his tiny kitchen.

Her car was on the fritz, as it turned out. She had gotten a lift to the meeting with a neighbour. Casually, he offered her a ride home. And when she accepted, he grinned to himself, wondering how many times over the last month she'd pulled this same scam, in the hope that he'd be there to take her home. He felt a great and protective tenderness for her then, imagining her disappointment when week after week, he hadn't shown up.

When he ushered her into the Lexus, it was as if she were the reason he'd bought the car in the first place. Other people had ridden in it, admired it. Lots of them. But it was her reaction he'd been waiting for. And she didn't disappoint him. At least, not much.

"What a gorgeous car," she said, sinking into the passenger seat. "Oh, dear. A person could go to sleep just sitting here."

And when he started the motor, its throaty purr sounded like sex. He was almost embarrassed, it was so palpable — a tiger-throated rumbling that spoke of sexual aggression.

"Wow," she said. "How fast does it go?"

He told her about the Lexus, recited all the way to her front door things about the car that he thought might interest her. He got carried away, of course. When he pulled up in her driveway she was looking slightly shell-shocked, like she'd been given more information than she could comfortably absorb.

"I'm sorry," he said humbly. "I'm kind of obsessed, I guess."

"That's okay. It's very interesting. Really. And it's truly a beautiful car." She opened the door before he'd opened his, and he had to hurry around the vehicle to help her out. "Thanks for the ride," she said. She looked up at him inquiringly. "I don't suppose you could handle another cup of coffee, could you?" she asked politely.

His heart broke loose and hung, quivering, in his chest. He closed the door. "I think I probably could," he said, smiling at her.

It was the beginning of the rest of his life, he thought, following her into her house, relieved to find that he could still walk.

Inside, he smelled a fragrance that was partly her perfume, partly furniture polish, and partly fabric softener. He stood just inside the front door with his hands in his pockets, suddenly nervous, and over and over he told himself not to rush it . . . *take your time, be cool, don't make assumptions, go slow oh for chrissake please please remember go slow. . . .*

"You take it black, right?" she called from the kitchen.

"Right," he said, and flushed with pleasure because already she'd begun memorizing his habits.

She returned to the living room. "I've put the kettle on. Instant's okay, I hope," she said, scooping into her arms a small black cat that had appeared from somewhere.

"Oh yes. Instant's fine."

"This is Tom-Tom."

"Ah."

"Sit down, why don't you?"

Carefully, he sat down. "This is an — an interesting house."

She laughed. "You don't need to be polite. It's a mish-mash. But it's kind of cozy. I like it."

It had started out as a three-room cottage, she told him, but rooms had been added over the years as families outgrew the place: a long, narrow one across the back that was now a kitchen-dining area; a square one on the west side, a combination office/guest room/storage area, which had two windows, one looking into the neighbours' side yard and one in the wall separating it from the living room; and a smaller room, her bedroom, which stuck out like some kind of growth on the opposite side of the house.

"I own it," she said proudly. She set the cat down and gathered her hair in her two hands, and he waited for her to lift it and twist it and pin it up at the back of her head, but instead she let it go and shook her head, causing it to fly off in all directions. "There's the kettle."

He didn't move while she got the coffee, although he wanted to. He wanted to cruise the house; he longed to stick his nose into every crack and crevice, to open every drawer and cupboard, to search out photographs and letters and clippings and all the things that constituted her life, that kept her private and sequestered. His hands trembled with the effort to keep still. He sat on them, to numb them, to prevent himself from *rushing things. . . .*

"Drink up and run," she said cheerfully, handing him a glass mug three-quarters full of black coffee. "Sorry," she added apologetically, "but I'm bushed. It's been a long day."

"Yeah," he said. "Me, too."

She sat on the sofa and the black cat jumped up beside her. All he remembered of the rest of the evening was the sight of her there, positioned as if he were an artist, painting her: her left arm resting on the top of the sofa; the cat in her lap, her right hand stroking him; her head bent in an attitude of such softness, such fragility and gentleness, that tears prickled at the backs of his eyes. He rubbed his palms hard against his thighs, against the coarseness of his denim jeans.

After a while, he cleared his throat. He wanted to empty his soul to her. He longed to tell her everything that lived in his heart. *Don't do it, don't do it, don't rush it, don't rush it. . . .*

"Better get going," he said, setting his mug down on the coffee table.

She got quickly to her feet, partly because she was a genuinely polite person and partly because she was tired; he could see this in her face.

"Thanks for the coffee," he said at the door.

"Thank you for the ride," she said.

He considered kissing her. On the cheek, since they had only just begun. But he listened to the voice in his head, which told him he couldn't screw anything up by going too slow, but he could sure as hell screw it

up by going too fast. And so he only smiled at her.
"Good night, Rebecca."

"Good night," she replied.

As he drove home, he thought that he had never been
so happy.

He dreamed about her, of course. Or maybe he lay
awake, and it was thoughts of her, flecks and flashes of
memory, that inhabited his restless night, gladdening his
heart, seducing him.

SEVEN

Matt Tomlinson, Eddie's next interview subject, was the detachment's intellectual. At thirty-six, he was also their oldest Member, a year older than Eddie. He was a recent addition to the Force, having taught sociology at the University of British Columbia for several years following graduate school at the University of Toronto. Gibsons was his first RCMP posting.

"What do you think is the most important characteristic you bring to the job?" Eddie asked him.

He grinned at her. "Have you been reading psychology texts, Sergeant?"

Eddie blushed, converted embarrassment into anger — and then didn't know what to do with it. She made slits of her eyes and waited.

"Sorry," said Matt. "Well. Let me think." His gaze travelled from Eddie's face to her desktop, to the filing cabinet behind her, to the bulletin board on the wall, and finally to the window, where weak winter sunshine trembled through the glass to fall upon the bare floor. "Curiosity, I think. I'm insatiably curious."

"What else?"

"I don't seem to have any fear," he said thoughtfully.

"That's handy," said Eddie dryly.

"But then I haven't been in many situations which might have called for courage," he confessed. "So I don't know for sure how true that really is."

"Hmmm," said Eddie. "You have a daughter, right?"

"Right. Sonia. She's twelve. She lives in Vancouver with her mother, but I see a lot of her." He hesitated, then added, "She's the most important thing in my life."

"What made you decide to become a cop?"

His face assumed an expression of utter blandness. "It was an abrupt decision," he said, "but not a sudden one. Hey." He leaned forward, tapped the edge of her desk with his index finger. "You wanted to talk to me about dogs, I think."

Eddie wrote in her journal, later, "He's self-assured. Intelligent. Someday in the not-too-distant future I'm going to get him to explain about his 'abrupt' but not 'sudden' decision to leave the academic life and get trained as a cop."

"You remember we're gonna lose Orsato in the new year," said Buster at lunchtime. He had eaten a Caesar salad, a bowl of minestrone, and a double burger (two patties) with fries. He popped the last french fry into his mouth and licked his fingers.

"I remember," said Eddie. She wondered again about Nick Orsato's sexual orientation, and she wondered if Buster and the others wondered about it, too.

She had finished her chowder long ago and was sitting at the restaurant table with her chin in her hand, watching Buster enjoying his food. He was completely absorbed in the eating experience. Eddie thought about his wife, Irene, and tried to guess what their weekly grocery bill might come to.

"Peck's up for promotion, too," said Buster.

"I know it," said Eddie irritably.

"He gets himself transferred, maybe some of the other guys'll have a better chance with the chicks around here."

"Married guys like you," said Eddie. "That's what we need more of around here."

Buster moved his plate to the edge of the table and flipped open a file folder with a sigh. "Okay. Down to business, eh, boss?"

Earl Chen, the proprietor, hustled over from the cash register. "All finished? Still working. You need more coffee." He whisked Buster's plate away and immediately returned with the coffee pot. "Nice atmosphere for work here. Better than the cop shop."

The back part of the café stood on stilts, suspended over the beach. Netting hung from the walls, with various marine-related objects clutched in its folds: a sheaf of dried seaweed, a battered oar, pieces of driftwood. Potted fig trees stood in the corners. The back wall was all windows, covered with horizontal venetian blinds that could be lowered against the sun when necessary.

"It isn't just the atmosphere, Earl," said Eddie. "Atmosphere by itself, that would never cut it with us guys."

"I know I know," said Earl, beaming. "It's the food. My food is very good. I know." He brushed crumbs from the table with the palm of his hand and hurried away, wiping his hand on the huge wraparound white apron that was his uniform.

Earl had once operated a restaurant in Sechelt, an establishment that still bore his name. But he'd found retirement intolerable. His new enterprise in Gibsons was so far nameless, except for the leftover sign above the door that read CAFÉ.

It was just after two o'clock, and Eddie and Buster were almost the only customers. A couple of middle-aged women sat at a nearby table drinking coffee and murmuring earnestly. A man Eddie recognized as a teller at the bank was sipping a Coke and paging through Vancouver's morning tabloid.

Earl kept a table for four in a corner by the window reserved for cops, but Eddie didn't like to occupy it when the place was crowded. Buster had complained loudly from noon onward that hunger pains were distracting him from his duties, but Eddie was implacable: they had agreed upon one-thirty, and one-thirty it was going to be. She ignored his bellyaching as long as she could, then, finally, yelled out to him to go buy himself a goddamn doughnut.

He was feeling much better now. He looked serene and complacent, sitting there opposite her. Without taking his eyes from the file folder, he lifted his beefy arms, stretching to loosen the constraint of his shirt sleeves, and rested his forearms on the edge of the table. "You're on for Christmas," he said.

"Right."

He looked up at her. "You don't have to be, you know."

"I know. I'm on."

"Okay," he said cheerfully. He tapped the file with his fingertips. "Bev and Jim, they've asked for days off. I suspect they're going to Regina, introduce him to her folks." He grinned at Eddie. "I say let's give 'em the days. They get back from Regina, then they can tell *us* they're engaged. Maybe we'll pretend to be surprised, maybe not."

"Yeah. Let them go."

"So how about Marlise to keep you company?"

"Sure," said Eddie, taking a sip of coffee. "Good. I like Marlise."

"She's been asking around about programs for teenagers."

"Yeah, I know. I think it's a good idea."

"Okay," said Buster comfortably, eyeing the roster. "That's that, then. And now, two on call. How about Hammond?"

Eddie thought about it. Glen hadn't asked for time off over the holidays, he was a bachelor. . . . "Why not?" she said.

"And . . ." Buster ran his finger slowly down the list. "Tomlinson?"

Eddie hesitated. "Who else is there? Maybe we ought to use him on New Year's, in case he wants to see his kid over Christmas."

"Chapman?"

Eddie gave an involuntary groan. Bert Chapman had developed a crush on her the instant they'd met. Eddie was finding this difficult to deal with.

Buster laughed. "He'll get over it. He's just never had a female boss before."

"Yeah, okay. Make Bert the second guy on call."

"Now," said Buster, flipping to a new page in his notebook. "New Year's. And then we're done here."

Eddie sighed, and gazed out the window at the water, and wished not for the first time that a big white yacht would miraculously appear and magically carry her away.

Ten down, two to go, thought Eddie wearily later that day, mustering a smile for Glen Hammond as he slid into her office and walked toward her with a lithe and easy stride.

"Sit down, Glen. I've got your file here, of course, but this is all official stuff. I need to know you a little better than that. Okay?"

"Sure. We want to get to know you a little better than the obvious, too." He eased himself into the diner chair, hands on its aluminum arms. "I have wondered as long as I've been here where Jablonski ever found this thing."

"Me, too," said Eddie, momentarily disconcerted. She was easily discomfited by Glen Hammond. Sometimes she thought she sensed resentment there.

He was about Eddie's height, slimmer than Buster Sheffield but not wiry like Nick Orsato. He had well-muscled thighs and forearms. Medium brown hair that fell across his forehead. Lustrous blue eyes. A prominent, bony nose.

"So," said Eddie, with a smile meant to be encouraging. "Tell me something important about yourself."

He sighed and lifted his eyes briefly to the ceiling. "Let's see. I'm single. Been on the Job for twelve years. I think I'm pretty good at it." He rubbed his forehead. "Most of the time."

The sun was struggling to shine through the overcast sky. Again and again, throughout the afternoon, the world had briefly brightened then darkened again.

"What are your ambitions, Glen?"

He turned from the window and looked directly at her for several seconds before replying. "Not sure yet. I've been in Gibsons since 1994. I've gotten to know it pretty well. I like it here. I like the fact that it's a small town, yet close to Vancouver."

Glen Hammond was thirty-four. He had come to Gibsons from Churchill, Manitoba, and before that had served in Ottawa and in southern Alberta.

"You've seen quite a bit of the country," said Eddie.

"Yeah. Time to settle down." He grinned at her. "Maybe."

Eddie said, "We've got you down for Christmas duty. That okay with you?"

He shrugged. "Sure. Fine."

Her journal entry read, "Don't know what to make of him. I don't think he likes me much. But it's only a feeling." She sat back and watched a splotch of sunlight fade from the floor. Then she went on, "He's smart. Personable. Attractive. His record's no more than adequate. Doesn't seem to have much drive. Was it ever there, I wonder? And he's been here for a few years now. You'd think he'd be getting restless, wanting to move on."

As she closed the journal and stuffed it in her desk drawer, she remembered a morning when she'd been in her office and Howard Peck and Glen Hammond had come in from the parking lot, through the door at the end of the hall. They'd been in the middle of a conversation about target practice; apparently they both needed — or wanted — extra drill with the new sidearm, the 9mm that had replaced the Smith & Wesson.

"When do you want to do it, Howie?"

"Let's check the roster Monday morning and work out when we're both off. Then I'll call Vancouver and set it up."

"Good," said Glen. "Good!" Eddie could almost hear him rubbing his hands exultantly.

She followed them into the main office with a sheaf of material to tack up on the bulletin board. She greeted them both as they shed their jackets. Howie sat down at his computer, leather creaking as his holster pressed on the chair back, and Glen went directly to the coffee machine.

Eddie, ripping outdated announcements from the board, overheard Howie making a phone call.

"Can't make it tonight, lover. . . . Ah, I know, me too. . . . Can't say, not yet. I'll get back to you, okay?"

When he got off the phone Glen was standing by his carrel holding a mug and grinning at him. "Is that a brush-off I just heard?"

Eddie was mildly surprised. Had she become invisible?

"Don't think so," said Howie thoughtfully, cranking up his computer. "Could be. Not sure yet."

"What's she like?" Glen wanted to know.

Eddie turned and gave him a pointed look, but Glen ignored her.

"Come on, Glen," said Howie. "Some other time, okay?" He nodded in Eddie's direction.

Now Glen looked at her. "Ah. Right. Inappropriate conversation for a squad room run by a woman." He smiled, brilliantly. "Sorry, Sarge."

"Not at all," said Eddie stiffly. "Don't mind me."

She turned back to the board and started tacking up the new stuff.

"I think I'm in love," Glen blurted.

Eddie rolled her eyes at the bulletin board.

Howie laughed. "Of course you are. I am, too. Always. But the question is, are they in love with us?"

There was a brief silence. Eddie glanced uneasily over her shoulder. They were lost in thought.

Then Glen placed a hand on his chest. "Of course they are. Always. For we are irresistible," he said solemnly.

"Forgive me, gentlemen," said Eddie, fastening the last message to the board, "but I am about to throw up." She retreated down the hall to her office.

A little later, Matt Tomlinson knocked on her door. She knew it was him because he had his own special knock. Besides, there was a pane of clouded glass in the door. She couldn't see faces through it, but by now she was able to recognize everyone by their silhouettes, their postures, their bearing.

She was expecting him. Olive Parfit had spotted her stolen books in the second-hand section of the local bookstore, whose owner had been unable to explain their presence there, and Eddie had asked Matt to look into it.

"Come in," she called.

"Okay," he said, coming toward her, notebook in hand. "I talked to the bookstore woman. Wagner, her name is. Helena Wagner. And the other one, the victim, Olive Parfit. This is a weird situation. Not sure what the hell's going on." He sat down and started thumbing through his notes. He glanced up at Eddie. His eyes reminded her of the young Paul Newman. "Vehement, Helena was. At first. Indignant. But she didn't keep that up for long. Couldn't, could she? Ms. Parfit was even

more vehement. They were definitely her books, handed down to her through her brother from her father —
her father's name was scrawled in every one of them. I
called the nephew she got them from, that's how thor-
ough this investigation's been. And so the bookseller
'fessed up to possession and sale of stolen goods." He
grinned.

"So how did she end up with them," said Eddie,
"these books belonging to Olive Parfit?"

"That's the weird part. She says they were left on her
doorstep. Literally. She comes to work in the morning,
there's a box outside the door of the shop. It's full of
books. There's nothing on or in the box to say where it
came from. The carton itself is new, it's got U-HAUL
printed on the sides.

"There are those inscriptions, of course, but they're
no help either. 'To Arthur' (that's Olive's dad) 'from
Margaret' (that's Olive's mom). So Helena decides she'll
hold on to them for a while, see if anyone claims them.
And this she does. And then she decides, 'Christmas
approaches, I'll see if I can make a sale or two.'"

Eddie glanced at her watch. It was fully dark outside,
and way past dinnertime. "So what have we got here?"

Matt looked at her reproachfully. "Be patient,
Sergeant. I'm getting to it. One day Olive wanders into
the store and recognizes the books. She also recognizes
Helena's description of the U-HAUL carton they came
in — the nephew got a bunch of them when he and
Olive were packing up her brother's house. So.
Somebody stole the box from Olive's car and donated it,
anonymously, to the bookstore." He lifted his shoulders.
"Now as for the *why* of it. . . . Haven't got a clue."

"What does Helena figure the books are worth?"

Matt referred to his notebook. "Somewhere between
twenty and fifty bucks, depending."

"Depending on what?"

"On the enthusiasm of her patrons for the works of Winston Churchill."

"So it wouldn't be worth it. She didn't do it. Steal the box."

He grinned again. "Probably not. For one thing, she couldn't have known it was there. In the car. Olive's car. On that Sunday."

Eddie levelled a steely glance at him. "You're enjoying this, aren't you?"

"I am. Yes."

"Soon I may strike you," said Eddie thoughtfully.

He laughed.

"Is there any reason to think that Olive might have — I don't know — misplaced the damn box?"

"Well, according to the nephew it was definitely in her car when she left Vancouver because he put it there. And she says she was tired, so she stayed in the car on the ferry, nobody could have taken it then." He held up three fingers. "She had three boxes. Two medium size, one smaller. That's the one with the books in it. All three in the back seat, *on* the back seat. She gets home, goes inside, puts down her purse, what have you, comes out, opens the back door of the car, hauls out the first box."

Eddie watched him, thoroughly exasperated.

"She takes it into the house, puts it . . ." He paused to check his notes. ". . . in the kitchen." He looked at Eddie. "There's kitchen stuff in it, you see. Dishcloths, napkins, that kind of thing."

"Get on with it."

"Right. So, the next box, that would be the second one, she fetches it, puts it in the living room. There's some books in this one, but mostly here there's what you'd call memorabilia, things. . . ."

"I said, get on with it, Constable," Eddie snapped.

"Right. Sorry. Now she definitely remembers, she says, that when she went out there for box number two, box number three was still there." Suddenly he was serious. He leaned toward her, resting his forearms on his thighs. "But listen, Eddie. It's dusk. It's getting cold outside. And the wind's come up."

She was looking at him skeptically. "How do you know the wind's come up? And what's that got to do with anything, anyway?"

"Olive told me," he said patiently, "that when she was inside with the second box, the wind blew the front door shut."

"Okay, so it's windy," said Eddie. "Wrap it up, will you? I want to get out of here."

"The point is, if somebody did steal the damn thing, he had to be out there watching her. And she wasn't dallying in the house. She'd carry a box inside, put it down, walk back out to the car for the next one. So he had two or three minutes, tops.

"Which means, if in fact some dude did swipe the box from the back seat of Olive Parfit's car — which I believe to be the case — he was hiding someplace very close to her while she was moving back and forth between her house and her car."

He was looking at her so intently that Eddie was uneasy.

"Just imagine it, Eddie. The wind's blowing. The sky's getting dark. Some guy's hiding in the bushes watching this woman. He sees there's one more box in her car — sees that because she's left the car door open. He emerges from his hiding place, takes the box, and disappears." He sat back, holding his notebook loosely in both hands. "What if she'd come out just a little bit sooner? What if she'd seen him, this guy who'd been hiding in the bushes, watching her? What might have happened then?"

Eddie, staring at him, imagined him telling stories to his daughter. She could just picture it. Ghost stories. He must have scared the shit out of the poor kid when she was little.

"It was probably some teenager," she said, breaking the spell. "There isn't enough for kids to do around here. I have that on good authority."

Matt shook his head. "I don't know. Maybe."

"I've gotta go," said Eddie. Her chair scraped against the floor as she stood up and headed for the hat rack on which she'd draped her cap and her jacket. "Thanks, Matt. Write it up, will you?"

He thought about her almost all the time — it was hard for him to concentrate on anything else — but it was when he was in bed, ready for sleep, that she really took over.

He was in bed now. It was midnight. His bedroom window was open and he could hear the metronomic swish of the sea on the gravelly beach.

He was planning their next date. And the next one, and the one after that. Christmas was only weeks away; there was a lot of arranging to do, a lot of discussing, decision-making. Was she a religious person? Would she want to go to a church service at Christmastime? Would she want to buy a tree, and decorate it?

And if so, where would they put it? They both had homes. His was only rented, but it was on the beach and he could hardly wait to bring her here, to walk along the sand with her and finally make that fucking beach his own. They could decorate the outside of his house, maybe, with those white lights that looked like icicles, and then go over to her place and put up a tree.

And what would they buy as presents for each other? He had to get to know her better, and fast, too. It had to be just right, his first Christmas gift to her, and although he knew everything about her that was important, had known all that from the moment he first laid eyes upon her, there were all kinds of extraneous things he hadn't the faintest idea about. What movies did she like? Did she read a lot? Did she like video games? What sports did she do? Did she travel a lot?

He wondered what his mother would have thought of her. He always wondered this, luxuriating in the knowledge that he'd never know. He'd never brought any of his dates home, not after the first time, and she'd always bugged him about it, mocking him. "What is it, then?" she'd say to him. "Am I not good enough to meet them? Or are you ashamed of them, maybe? Are they whores, these dates of yours?"

He'd brought the first one, Emma, home because he wanted his mother to see that some other female person had a straightforward, uncomplicated affection for him.

She was standing on the porch when they pulled up in front of the house in the '55 Chevy that he'd bought on his sixteenth birthday, six months earlier.

"I'm nervous," said Emma, with a little smile. "See? My hands are all sweaty."

"There's nothing to be nervous about," he said, but his own heart had speeded up and he felt like his feet were too big for him: he tripped over them as he climbed out of the car. Emma wiped the palms of her hands on her skirt and took a deep breath. He felt a whoosh of pride because she was so pretty. He took firm hold of her hand and side by side they proceeded up the walk toward the house.

His mother smiled at them as they approached, and held out her arms.

"Welcome," she said, and she put her hands on their shoulders and kissed their cheeks, first Emma's, then his. He was very surprised.

His mother held open the front door and ushered them inside, into the living room, where a jug of lemonade and three glasses sat on a tray on the coffee table.

"Sit down," she said, and they did, side by side on the sofa. His mother dropped gracefully into an overstuffed armchair and crossed her legs. She stroked the arms of the chair and he felt an ache in his chest; she had done this so often over the years that the fabric had worn thin and shiny.

"This is a lovely house," Emma offered.

"Thank you," said his mother. "Lemonade?" They murmured yes, and she poured three glasses. "Use the coasters, please."

The silence was like a separate, stronger presence in the room. It was unaffected by the clink of ice in their glasses, the sighing of the sofa as Emma adjusted her position. He felt like the silence was trying to tell him something. He was becoming more and more tense and he knew that Emma was, too, but his mother seemed unmoved. She watched them curiously, as if they had come to her to make an announcement, or a confession. Her eyes never left their faces, even when she lifted her glass to her mouth to drink. His discomfort continued to grow, threatened to become anger. Would he ever ever be able to make casual conversation, to smooth over potentially awkward situations with small talk? What a dork he was, he thought dismally.

"Where's Dad?" he said finally, desperate.

His mother shifted her gaze from Emma to him and considered this. "I don't know."

He nodded, as if she had given him real and valuable information. He thought his face was getting red.

"How serious is this thing between the two of you?" said his mother.

"Oh gosh," Emma blurted. "We're not serious." She put her glass down and rubbed her hands together.

He didn't dare look at her. He stared at his mother.

He knew his face was red now; he could feel it burning. He couldn't think of anything to say, and so he just nodded.

"Well, that's probably good," said his mother. He thought he saw amusement in her eyes and didn't know how to interpret this. Was she teasing them? Or mocking them?

"We'd better go," he said abruptly.

They got to their feet, all three of them, and his mother preceded them to the front door. She was the same height as Emma, he noticed. She had probably been prettier than Emma, when she was young. He wondered if she'd been as unpredictable then as now, if she'd made her boyfriends nervous.

"Have a good time," she said warmly on the porch, but he saw no warmth in her eyes and for a moment he felt sick to his stomach.

That night he was in his room getting ready for bed when she tapped on his door.

"Come in."

"She's a good-looking girl," said his mother, leaning against the door frame.

He sat on the edge of the bed.

"Seems nice enough."

"She is."

"Does she get good grades?"

"Better than mine."

"Are you having sex?"

His face flushed and he looked at her helplessly, resentfully. She folded her arms and looked back at him, curious.

"I've had that talk," he said, pushing the words past a large, painful lump in the back of his throat. "With Dad." He thought he must be beet red all down his neck by now. His whole body was probably bright red. Like a goddamn traffic light.

His mother nodded thoughtfully. "Good night," she said as she stepped out into the hall and softly closed his door.

Emma was sweet but he'd never been serious about her. He'd never been serious about anyone, as long as his mother was alive.

He linked his hands behind his head and listened to the sea, which was quiet tonight, and he was utterly content. Because of Rebecca. Because he'd found Rebecca.

He could tell that what he felt was a mature passion because even though his work schedule hadn't permitted him to attend the last couple of meetings, he'd been content not to see her. In fact, she managed to fill his mind and his heart so completely when she wasn't even with him that he sometimes wondered if he could bear to be in her presence day in and day out.

His brain overflowed with images, both real and imagined: she lifts her hair above her head, smiling at him; she picks up the black cat, cuddling it in her arms; she hands him a mug of coffee, her bright eyes dancing; she runs, laughing, her shoulder bag bouncing, lifting in her hands the long skirt she's wearing, with a sleeveless T-shirt on top; she sits on the beach, on a piece of driftwood, looking dreamily out to sea; and now she's in his kitchen, her hair piled on top of her head, cooking breakfast for them, wearing only a bra and panties.

He shuddered and took hold of himself, tried half-heartedly to control himself, but "Fuck it," he said. . . .

Later, he turned over and stretched, seeking cool places between the sheets. The curtains at the window seemed to flutter, beckoning him. Outside, the sea murmured plaintively.

They needed to talk, soon. And seriously. There were things he had to know. Did she plan to continue working after marriage? Did she want children? What kind of people did she have as friends? What kind of a family did she come from? He wanted to know them — wanted them to adopt him.

He sighed, his eyes closed, and he fell asleep smiling.

Eddie had been dreading her interview with Bert Chapman, a twenty-seven-year-old constable who had been with the detachment for two years.

"Your record is excellent," she told him when they sat down together the following morning. "You like your job, don't you."

"Oh yes. Very much. This is the life for me. No doubt about that."

His eyes followed her every move. They never left her face, big brown eyes with thick lashes. He bent toward her, his hands clutching the aluminum arms of the red chair so tightly it was as if he was trying to prevent himself from falling at her feet.

Eddie was physically weary after only ten minutes of Bert Chapman. She wondered if she ought to bring it up, but decided once again not to. She would continue to ignore the fact that the young man seemed dazed yet giddy in her company. She had observed him, unnoticed, on the job and in conversation with other people and had been relieved to see that he behaved then in a perfectly normal manner.

"You've got flaws," she said to him. "Everybody has. Tell me what your biggest fault is, as a police officer."

"I'm too quick to judge. But I'm working on it," he told her earnestly, grasping the chair arms, his body straining forward; Eddie felt herself leaning backward in response.

"And what do you do well?"

He gaped at her, then scrambled to recover himself. "I think I'm fairly observant. A fairly good observer. Yeah, I think I am."

Eddie nodded. "Good. Good." There was a long, painful pause. "You and Maryanne," she said finally, "you've been married how long?"

"Almost a year," he said absently. "I think it's about a year."

Her journal entry read, "Please god, make this infatuation go away. I hope it isn't a sign of things to come. I can imagine him lusting after colleagues — perps — witnesses. But that's ridiculous. He's a good cop, smart and confident. This thing he's got, this virus, it's going to be short-lived and a-bloody-typical."

He didn't know why he hadn't called her yet. He'd look intently at the phone, a slim, black instrument with all the bells and whistles, call forward, call waiting, caller ID, you name it. He'd pick it up and press her number. She was on his speed dial, of course, right up there at the top — Number One, Rebecca. And then he'd push the off button before the phone had rung even once.

He couldn't figure it out. He had every reason to call her. Hell, she'd be wondering every day why he *wasn't* calling. But he just couldn't bring himself to do it.

Maybe he wanted to keep her guessing. Could that be it? Was he really that much of a sonofabitch?

Or maybe he just wanted to enjoy these last days as an unattached guy, savouring his freedom while at the same time impatient to give it up. Who the hell knew.

This must be love, he told himself, as for the hundredth time he placed the phone carefully back in its cradle. A blur of lust and confusion, faith and uncertainty.

He dressed meticulously for the next meeting, showering first, wielding the blow dryer expertly, rolling on deodorant, shaving, slapping on cologne. Once again, he wore a shirt that accentuated his eyes and a pair of jeans that clung to his butt and his thighs. He tossed the keys to the Lexus in the air and watched himself in the mirror as he caught them. He knew he looked good.

This time he was almost the last to arrive, and the first thing he noticed was that she hadn't saved a seat for him next to her.

The meeting got underway.

She refused to meet his eyes. Shit. She was punishing him for not having called her. She was hurt. The coffee date had meant so much to her, and she'd thought it had meant the same to him — which of course it had. But he hadn't called, and what could that possibly mean, except that he'd lost interest in her?

He felt a painful spasm in his chest. He willed her to look at him. And eventually she did. She was responding to something someone else had said and her eyes swept the entire group, including him. With a cold, stark shock he realized that her expression did not change when she looked at him, her eyes did not linger on his.

She is really mad at me, he thought, awed. And he sat back to wait out the rest of the meeting, sipping absently at his coffee, patiently biding his time.

Finally, chairs were pushed back, mugs were rinsed and placed upside down in a dish drainer, and people collected their possessions and headed for the door. He made sure he was right behind her as she hurried into the parking lot, digging in her bag for her keys. She was extraordinarily beautiful again tonight and he was looking forward to telling her so, eager to apologize for his neglect of her. She would be snuggled next to him on the sofa — either his or hers, he didn't care which — her hair a fragrant cloud against his cheek, his hand linked in hers. He could hear his voice, both reassuring and seductive. They would make love tonight. He was sure of it. . . .

She was unlocking her car when he said, "I'm so sorry, Rebecca."

She looked up at him, smiling a little. "Pardon?"

He smiled and leaned across the roof toward her. "I should have called you. I'm sorry."

She frowned. "Called me about what?"

He searched her face for clues but saw only bewilderment. No hurt, no hostility — no *fondness,* could he find there. "How about some coffee?" he said. "At my place, this time. Or yours," he added desperately. "Whatever you like."

"That's nice of you," she said, glancing at her watch, "but I can't."

He heard himself blurting it: "Why not?"

She grinned at him, across the roof of her car, almost conspiratorially. "I've got a date." She gave him a little wave, climbed into her car, and drove away.

EIGHT

It was early evening, New Year's Eve. Olive was enjoying a cup of coffee, having just finished her dinner — only two pieces of buttered toast and a bowl of canned peaches, since she would be eating a full meal later, at midnight.

She was sitting at her kitchen table, listening to the radio. The broadcaster was remarking upon the fact that nothing untoward had occurred so far, as the world moved from the twentieth century into the twenty-first. Olive thought he sounded disappointed. She was reminded of an acquaintance at the senior citizens' hall who had asked her recently if she thought the universe knew about the coming of the new millennium. Olive, after a moment of incredulity, had decided despite herself that this was an interesting question.

But no, she decided now, carrying her dishes to the sink. It was most unlikely that anything beyond the skein of citizens spread thinly upon its very own globe knew or cared anything about the passage of time, even when a certain moment in this passage seemed to human beings to be symbolic. She found this ineffably sad, as if humankind were an orphan that had been abandoned at birth by — by what? In her mind, Olive fashioned a sea creature of mythical proportions, a cross perhaps between a dragon and an alligator, saw it eons ago opening its gigantic mouth and vomiting onto the land a gaggle of tiny, rubber-limbed people who scrabbled upon the beach like a bunch of maggots, making desperate mewling sounds as their mother slipped back beneath the water and disappeared forever.

Olive rinsed her dishes and stacked them in the dishwasher, and wiped the table and the countertops. It was the last time she'd tidy her kitchen this year. The last time in this century. In this millennium.

She wondered why she hadn't given much thought during her lifetime to this auspicious event. She remembered once working out how old she would be and thinking that she'd probably make it that far, but that she would be too old and decrepit to appreciate or participate in the festivities. She must have been very young, when she had embarked upon these calculations.

And then she hadn't thought about it again until last New Year's Eve, which she had spent alone, as had become her habit. During that evening, though, watching television because she couldn't think of anything else to do, she had decided that next year, on the night during which 1999 became 2000, she didn't want to be alone.

She was to join acquaintances at the hall for an evening of dancing and conversation and a midnight supper. At the moment, however, she was feeling weary and slightly melancholy, and was not looking forward to the occasion, was in fact considering staying home after all, when the phone rang. It was Danny, calling from Vancouver to wish her a happy New Year.

"I've been watching the TV, have you?" he asked. "And it looks like nothing's collapsing anywhere. It's going to be the Y2K bug that wasn't," he said, chortling comfortably. "What're you doing with yourself tonight, Olive?"

She had finally gotten him to stop calling her Aunt Olive. She felt that this had brought their relationship

onto a new, sturdier footing — that of affectionate
friends. She liked this, because people were stuck with
their relatives but they got to choose their friends.

"I'm supposed to go to a thing at the seniors' hall,"
she told him. "But I'm not feeling much like going out,
just at the moment."

"What's your weather like?"

"It seems to be alright," she said reluctantly, peering
through the gap between the curtains over the kitchen
window. "Cloudy. But not raining, as far as I can tell."

"It's very mild," Danny offered. "Not likely to snow,
or even freeze."

"No," said Olive dryly, "I can't use the weather as an
excuse, that's for sure."

"Maybe it's just the getting there that you don't look
forward to," he suggested. "I mean, once you're there,
you'll most likely have a good time, right?"

"Right," she said wearily. "I'm sure you're right."

"And if you stay home, Olive," he added seriously,
"you'll probably regret it, don't you think?"

Olive laughed, capitulating. "Right again." She
inquired about Danny's plans.

"I've been invited to a house party. And I'm going,"
her thirty-seven-year-old divorced nephew said bravely.
"Who knows? Maybe I'll meet an interesting, unattached woman. All things are possible, aren't they? On
the eve of a new millennium."

Olive hung up the phone feeling considerably cheered.

She had selected three possible outfits to wear to the
seniors' do, and now she took them from her closet, laid
them upon her bed side by side and studied them critically. She eventually chose a lavender-coloured dress,
empire-line, that came to mid-calf. It had long sleeves
and a V-shaped neckline. With it she would wear
silver earrings and a wide silver bracelet that had
belonged to her mother.

Olive had only recently begun to attend events at the seniors' hall. She was among its youngest patrons and didn't yet feel entirely comfortable there. She had offered to transport some of the older people this evening, but by the time she got around to doing this everyone had already made arrangements.

The event was to begin at nine o'clock, but Olive thought three hours of socializing before dinner was excessive, even if it did include some dancing. She hadn't been to a dance there yet, and she was rather apprehensive about what constituted dancing among senior citizens.

She would leave her house at nine-thirty, she had decided.

It was now just a few minutes before nine.

Olive poured herself a small glass of sherry and sat down in front of her television to wait.

He got home late in the afternoon carrying a bunch of lilies he'd picked up for his New Year's Eve hostess. He wished he could dredge up some enthusiasm for the new millennium. But this New Year had turned out to be no different from any other. Less than a month ago he'd been riding high, drunk on love and the future. No more.

He put the lilies in water and stashed his groceries in the fridge, then gave in to a tiredness that had been growing in him all day, creeping up his body like moss up a tree trunk. He lay down on his bed, indifferent to the crumpling of his well-pressed pants, his tailored sports jacket.

He had turned on no lights, but the bedroom curtains were open and the grey light of the dying day seeped in, its complexion that of dirty dishwater. He felt a sudden depression. He thought he might never again be able to move his body, which felt as heavy as a hulking marble

statue, or one of those pyramids in Egypt. He tried to
stir upon the bed, and couldn't, and closed his eyes, giving in to it, letting despair take hold of him, feeling its
enormous claws pressing with a strange affection upon
his chest. He struggled to breathe, but was otherwise
submissive.

He lay there for a long time. It was the cool, impas-
sive touch of tears upon his face that finally shamed him
into consciousness. He blinked his eyes open, and saw
that darkness had claimed the day.

He sat up and swung his feet to the floor, remaining
for a moment on the edge of the bed, looking up at the
window; from this angle he could see only the sky, dark,
starless, moonless. He stood and leaned on the window
ledge, looking out onto a chunk of weedy lawn, a strip
of sand, and the sea. Across Shoal Channel was Keats
Island, many of its houses brightly illuminated with
strings of holiday lights. To his right, although he couldn't
see it from his window, the marina. And beyond
the marina, tucked with others along the curve of the
bay, was her house.

He thought about this, resting his forehead against the
cool window glass, warming himself with the thought of
her, needing at the moment not to see her, but rather to
breathe in her scent. He shook his head slightly and tried
to laugh. He pushed away from the window, pulled the
curtains closed, and made his way through the dark bedroom, across the hall, and into his kitchen, where he
turned on the light over the stove.

Resting his hands on either side of the electric range,
leaning again, apparently studying the four cold black
burners, he wished that the damned New Year's thing
was over, that his days off were over and he was back at
work, back in the normal goddamn world. He hated the
aimlessness that accompanied holidays, the painful rup-
ture in the routine that nurtured and stabilized him.

But it was almost over. Tonight, tomorrow, Monday — then, the real world. Tonight he'd go to the damn party. He'd been invited to two, and had promised to show up at both of them, though he probably wouldn't.

Tomorrow he'd wash the Lexus and take it out on the road for a while. Look up Jemima in the chat room. Spend some time with his favourite car-chase video game. Plus he wanted to add to his pitifully small CD collection — he'd download some stuff from one of the sites he'd read about.

And on Monday, if the ferry situation wasn't too chaotic, maybe he'd slip over to Vancouver, see a movie, have dinner in a good restaurant.

Yeah, he thought. I can do it. I can get through it.

He opened his fridge to see what was available for dinner.

Rebecca Wilson had spent the day removing all traces of Christmas from her small house. The tree was down and had been carried out to the backyard. One day next week she would take it to a free wood-chipping event that was held every year by a local nursery. The decorations had been packed in their boxes and put away on a shelf in the storeroom. She had slapped an elastic band around a stack of cards that now sat on her desk; eventually she would go through them carefully, sending notes to people who had written her lengthy or significant messages. And she had energetically swept and vacuumed, removing pine needles shed by the Christmas tree and tracked by Rebecca and her holiday visitors — and the cat — into far-flung corners of the house. She had bought a shallow bowl of spring bulbs — mini-daffodils, a primula, a hyacinth, and a couple of small tulips — and this sat in the middle of her living-room coffee table: a cheerful, fitting symbol, Rebecca thought, for the dawning of a new era.

Her housework completed, she was too keyed up to
think about getting herself some dinner, and found herself whirling from room to room, feeling much younger
than her thirty-some years, longing to turn cartwheels,
wishing herself upon a huge sunlit lawn, or in a gymna-
sium. She felt the cat watching her from the bed, yawn-
ing hugely from time to time, following her comings
and goings in and out of the bedroom with equanimity.
She knew he was hoping she'd be able to resist the urge
that frequently possessed her to pick him up in her arms.
Tommy hated being picked up.

She decided that if her host and hostess hadn't
planned to clear the living room for dancing, she would
do it for them.

But the party was still hours away. She really must eat
something, make herself a bowl of soup at least. Then she
would shower, blow-dry her hair, dress up to the nines,
and be off.

He stood under a willow tree, partly hidden by its cas-
cading branches. They were almost completely bare,
though, and he knew he'd be easily visible to someone
looking for him.

He didn't know what he was doing there. It worried
him that he'd come. There was a chalky taste in his
mouth and his body was stiff with tension.

Leaves from the willow tree had piled up around its
perimeter in an almost perfect circle on the lawn. The
grass near the tree's trunk was muddy, squishy with the
rain that had fallen for days.

He was wearing his best clothes. A dark grey overcoat
over a dark grey suit, a white shirt, a tie in tasteful shades
of olive and maroon, black socks and shiny black loafers.
Oh, if his old mom could see him now.

The willow tree stood between the street and her
house. Music drifted across the water behind the house

from one of the yachts moored in the marina, their masts and rigging edged with Christmas lights, creating glittering silhouettes.

His breath came from his mouth in small, white clouds, fragile, almost unsubstantial. He concentrated on this, listening to himself breathe. The house was dark except for a porch light above the door, and the nearest streetlight was too far away to shed light upon the willow tree.

His gloved hands were in his pockets. His shoulder was almost touching the trunk of the tree. In the sky above, the moon had appeared, but it was frequently obscured by quick-skidding clouds. The world was restless.

He was amazed at himself. What was going on here?

A byway, a lane of sorts, led from the street parallel to her driveway, alongside her house and backyard, straight down to the water. He thought it was probably used as a boat launch.

He shifted his position slightly and felt under the soles of his dress shoes, below the mushy layer of mud and grass, the hard roots of the tree pushing up through the soil.

He was waiting, under the willow tree, although he didn't know why. She had obviously left the house: the place was empty. So why was he standing there staring at it? Did he plan to stay there until she came home? To see if she came home alone?

He'd hung about her house that other night, waiting under a tree across the street for her to show up with her fucking "date." Waited until he was cold and wet and as pissed off as he'd ever been. They'd blown into her driveway in her goddamn Accord about one o'clock in the morning and although he'd waited outside under the fucking tree for another three hours the guy had never come out.

In a house up the block and across the street, a party was in progress. Music blared forth every time the door was opened to admit a new arrival, clashing with whatever was currently emanating from the speakers on the yacht in the marina. Another car pulled up in front of the party house, blowing its horn, and four people who were waiting on the porch turned and waved. He saw smiles on their faces, huge and distorted. There was nowhere to park near the party house. Cars were jammed in bumper to bumper on both sides of the street. It was a small house, he thought, to hold so many people. The car trundled on past, in his direction, and pulled into the byway that led to the water to get turned around. He pressed his back against the tree trunk, hiding as best he could, feeling like a goddamn idiot. He had seen the driver, a blond man of about his own age, and the passenger, a dark-haired woman. He didn't know whether they'd seen him. The blond man backed his car out of the byway and headed slowly back past the party house, disappearing around a bend in the road.

He'd never seen the guy again, her fucking "date." He'd finally worked it out that he must have come over on the ferry as a foot passenger, and had gone back the next day to wherever he'd come from.

He continued to wait. He heard a car door slam, and the sound of laughter, and a few minutes later the blond driver materialized, on foot, in the middle of the street, his passenger clinging to his arm. She nuzzled his neck as they mounted the steps to the party house, and on the porch, he bent to kiss her before ringing the doorbell.

Really, he didn't give a shit about her "date." The point was, he'd misread the signals again. Gotten it all wrong. She didn't love him, had never loved him. She'd flirted and teased and trifled with him and she'd never loved him.

He watched as the door was opened, music rushed out, and the new arrivals were ushered indoors. He looked at his watch: it was almost ten-thirty. He moved from under the tree and crossed the lawn to the street. He walked four blocks to where he had left the Lexus and circled it slowly, inspecting it carefully for dents and scratches and spots and smudges. It was pristine.

He sat behind the wheel for several minutes, watching through his new windshield as if expecting her to appear. She didn't, though. Finally, he started the motor and drove away.

NINE

New Year's Eve, 1999, and Eddie was, by choice, at home alone.

She considered herself a social creature. Why else would she have chosen the police force as a career? Bottom line, a police officer had to like people, to possess a certain basic faith in humanity. Her job, as she saw it, was to encourage this humanity — which she might have described as an instinct for goodness, and justice — and to deal firmly with those in whom this instinct was permanently or temporarily absent. Yes. A social and sociable creature. So why had she decided to spend the dawn of the new millennium alone? She could be celebrating with Cindi, or with her neighbours, the McKechnies. And Buster Sheffield was having a party in Gibsons; the whole detachment would be there, except for people who were out of town or on duty.

She peered through the living-room curtains at the Mercedes, parked in front of the house. She knew it deserved a garage. She tried to make up for this by caring for it lovingly. She'd considered getting a cover for it but thought that might attract too much attention to the car, and to the fact that it was precious to her.

Nick Orsato had permanently endeared himself to her on Thanksgiving weekend when he'd burst into Earl's café and headed straight for the table Eddie was sharing with her father, who was visiting from

Vancouver. "Sarge," he pleaded, "tell me that's your vehicle out there. The Mercedes. Please."

"That's my vehicle out there," said Eddie smugly. "The Mercedes. The green one."

"I can't believe it." His face was positively glowing.

"Dad," said Eddie, "I'd like you to meet Nick Orsato. Nick, my father."

"Mr. Henderson," said Nick. "It's a pleasure. Can I join you?" he asked Eddie. "Just for a minute?" He glanced at the till. "I'm getting a take-out."

"Sure," said Eddie, and Earl brought him a coffee to drink while he waited.

"So tell me about it," said Nick. "The Mercedes."

"It's an '85," Eddie began. "Automatic."

"A 300D," said Nick.

"Right. I saw it two years ago in the ferry lineup. There was a FOR SALE sign in the window." She had prowled around the empty vehicle for several minutes, looking for flaws and finding none. "The next day I called the phone number on the sign. The guy lived in the Fraser Valley. He wanted $12,500, I offered $12,000, and he took it."

"It's a great car."

"It's rather like riding in a tank," said Eddie's father dryly.

"I didn't know you were into cars, Nick," said Eddie.

"Oh yeah. I am. A sports car," he said wistfully, "that's what I lust after. A Mercedes SLK, black. A yellow BMW Z3."

Eddie laughed. "Or a fire-red Porsche," she offered.

Her father had clucked his tongue at this exchange. "Those are dangerous automobiles, aren't they? And expensive. And don't they seat only two people?"

Eddie turned from the window. She wondered what the guy in the Valley would have to say about her parking the Mercedes on the street.

I'm definitely getting myself a dog, she thought.

In lieu of a Christmas tree, she had enveloped the large fig tree that lived in a corner of her living room in a multitude of tiny white lights. A row of candles glowed from the narrow mantel. A three-hour fake log sat in the fireplace, ready to be lighted. A split of champagne was cooling in the fridge, next to ingredients for her favourite dinner.

Eddie showered and washed her hair, leaving it loose to dry into a crinkly cloud that would be unmanageable but pleasing; she liked the feel of it against her bare neck and shoulders. She put on nightclothes: a silky, sleeveless, sun-coloured T-shirt and matching panties, a deep rose, lounging robe and a pair of slippers.

The television set was already on in the living room, pursuing the year 2000 around the globe. Eddie prepared her dinner, served it, and put the plate down on the coffee table, along with a linen napkin, a knife and a fork, and a glass of red wine.

While she ate, she watched dancers materializing out of the sand, somewhere in the Pacific. Wall-walkers in Australia. The Dragon Dance on the Great Wall of China. Kiri Te Kanawa singing from New Zealand. An endless explosion of fireworks up and down the Thames. In Paris, a long shuddering of lights kindled the Eiffel Tower, then fire burst from its torso and it seemed to begin to move; its exultant straddle, powered by light and fire, threatened to become a stride, as if it were Mary Shelley who had flung the millennium switch.

Eddie watched, oddly proud, as the planet's human population greeted the new century, the new millennium, together. She was grateful for television, which made it possible for people to see that around the entire globe an event was being joyously and simultaneously celebrated, oblivious of the boundaries of geography,

culture, race, religion, age, and gender that customarily
separated Earth's peoples.

"Hot damn," said Eddie, pouring a second glass of
wine and returning to her dinner: a T-bone steak, a
baked potato with butter and sour cream and chopped
green onions, fried mushrooms, and oven-roasted asparagus with parmesan cheese.

Yeah, she thought. I need a dog. Matt Tomlinson, who
apparently had had nothing to do with acquiring his
daughter's pet, had suggested that she call somebody at
the dog squad for advice. She'd do it next week.

Adult or puppy? Male or female? Should she get a
purebred, or rescue some poor creature from the SPCA?
She pondered this as she finished her dinner and waited
for the millennium to glide into her own time zone.

He arrived at the home of his friends Fred and Pepper
Halliday shortly before eleven. He liked their home,
which had an interior courtyard that was about the size
of an ordinary living room. The courtyard wasn't particularly inviting in winter but he thought it still must be
good to have your own personal chunk of parkland
inside your house. He noticed that they'd draped the
bare-limbed birch tree out there with coloured lights,
and backlit some of the shrubbery. On the garden bench
sat a life-size stuffed Santa Claus. He found this unnerv-
ing, probably because no kids lived here.

Fred was a large man, pink-faced and perspiring, with
a deep, mellow voice, a life insurance salesman whose
wife Pepper was also large, a smiling woman with a mass
of curly brown hair. He didn't know how she'd come to
be called Pepper but connected it with the freckles that
were spattered across her face and hands. Now, as she
welcomed him, thanking him for the flowers, taking his
coat, smiling, he tried to imagine her naked. Would there
be freckles all over her body? Or only where sunlight

regularly touched her? He shook himself out of his fantasy and accepted a glass of wine from Fred, whose forehead was studded with beads of sweat.

The living room, which opened onto the courtyard through sliding glass doors, was crowded with people. He knew most of them slightly and didn't want to get to know any of them any better. If it wasn't for the damn Santa he'd wander outside and sit on the garden bench for a while, watching his breath become fog, scrutinizing the drizzle on the slim branches of the birch tree, which was gleaming like something incandescent.

Pepper loomed suddenly next to him, a vessel seeking harbour, offering a tray laden with pastries. "Empanadas," she said, winking at him. "Have one. Have two. Have several." She tossed her head back and laughed, and he took one of the pastries, plastering a grin on his face. At that moment he knew he couldn't stay there any longer.

Pepper sailed off into the throng. He demolished the empanada in two bites, feeling eyes upon him. He glanced across the room and saw a young woman studying him. He couldn't remember her name, and he didn't like the purposeful expression settling on her face. Casually, he put down his glass and eased himself around a group of chattering guests and into the hall, where he began rummaging through the coats that were draped on hooks or lying on the floor by the front door.

"Oh, you're not leaving, are you?"

He swung around, gripping the collar of his overcoat. "Yeah, I'm afraid I am," he said, smiling at her, the redhead who'd been eyeing him. She looked a little the worse for wear. Her lipstick was smudged and her elaborate hairdo was slightly out of whack. He thrust himself into his coat.

"I was hoping we could become better acquainted," said the redhead, articulating fussily. Her right elbow was cuddled into her waist. Her arm flared out to the side, her hand clutching a glass of something tea-coloured.

"I promised to drop in on another bash," he said, diving into his pockets in search of gloves. But he knew he wasn't going to the other party. He didn't feel like seeing anybody from work.

"Take me with you," said the woman. "I'm good company." She laughed.

"Sorry," he said. He opened the door and backed out into the night. "Another time, maybe."

He strode to the Lexus through thickening fog. What now? What now?

He suddenly saw himself back in Fred and Pepper's house, creeping stealthily through the crowd, through the sliding door into the courtyard, grabbing the stuffed Santa by the neck, and shaking him into small pieces, choking him until his head fell off. He even felt his hands twitch and stopped walking and lifted them, examining them. He had strong hands, square, strong hands. He looked at them as if he'd never seen them before, looked in amazement at those hands.

What have I been doing with my life? he asked himself. Frittering it away, that's what. Living each day like it was a bloody preamble.

Well no more, he said to himself, and then he said it again, out loud this time: "Well no more, no damn more."

The fog was a cloud fallen from the winter sky, smelling of winter, of earth and rain and dormancy.

Twenty minutes later he was once again standing under the willow tree. He took a deep breath and moved from the protective embrace of the narrow, leafless strands that served as its branches, and crossed the lawn to the side entrance of Rebecca Wilson's house. It was almost eleven-thirty. He tried the door, which was locked.

The night she'd invited him in for coffee she'd forgotten that her house key was on the same ring as her car key, and that was at the garage where her car was getting fixed. And so he knew where she kept a spare. He plucked it from under a large rock at the edge of a flower bed. It was cold, and slippery with damp soil. He wiped it clean with his handkerchief, unlocked the door, and slipped inside.

The fragrance in the house that he'd found so intoxicating was still present. He took a deep breath. He thought he could smell flowers tonight, in addition to perfume and fabric softener and furniture polish. He dropped the house key into one of his coat pockets and his handkerchief into the other, gazing around the darkened living room, waiting for his eyes to adjust. Eventually shapes emerged. In the faint light seeping through the drapes that were drawn across the window, he moved around the room, touching the back of the sofa, running his hand across the surface of the large, glass-topped coffee table, fingering the music that was open on the piano.

He moved into the dining area and looked through the french doors at the boats in the marina. The music he'd heard earlier in the evening had gotten louder, and he imagined the house trembling in the racket once midnight arrived. Some leaves still clung to the branches of a tree in the yard next door, large leaves hanging limp, tattered and morose, looking like abandoned decorations the morning after.

His overcoat rustled as he folded his arms, and he heard himself sigh. He rocked back and forth, heels to toes, and inhaled the scent of her perfume, her home.

He opened drawers and cupboards, went back to the living room and rifled through a pile of magazines on the coffee table, and finally went into the bedroom, where her cat was curled up on one of the pillows. The cat looked at him suspiciously, its eyes glowing eerily, reflecting light from the marina that entered the room through a large, uncurtained window.

Suddenly he heard a raucous cry, and through the window he saw people gathering on the deck of a sailboat, leaning over the rail, talking excitedly and pointing at the water. Someone's fallen in, he thought. He stopped himself from rushing outside to help. People had emerged onto the decks of some of the other boats and there was shouting back and forth. A dinghy was lowered from the stern of a yacht blazing with lights; there was even a decorated Christmas tree on one of its wide decks. He watched two men in tuxes — their white shirts bright and gleaming, streaked briefly with red and green as they hurried beneath the coloured lights — clamber down an aluminum ladder on the side of the boat into the dinghy, which they manoeuvered quickly toward the person in the water. He couldn't see the guy until he was hauled into the dinghy and the people ogling from the other boats started cheering and applauding. The guy looked to be about twenty, and he had on only a white T-shirt and a pair of jockey shorts.

He turned from the window. The cat was still watching him. He wanted to pick it up, carry it outside, and dump it into the bay. Not because he hated cats. He didn't give a shit one way or another about cats.

It was because it was *her* cat. Rebecca's.

He crossed to the bedroom doorway, studying the cat. At least he knew what was going on now.

The cat was staring at him. He thought it had probably read his mind. He shook his head, looking at it. There was no way that cat would ever let him get his hands on it.

He prowled the house feeling strangely liberated now that he'd figured out why he was there. He was there to bring pain into her life.

He stood in the middle of the living room, frustrated and irritated. What a boring room this was. A boring house, a boring woman. Why was it so important to hurt her? A boring bitch, nothing more, he wanted only to get her out of his fucking life.

The cat remains on the bed. It is a double bed with two pillows. It is made in an old-fashioned way, with blankets and a bedspread, the top of which folds back to enclose the pillows. And this is where the cat lies, in the indentation between the pillows. He has warmed it up and doesn't want to leave it.

The man is standing again in the bedroom doorway. The cat has seen him before, but never here in this room. The cat sinks deeper into the pillows, as if he might disappear, become part of the bedspread. He has been uneasy since he first heard the man outside, crunching his feet upon the sidewalk, then opening the door and coming into the house.

The cat cannot recall when he's seen him before. His memory of him is indistinct. He lifts his head, invisible antennae quivering, seeking signs — warnings. He regards him, immobile in the doorway, as a danger to himself and to cats. And the cat gathers his feet beneath him, preparing to spring and run.

He hears a sigh from the man, who turns his head away, looking through the window into the increasingly clamorous night. The man takes his hands from his pockets, holding a pair of gloves, and slaps the gloves distractedly against his thigh. He steps backwards, out of the cat's sight.

The cat hears him moving around in the house again, occasionally muttering under his breath. The cat considers following him, keeping an eye on him, but doesn't. He doesn't want the man's eyes upon him again, large eyes, the whites luminous, wishing pain upon the cat. He opens his mouth in a silent meow as he listens to the man pacing.

Suddenly the man is in the doorway again, looking not at the cat but at the chest of drawers in the corner. The cat creeps to the edge of the bed and descends to the floor — he is a grey ripple, like water over a dam — and slips under the skirt of

*the bedspread. He vaults over to the wall and crouches imme-
diately below the hollow he's made between the pillows, a hollow that retains his body warmth, the hollow to which he will
return as soon as this man has left the house. He listens,
pressed against the wall, paws flat on the floor, tail coiled
around his body, ready to rocket out from under the bed in an
instant should the man lift the bedspread and aim his eyes at
the cat. He knows just where he'll go, too — somewhere the
man can't reach — and he'll get there so swiftly the man won't
see him hide.*

*Suddenly there is a lot of noise outside. Car horns honking
and people shouting and whistles blowing. But the man pays no
attention. The cat hears the sound of furniture being opened,
moved around, kicked. And this increases his unease. But what
causes the hair on his back to rise is the man's babbling, a plain-
tive susurration that becomes louder and angrier until he is bel-
lowing, producing a shocking racket, punctuating it with sobs.
The cat doesn't move. After a while the man grows silent. He
sits on the edge of the bed — the cat can see the heels of his
shiny black shoes — and it's quiet in the house again, except
for the slight squeaking of the mattress whenever the man
adjusts his position. The cat wishes the man would leave.*

And finally, he does.

He stood in front of the house pulling on his gloves,
thinking that the meetings were almost the only times
he'd ever seen her. Except for when she'd invited him
into her house, of course. And that time right after they'd
first met, when he'd gone out for a run and happened to
pass her house. She'd been bringing in the morning
paper and he had stopped to catch his breath and watch
her. And then he'd called out to her and waved, and she
turned and waved back.

She was imprinted in his mind forever as she'd
appeared that late summer morning, clutching a powder
blue robe around her slim waist, the same robe that was
hanging now from a hook on the back of her bathroom

door. Her feet were bare, her hair was a mess as she
reached for the newspaper. When she looked across the
street at him her face was completely open, because he'd
caught her by surprise. And even though she'd quickly
hidden herself behind an expression that was polite but
watchful, he had seen her real self, and she *knew* he'd
seen it.

And this was the bond between them.

It was so *clear* to him.

He strolled the several blocks to his car, wondering if
she'd talk about it at the next meeting, about the guy
who broke into her house on New Year's Eve.

Some party-goers waved to him from a front porch.
"Happy New Year!" they called. He looked at his watch.
The world was half an hour into the new century. He'd
missed the millennium moment.

As he got near the Lexus, he pulled his gloved hands
from his pockets and heard a tiny clatter as something hit
the street. He stopped, looked down, and bent to pick it
up. It was her house key. He looked for a moment in the
direction of her house, then pulled his wallet from his
pants pocket and tucked the key inside.

TWO

Eddie knocked on the McKechnies' front door late the next afternoon and when Alvin opened it, she held out a bottle of champagne. "Happy Year 2000," she said with a smile.

"Happy New Year," he said, taking the champagne with one hand and giving her a clumsy hug with the other. "Come on in, I'll open it right away."

In the small foyer, Eddie shucked her jacket and toed off her shoes. Then she joined Alvin and Bev in the living room, where Bev, sitting in the rocking chair, was closing a library book and Alvin was taking champagne flutes from a glass-fronted cabinet.

"Hi, Bev," said Eddie, bending to kiss the older woman's cheek.

"Sit down, Eddie. Thanks for the bubbly. Can you stay for a while? Pâté and crackers?" She set the book down on the floor beside her chair.

"No thanks, I know you're going out. I'll just have a drink with you, then I'll be off."

Alvin — round-faced, big-bellied, short, and balding — carefully poured the champagne and offered it around to Eddie and Bev, who was tall and slim, with a face so lined and weathered she looked more like a former seaman than her seaman husband did. "It's gonna be a good year," he said, lifting his glass.

"To the New Year," chorused Eddie and Bev, and they drank.

"I've got a proposal for you two," said Eddie a few minutes later, looking from Alvin to Bev and back again.

"Propose away," said Alvin expansively, settling himself in one of the easy chairs that flanked the fireplace.

That evening Eddie met Cindi in the pub for a drink before dinner. Cindi was still sulking because Eddie had refused to party with her on New Year's Eve, and had been only partially mollified when Eddie told her she'd made dinner reservations for them at the only restaurant in Sechelt that was open January first.

They were very comfortable in the pub. Everyone knew who they were, of course, and they were seldom hit on. The guy had to be very, very drunk who would hit on an RCMP sergeant. Drunk and probably hostile. When he was a hostile drunk the bartender took care of him, which Eddie accepted because after all it was his responsibility. And besides, why should she have to take somebody on when she was off duty?

Eddie was pushing her beer glass in slow circles through a puddle she assumed was the result of the glass sweating, trickling moisture down the sides, creating this damn pool on the table in front of her. She was thinking about Matt Tomlinson. About his investigation into the stolen books. Wondering how seriously he took his job. It seemed to have his full attention — but what did he do with his conclusions about things? Did he rearrange events, occurrences, in his own head for his own amusement, or did everything happen precisely as he described it? Was his apparent compassion genuine? Was his sporadic impassivity under his control? Eddie was intensely curious about why he'd decided to ditch an academic career and join the RCMP.

She remembered a call Matt had picked up a month or so ago that had come from the Gibsons pub at the bottom of the hill: an intoxicated customer was insisting that he was sober enough to drive.

"I'll go with you," Eddie had said, grabbing her jacket.

"You sure?"

"Sure I'm sure. Let's go. You drive."

Matt sped down the hill and pulled up swiftly but silently into the parking lot, and he and Eddie got out of the car. A small crowd had gathered.

The inebriated patron had climbed into a dark blue pickup and was kneeling on the driver's seat while an employee of the pub tried to persuade him to get out of the truck.

"I think he's right," said Matt, ambling toward the pickup. "You ain't fit to drive, man."

Eddie was hanging back a little, eyeing the crowd, which included several other people who weren't entirely sober. She wondered where their loyalties would lie. Sometimes the citizens were on your side. Sometimes they weren't.

"How about waiting a while?" Matt suggested to the drunk. "Have a coffee before you go. The burgers here are good, too."

The guy was trying to focus, frowning in the direction of Matt's voice.

A restless teenager in the crowd was bouncing from one foot to the other and shaking his hands in the air in front of him. Eddie eased toward him.

"Who the hell're you?" said the drunk.

"I'm a cop," said Matt. "Who're you?"

There was a giggle from somewhere in the crowd.

"He's a cop," someone called out and laughed.

Matt ignored this. "What's your name, pal?" he asked the drunk.

"I don't think he's your pal, Jerry," said the restless teenager. "He's a cop, for fuck's sake."

The assemblage waited impassively.

Eddie waited.

Then the drunk passed out. The top half of his body fell through the open window. "Whoops," said Matt, supporting him.

The crowd sighed, and began to disperse — all but the teenager, who covered his face with his hands and wept. Matt got the drunk out of the truck and he and Eddie stashed him in the back of the patrol car.

"Can we drop you somewhere?" said Matt gently to the teenager.

The kid shook his head.

Matt murmured to Eddie, who hesitated, then nodded.

Matt said to the kid, "Do you want to come with us to the detachment, wait there for him to sober up?"

The kid thought about it and slowly nodded.

"Okay. Come on then." Matt had put his arm around the boy's thin shoulders, steering him to the patrol car. "It's gonna be okay."

"What're you thinking about?" asked Cindi. Eddie knew she hated it when a companion's mind wandered.

"Dogs," said Eddie.

"So you're on about that again. I can't believe you're serious. What are you going to do with a dog when you're away at work all day?"

"I've made an arrangement with my neighbours. Alvin and Bev. They said they'd look after him for me. I'm going to pay them. They don't want any money, but I'm going to pay them anyway."

"You better not get a puppy, then. It'll bond with your neighbours instead of with you. The first months are crucial." She drained her beer glass and waved at Chloe, the barmaid. "What kind of a dog?"

"Twice again?" said Chloe, whose long red hair made Eddie think of Anne of Green Gables. She was exceptionally tall and willowy, and she wore tight jeans and cowboy boots and let her hair hang straight and loose.

Cindi looked inquiringly at Eddie.

"What the hell," said Eddie expansively. "Why not." Chloe put their empty glasses on her tray and moved away, swinging her insubstantial butt. "I'm not driving," said Eddie to nobody in particular.

"If you're going to get a dog," said Cindi, "you ought to rescue some poor mutt from the pound."

"Can't," said Eddie, watching Ted behind the bar. "Thought about it. Can't."

"Why not?" asked Cindi accusingly, scrabbling up the last broken peanuts from the bowl in the middle of the table.

"Because I wouldn't be able to choose," said Eddie. "Because I'd end up taking all of them. No." She shook her head firmly. "I'm going to talk to somebody in the dog squad, next time I'm in Vancouver. I'll probably get a German shepherd."

Chloe returned with two more glasses of beer and a full dish of peanuts.

"My turn," said Eddie, paying for the drinks. "Or maybe a Lab," she said.

"So how many unattached guys work for you?" Cindi wanted to know.

"You've asked me that before. I've answered you before."

"Yeah, well, refresh my memory."

"Five. One of them's a woman. And one of them I'm pretty sure is gay."

"So three."

"Yes."

"Tell me about them," said Cindi hungrily, sipping her beer. Her brown eyes above the rim of the glass were wide and dreamy — rather like a cow's eyes, Eddie thought, and she giggled.

"It's not funny." Cindi put the glass down hard and sat back, crossing her arms in front of her. "What the hell am I doing here, Eddie? Answer me that."

Eddie looked around the pub. "Well . . ."

"Not *here* here," said Cindi irritably. "In *Sechelt*. What am I doing in *Sechelt*?"

"Well," said Eddie, "you're getting journalistic experience, I guess. Next stop, Kamloops, maybe. Kelowna. Penticton? Eventually, Vancouver. Maybe Toronto. Or Montreal. Except you don't speak French, so scratch Montreal."

"I want to be a foreign correspondent," Cindi confessed.

"Then you probably will," said Eddie.

She was depressed all of a sudden. Angry, too. Where the hell was her own ambition when she needed it? She felt — vague. Unfocused. Un-bloody-satisfied.

She remembered overhearing Beverly Brooks and Marlise Beyer in the Gibsons pub one night. She'd been hunched over in a booth, making notes — she couldn't remember why, now, probably it was just cover, looking absorbed in something so nobody would decide to join her.

"Well there's no big bucks in the damn job, that's for sure," Beverly had been saying. "But I gotta admit, there's tons of gratification."

"It's still mostly a man's field, though," said Marlise.

"Yeah, it is," said Bev cheerfully. "You're gonna get some persecution. You gotta give it right back."

"Hmmm. I'm not too good at that," Marlise admitted.

"You'll *get* good at it, believe me. Another thing." Bev leaned closer to her; Eddie figured she was a little bit drunk. "I make it a point to get to know the wives. 'Cause when they see you're not interested in hopping into the sack with their hubbies, I mean, that mollifies them, to some extent."

"So you've never been attracted to a married guy you worked with?"

"Oh yeah, I have, sure," said Bev. "But you can't let it

happen, that's my philosophy. Hey, things are tough enough out there, right?"

"So I know you and Jim are — a couple," Marlise began.

Beverly whispered something in her ear, and Marlise smiled. "Really? Congratulations, that's great."

"But nobody else knows," said Bev, wagging a finger under Marlise's nose.

"I won't say a word. But listen, apart from Jim, what do you think of them? The guys?"

Bev pursed her lips and gazed into space. "They're a pretty sexy bunch, is what I think." She and Marlise took refuge in laughter. "Seriously," she went on. "Seriously. Well, Howie, he's full of himself, very offensive — until he starts making nice, and then you're a goner." She contemplated the empty beer glass in front of her. "Nick Orsato, he's a real cutie."

"He is, yeah," said Marlise, shaking back her shiny black hair. Eddie wondered if she knew how many men in the bar were taking a subdued, and not so subdued, interest in her.

"And there's Glen, of course, keeps himself to himself, does our Glen, but I've heard rumours." She gave Marlise an exaggerated wink. "Sexy hunk, our Glen." She held up a hand. "We don't discuss Jim, because he's mine. Or Buster, or Johnny, because they're married."

"There's Matt, though."

Eddie's waning attention had sharpened then.

"Oh yeah. Matt," said Bev dismissively. "Well he's a whole 'nother story, Matt is." Here she glanced over at Eddie, who realized with a slight shock that they'd been aware of her presence all along. "I'd really like more beer," said Bev. "But I've got a feeling I've had enough."

Eddie had burned with curiosity all the way home from Gibsons.

"I want to go home now," she said to Cindi now. "I'm
incredibly depressed, all of a sudden."

"You can't," said Cindi, dismayed. "We've got a reser-
vation for dinner, remember?"

"Oh yeah," said Eddie wearily. "I forgot." She checked
the time. "We'll have to be going soon."

"We've got ten minutes," said Cindi. "So listen. Who
are they? These three guys."

Eddie looked at her blankly for a moment. "Oh
yeah." She took a drink of beer. "My unattached troops."
She sighed. "What do you want to know about them?"

ELEVEN

His mother, having been only a memory for years and years, had begun insinuating herself into his living life, which was pissing him off. He started recalling things he had no interest in recalling. Like the way she had announced her mood at the start of every day by either pounding fiercely on his bedroom door or giving it a friendly tap. He had eventually learned that if she pounded, he had to just get the hell out of there, as quick as he could. Dress fast, grab school books, snatch an apple from the bowl on the counter and his jacket from the hook by the back door and get the hell out of there. "Hey," his father would say, reproach and dismay in his voice, and he knew the first was fake and the second real but he didn't care, and his mother would be banging the frying pan around on the stove and she might swear at him as he fled, but she wouldn't try to stop him.

He was very glad when he became old enough for her not to try to stop him. He didn't know exactly when that had happened but it was a big relief not to have to sit there while she stalked around the kitchen, smoldering, her fuse lit, and him wondering if he could get out of there before she went off. Usually, when he was little, he couldn't. Usually he'd get at least one smack on the side of the head. And these smacks were really, really embarrassing because they made his eyes water, and that looked like she'd made him cry, which she fucking hadn't.

Even when the day began with a tapping rather than a pounding on his door, he still went downstairs warily, spoke only when spoken to, and stayed out of her way, and finally, when she'd sat down with a cup of coffee and her first cigarette of the day, he was able to relax.

When he'd started to date, while he was still trying to believe that the joy of sex was the same as the joy of finding your soulmate, sometimes he'd try to confide in his dates. . . . well he wasn't quite sure what he wanted to confide, he just wanted to talk, aimlessly, in the hope that he'd eventually say something that would surprise him with its truth.

"My dad — I guess you'd have to call him ineffectual," he'd told one girlfriend. "He let her rule the roost. And when he realized that things had gotten out of hand, it was too late."

"What do you mean, gotten out of hand?" she asked. He wondered if she was genuinely interested or only being polite.

"I guess when I was little, things were okay. I was easy to handle."

"Never," said the girlfriend teasingly, resting her hand on his thigh.

They were in his Chevy, parked by a reservoir. It was supposed to be a romantic place but that night it had been dark as shit. There wasn't a star in the sky, and no moon to shine down and glitter on the water; you couldn't even tell there was any water out there. Her face was a soft, glowing circle. He was amazed that he could see her at all.

"But I got older," he said, "and caused her some grief, I guess."

"You were a kid," she said. "That's what kids do."

"Not my mom's kid." He was glad of the darkness, though. He didn't know what happened to his face when he talked about his mother. Maybe he wouldn't want this new girlfriend to see whatever expression he was wearing. He made a mental note to talk about his mother while studying himself in a mirror.

"She'd get pretty mad," he said, "slap me around some. My dad knew about it. He came in once while it was happening. I remember he said, 'What's he done now?' And he sounded — just real tired."

"How bad *were* you?" said the girlfriend. "Were you, like, doing drugs or something?"

He laughed. He turned to her. She was leaning close, her hand higher up his thigh now, and he could see her quite clearly, saw her curiosity and in her voice heard hunger purring. "No. No drugs." He put his hands on either side of her face. "Let's fuck," he said softly.

Just after ten Tuesday morning Eddie was hanging out at the marina with her friend Marjorie Gillam, watching a sailboat make slow circles as it crossed the harbour. They had eaten breakfast at Earl's, where Marjorie had scarfed down her scrambled eggs with a keenness that suggested she hadn't eaten in some time. Eddie had watched, unaccountably irritated.

"Let's get out of here," she had said when Marjorie had finished, and they'd wandered along the street and down to the marina.

"Jesus," said Marjorie, admiring the view. "You've got yourself a little bit of paradise here, haven't you?" She was a tense, wiry woman with hair that Eddie envied because it was thick, dark brown and gleaming and it hung straight almost to her shoulders, turning under at the ends. No-care hair, unlike Eddie's own.

"I'm thinking of getting my hair cut very short," Eddie said sulkily, staring down into the water. Marjorie darted a glance at her and then hooted. "I'm serious," said Eddie.

"It'll never happen," said Marjorie confidently.

It was an exceptionally mild day, with frail sunshine that was warm enough to be noticed and strong enough to delicately finger aside the clouds. Between the marina and the shores of Keats Island, the sleek sailboat glided and tacked. Halyards clanked musically on the boats that remained tied to the jetties.

"So tell me about your life," said Eddie.

"I'm applying to take a couple of courses in Ottawa." Marjorie pushed herself away from the fencing she'd been leaning on and turned around, facing up the long wooden incline toward the village.

"What kind of courses?"

"Profiling. Geographic profiling," said Marjorie. "Among other things."

"You're kidding," said Eddie. She saw a small white dog emerge from the cabin of a powerboat. He looked skyward, then in Eddie's direction, and barked sharply. "That sounds fascinating."

Marjorie, squinting against the sun, said, "I won't know for a while if I'm in or not."

The dog shook himself, jumped from the boat, and hurried along the jetty toward them, his short legs pumping.

"Let's get down to cases," said Marjorie, checking her watch.

"You've got plenty of time," said Eddie as the dog drew near, swerved around them, giving them a suspicious glance, power-walked up the incline, and disappeared around the corner into a lane.

"How much?" said Marjorie. "I'd like to take a look at your new digs before I get the ferry back." She grinned. "My camera's in the car. I want a picture of you, in your office, sitting behind your desk. You do have an office of your own, don't you? And a desk?"

"Oh yeah," said Eddie. "You won't believe my desk."

"So." Marjorie turned and rested her arms against the

fencing. "Is it true? Are you going to lay a harassment complaint against Alan?"

"I want to know what makes you think I am."

"It's sort of getting around."

"Who told you?"

"You know, Eddie, I can't even remember."

"Don't believe you, Marj." Eddie looked steadily at her friend. "Was it Alan?"

Marjorie sighed.

"What did he say, exactly?"

"Oh I don't know for godsake. That you were siccing the dogs on him, something like that."

Eddie looked out across the water and remembered lunches in Sechelt, with Cindi, sometimes with Alberg, gazing out at the waters of the bay, no land directly ahead except the blue-haze ramble on the faraway horizon that was Vancouver Island. Here, only a hop, skip and a jump away across Shoal Channel was Keats Island. It was a no less pleasing sight, just different, but for a moment she was paralyzed with homesickness. An odd feeling, since she still lived in Sechelt and had visited that very restaurant just the previous evening, with Cindi.

"I taped the bastard," she told Marjorie grimly. "Screaming at me on the phone. Me screaming back." She glanced at her friend. "He threatened me, the stupid sonofabitch." She dug in her shoulder bag and hauled out a pair of sunglasses, smudged and dirty; it had been weeks since she'd needed to wear them.

"How long has this been going on?" asked Marjorie quietly.

"Can't remember, exactly. I think it started soon after I got to Sechelt. Finally I told him I'd report him, and it stopped." She looked closely at Marjorie through the sunglasses, examining her face intently, as if determined to memorize every feature. "I'm afraid that if I don't report him, it'll start again."

Marjorie nodded.

"So what do you think?" said Eddie. "What's your opinion?"

"My opinion," Marjorie said slowly, "is that you ought to hold off."

"Huh," said Eddie. "But that sonofabitch. It just *galls* me, to let him get away with it."

Marjorie put her hand over Eddie's. "I know. And theoretically, hauling him onto the mat wouldn't get you in any trouble. But the truth is, it's gonna slam some doors on you. And you're ambitious, Eddie, even if you haven't quite decided how."

Eddie looked at her in surprise.

"I know you sometimes think about joining the suits."

"Do I?" said Eddie.

"Well, don't you? And if you don't go that route, you'll be looking for bigger and better detachments, more promotions, right?" She waited again.

Eddie sighed. "Yeah. Sure." She gave a little shrug.

"It's just not worth it," said Marjorie, as if she knew this for certain.

"But if it starts up again . . ." Eddie shook her head. "I'll have to take some kind of action if it starts up again."

The dog reappeared at the top of the incline. His ears stuck straight up in the air; Eddie thought they were far too big for the rest of him. He checked out the two women closely and then headed cautiously toward them, swinging away before he reached them to scoot back down the jetty to his boat, looking back over his shoulder every so often, making sure they weren't on his tail.

Rebecca parked on the street in front of the detachment and hurried up the walk. Inside, she approached the receptionist's window and saw that the desk behind it was empty. At the far side of the room an elderly man was replacing a stack of folders in a filing cabinet, moving slowly, gracefully, absorbed in the task.

"Excuse me," said Rebecca. She had to call out several times, more loudly each time, before the man turned and saw her. She waved to him and he approached stiffly, a folder in his hand. He was a tall, thin person with a fringe of white hair and thick eyeglasses.

"Hi," said Rebecca. "I'd like to see the sergeant, please."

The man tilted his head in a manner that suggested he was having trouble hearing her. She opened her mouth to repeat herself.

"Good morning, ma'am, my name is William Kirkpatrick. You'll be wanting to talk to our receptionist, who has just stepped away from her desk for a moment. If you'd like to sit down, I'm sure she'll be back very soon." He wore dark blue suspenders over a white shirt, and a pair of khaki trousers. He gestured in a courtly fashion, and Rebecca turned around to see a bench against the wall. William Kirkpatrick smiled at her and returned to the filing cabinet.

Rebecca peered through the glass that separated her from the detachment's main office, hoping to spot a cop she knew. She heard laughter issuing from behind the reception area but nobody appeared: the office remained empty except for William Kirkpatrick, patiently filing. She looked at the clock on the wall, and at her watch, and turned to look first at the bench, then at the door. Maybe she'd leave, maybe she'd come back later — maybe she shouldn't be here at all.

"Can I help you?"

Rebecca turned swiftly. "Hi," she said to the receptionist. She knew that the woman was called Beatrice, but couldn't remember her last name. "I'd like to see the sergeant, please."

Behind Beatrice, Johnny Grieg sauntered into the office, a coffee mug in his hand.

"Oh, I'm afraid the sergeant isn't in," said Beatrice. "What's the nature of your business? Perhaps someone else can help you."

But Constable Grieg had spotted Rebecca and was approaching. "Hi, Rebecca," he said with a smile. "You got some juvenile offender out in your car?"

"Hi, Johnny. No, I was hoping to see your sergeant, actually."

"Who's out," said Beatrice.

"Nope. She just drove in," said Johnny Grieg.

Eddie had removed her jacket and hung it on the hat rack when her phone buzzed.

"There's someone out here wants to see you," said Beatrice Fitzgerald. "I told her first, you're out, but then I find out you're in, and I tell her, we've got procedures here, we've got a duty officer on duty, but oh no, she's got to see the person in charge. So what do you think? Do you want to see her? I personally wouldn't recommend it."

"I'm not doing anything that can't wait. Send her in," said Eddie, hauling a notebook from her desk drawer.

Beatrice held open the gate so that Rebecca could pass through. "Follow me," she said, and Rebecca did, trailing after her around a corner into a room that contained PC cubicles, bulletin boards, a large coffee-machine station, and several uniformed officers, only two of whom she knew. She greeted them distractedly, hurrying to keep up with Beatrice, who led her briskly down a short hallway. The receptionist pushed open a door with a small glass pane in the top half. "Sergeant Henderson," she said stiffly, "this is Miss Rebecca Wilson."

"Ms.," said Rebecca Wilson, striding across the room, her hand outstretched. Eddie stood and shook it. "I would like to report a crime," said Rebecca. "She told me I'd have to fill in forms. I don't mind filling in forms, I do it all day, I've got nothing against forms. But I also want to discuss this matter with the person in charge. It's nice to see you again. I don't think I realized when we met before that you were the new head guy around here. I'm happy that you're a woman."

"Well. Good." Eddie glanced into the corner where two straight-backed chairs sat primly on either side of a small table. She had found the chairs and the table at three different garage sales in the fall, and just before Christmas she had stripped and sanded them and painted them dark blue. The arrangement reminded her of those areas found in doctors' and dentists' waiting rooms, and in some restaurants that were outfitted for children, with mini-chairs and boxes of sturdy, bright-coloured toys. She had placed a large glass ashtray on the table, but Beatrice had removed it, reminding Eddie of the new law that had just taken effect, forbidding smoking in the workplace. Eddie had reservations about this law. She wondered if it would be applied in psychiatrists' offices, for example. Or at mortuaries. "Well, give it back to me at least," she had said irritably, and when Beatrice returned the ashtray to her, Eddie stowed it away in a desk drawer.

Rebecca Wilson didn't looked like a smoker, although this conclusion set Eddie to thinking about what a smoker ought to look like: she imagined a grey-faced person, limp hair tied back with a piece of wool, slightly stooped, her face deeply lined; she was hooked up to a portable IV, hanging onto it with one hand and holding a cigarette in the other, puffing on it hard, causing her cheeks to get so hollow Eddie could see her skull. . . .

Eddie ducked her head and began rearranging things on her desktop: the IN and OUT baskets, the mug that held pens and pencils, a stapler, a tape dispenser, a calculator. She really had to do something about her penchant

for imagining stuff at inopportune moments. Rebecca
Wilson was prattling on nervously, and Eddie let this
continue for a while until the image of the death's-head
smoker had retreated.

"Excuse me," she said. "Let's sit down over here,
shall we?"

The woman immediately stopped talking. She
watched Eddie move toward the corner and gesture to
the two chairs. "Alright," she said, and sat down, and so
did Eddie. "You could do with a rug in here," she said,
looking critically at the bare floor.

"You're right," said Eddie modestly. "And a couple of
non-official-type things on the walls."

"Yeah."

"I'll get around to it eventually. Do people call you
Becky?" Eddie asked her.

"Good god, no. Becky is a child's name," she said
loftily. "It makes me think of bony knees and freckles."

Eddie laughed. "What happened to the little girl?"

Rebecca had to think for a moment. "Elizabeth.
Perkins." She looked up at Eddie. "She's been taken into
care. She's with foster parents. I think she's doing pretty
well." She looked away, frowning. "As well as can be
expected."

After a moment, Eddie said, "What can I do for you,
Ms. Wilson?"

"My house got broken into," said Rebecca indignantly. "On New Year's Eve, for heaven's sake." She
looked upward with a grimace. "Not broken into, exactly. Entered, without my permission." She cast a furtive
glance at Eddie. "It's like a rape," she said miserably. "It's
like somebody raped my house."

"When did this happen?"

"On New Year's Eve. Shouldn't you be writing
things down? I don't mean to tell you how to do your
job, but . . ."

"No problem," said Eddie. She fetched the notebook and a pen from her desktop and sat down again. "Why didn't you report it right away?"

Rebecc, had set her handbag on the floor. She stared at the filing cabinet. "I know. Everybody's been telling me that." She looked at Eddie, her face flushed. "I don't know why. Maybe — no one was hurt, nothing was damaged. I thought you'd have more important things to do, maybe? I don't know, Sergeant."

"Okay. Tell me about it," said Eddie.

"I went out at about nine and got home very late, four-thirty, maybe five in the morning. Somebody had emptied my chest of drawers all over the bed. Underwear, socks, nightgowns — just thrown onto the bed, every which way, the drawers hanging open. They looked like they'd vomited my stuff out of themselves, you know? And the stuff hanging in the closet wasn't hanging anymore, it was on the floor, in heaps, in piles." She lifted her hands to sketch dramatic circles in the air, then sat back and crossed her arms.

"Is anything missing?"

"I don't think so."

"Was anything else disturbed? Any of the other rooms in the house tossed?"

"No."

"You said it wasn't a break-in. So what was it?"

Rebecca looked away. "I keep an extra key under a rock near the side door. He must have used that."

"Hmmm." Eddie scribbled for a while in the notebook, then snapped it shut. "Any idea who it was?"

"No," said Rebecca promptly. "Of course not."

Eddie regarded her kindly. "I'm sure it's obvious to you that it's someone you know."

"I don't think it's obvious, exactly," Rebecca protested.

"He knew there was an extra key," said Eddie. "He knew where it was. He created chaos in your house, but he didn't steal anything." She waited until Rebecca's restless gaze had settled reluctantly on Eddie's face.

"Rebecca, he was playing with your underwear, for godsake. What on earth makes you think it could possibly have been a stranger?"

Rebecca winced, but remained stubbornly silent.

It would be good if they could find the guy quickly, Eddie thought. Before he got any bolder. Rebecca *had* to know more than she thought she did. "Have you dumped anybody recently?" she asked. "In the last six, twelve months?"

Rebecca shook her head.

"Have you rejected anyone? Has somebody come on to you, and you've kissed him off, however nicely?"

"Of course not," said Rebecca indignantly.

"Okay. How about regular boyfriends?"

"I don't have a boyfriend at the moment."

"Tell me about the last one."

"For heaven's sake, Sergeant, I haven't had a single damn date since last summer, if you can believe that. Except for . . ."

"Except for who?"

"It's nothing. An old boyfriend from Vancouver, sometime in November, I think it was. It was just a lark. An impulse. He called me up, came over in the afternoon, as a foot passenger. I took him back to the ferry the next morning." She looked defiantly at Eddie. "It was nothing. Believe me. We hadn't seen each other for a couple of years, and it'll be years before it happens again. If it ever does. He just wanted to see my house, mainly."

"We'll check him out."

"Oh *puleeze*. . . ." She dropped a hand over her forehead, shading her eyes.

Eddie looked her over. "Has anything like this ever happened to you before?"

"Of course not."

"It's happened to me."

Rebecca looked up from under her hand.

"I knew who it was, that's the difference."

"And why? Did you know why?"

"Yeah. I'd dumped him."

"But I told you, I haven't dumped anyone!" Rebecca cried.

"And I believe you. But you've done something to this guy. You just don't know what. And that's what I want you to think about. Offenses. Large, small, tiny, infinitesimal. Anything that somebody who's serious about you could take seriously. Okay?"

The lines bracketing Rebecca Wilson's mouth seemed to have deepened in the half-hour she'd spent in Eddie's office. Eddie felt a pang of sympathy. She reached across the table and patted Rebecca's hand. "Okay?" she said softly.

"Okay. I'll try."

"And meanwhile — get your locks changed."

Rebecca Wilson worked in an office with four other people: Peter Stevens, her supervisor; Corinne Hatchfield, another social worker; Gloria Hyde, the office secretary; and Linda Wickerson, the receptionist. Rebecca was late getting to work this Tuesday morning, because of having visited the RCMP. But she had called to tell Linda about this first thing in the morning, and so she wasn't expected to show up on time. She ran a couple more errands, hurriedly, things she'd scrawled on a list before leaving the house: Police. Bank. Drugstore.

"Is something wrong?" asked Anna-May, the teller at her bank. "You look kinda funny." She peered closely at Rebecca. "Rattled, maybe."

Rebecca laughed, a tinny sound, and glanced behind Anna-May at Teddy, the assistant manager, who was slowly cruising among the desks with his hands behind his back. He caught her eye and smiled. They were acquaintances, after all, he had every right to grin at her if he felt like it. But the skin on the back of Rebecca's neck crawled and she didn't smile back, because maybe it was him, she was thinking, maybe it was the assistant bank manager who'd insinuated himself into her private space.

She shook her head. "I just — I forgot to pay this," she said, thrusting her cable-TV bill across the counter at Anna-May. "I'm afraid they're going to cut me off or something."

At the drugstore she avoided the pharmacist's eyes when she picked up her prescription. "Address?" he said, consulting his computer. "Here you go," he said cheerfully, dropping the birth control pills into a small white bag. He handed it to her with a smile.

He had blue eyes, she remembered, not looking at him, and he kept his hair cut very short, and he was an acquaintance, too; but she couldn't imagine him . . . Suddenly she raised her head and looked directly into his face. His smile faltered. He gave her a look that was both wary and expectant.

"Never mind," said Rebecca incongruously. "Forget it." She snatched the bag from his hand and hurried out of the drugstore.

The whole world looked different to her now. The grey skies weren't merely gloomy, they were positively threatening. The cold breeze from the ocean wasn't simply evidence of winter, it was a foreshadowing of something terrifying. When she parked in front of the office, she actually locked her car. Rebecca hardly ever locked her car, not in Gibsons, not unless she had left something conspicuously stealable in it. And today it was empty. Well, virtually empty. There were maps in the door pocket, and a few tapes in the compartment under the seat divider, and a quarter and a loonie in the circular depression meant to hold a coffee mug. Nothing that anyone would want to steal. But she locked the door anyway.

She had a home visit to do that afternoon. She needed to calm down, get focused. Hurrying up to the office door, she decided that she would collect the pertinent file, look it over at her desk, make a few notes, and flee. She would grab a sandwich and a coffee and park somewhere to eat, quietly, while she tried to get rid of her jitters. She had to concentrate. She couldn't do her damn job properly in this condition.

Goddamn him, she thought fiercely. Goddamn him, whoever he is.

She knew it was a man. She was convinced of it. Not for a nanosecond had she considered that it might be a woman who had broken into her house, violating her privacy and probably scaring the hell out of her cat.

She was going through the office door now. The first face she saw was of course Linda's . . . and suddenly she was imagining *Linda* doing it, plucking the key from beneath the rock, unlocking Rebecca's door, sidling inside.

Rebecca stopped moving, as abruptly as if she had run into a wall, and stared at the receptionist. Who smiled at her. Whose smile became uncertain, under the unblinking vehemence of Rebecca's scowl. Linda moved slightly, so that a vase of yellow tulips sitting on her desk effectively blotted Rebecca from her line of vision.

Rebecca gave herself a shake and made her way to her desk, one of two that occupied the back half of the main office, surrounded by filing cabinets.

Corinne turned from her computer. Rebecca had called her on New Year's Day about the break-in, and Corinne had convinced her to report it. "So how did it go at the cop shop?" she wanted to know. She was in her mid-forties, married to a millwright. They had three cats, two dogs, and seventeen-year-old twin boys. Despite this, or perhaps because of it, Corinne was the most serene person Rebecca knew.

Rebecca put her purse in the bottom drawer of her desk and sat down. "Oh I don't know. I don't know," she said miserably. She glanced over at Linda and whispered, "They said it's got to be someone I *know*."

"Of course. You must have figured that out for yourself." Corinne's eyebrows shot up and her eyes widened behind their glasses. "What, you thought it was some ordinary burglar? Oh Rebecca. He used your *key*."

"But somebody could have seen me get it out from under that rock," Rebecca argued. "Some stranger. And remembered it."

"I don't think so," said Corinne gently. "What else did they say? The cops."

"She," said Rebecca. "Sergeant Henderson. She's the new boss over there. Well, nothing. She said it's somebody I know. Somebody who's — she said it's somebody who's plenty mad at me." She hadn't wanted to say this aloud, and now she knew why, because saying it aloud had made it real.

But it was real before, she told herself. I just didn't want to believe it.

She turned a blind, naked face to Corinne and thought that if she were to see herself in a mirror at that moment she would not recognize herself.

"Oh, Rebecca," said Corinne again. "Have you got any idea . . . ?"

"No," said Rebecca, and it was almost a wail. Linda at the reception counter began to turn around, then changed her mind.

"Listen," said Corinne. "Let's go someplace for lunch. Bring a notebook. We'll make a list of everybody you know. Try to figure out who it might be."

"Rebecca," Linda called out. "Line two."

"Got it," Rebecca called back. She reached for the phone. "Yeah, okay," she said to Corinne. "It'll have to be late, though. I've got a one o'clock appointment."

"It's Eddie Henderson, Miss Wilson."

"Who?"

"Sergeant Henderson. RCM Police."

"Oh yes. I'm sorry. I forgot your name for a minute."

"Did he put the key back?"

Rebecca grasped for comfort from her immediate surroundings. Corinne's coffee, steaming. The file on her desk, waiting. The glass frog on her TO DO pile, glinting.

Like a gopher in its hole, she thought bitterly. And it was false comfort, anyway. Nowhere was she safe.

"Pardon?" she said politely into the phone, needing time.

"Was the key put back under the rock? I forgot to ask you when you were here earlier."

"Well, what the hell," said Rebecca, standing up. "I mean, what difference does it make?"

"Rebecca?" said Corinne from the next-door desk, alarmed.

"So I get the locks changed," said Rebecca to Eddie Henderson. "He can still get in. He could break a window, easy, get himself in that way." She sat down, opened the drawer that held her purse, slammed it shut. "I don't know. I didn't look." She concentrated on the back of Linda's head, where Linda's chestnut hair was held fast by a silver-coloured clamp. "I didn't look. I'll go home and look."

TWELVE

There were two kinds of bright winter day in this part of the world, observed Olive Parfit that same morning, gazing through her kitchen window. One kind was brilliant — exuberant with shimmering sunlight and a deep blue firmament, the snow-burnished mountains blazing against the sky; the world sparkled and made the heart pound. The other kind — like today — was a pastel sort of a day. The sky was a dreamy mix of blue and shallow shades of grey, and the sluggish sap had flushed tree branches and underbrush a pinkish colour that looked like flesh.

Olive stepped outside, pushed the wheelbarrow aside, and walked to a large poplar that grew not far from her back porch. Stooping, she carefully brushed aside the drifts of autumn leaves, looking for the pale shoots of snowdrops and crocuses. It was too early, though.

She stood and surveyed her garden. After the crocuses, grape hyacinths. Then daffodils. And tulips. Olive, dreaming of spring, nonetheless felt melancholy on this early January morning, as if some part of her brain or body had received unpleasant information and was withholding it, for the moment, from the rest of her.

Her backyard, although small, was terraced, because it sloped sharply downward. A rock wall dividing it roughly in half was almost entirely covered by periwinkle plants; Olive loved its blue-studded look in springtime. In the middle of the wall, a set of steps led to the lower half of the yard, which Olive had let go. Someone years ago had planted bamboo and forsythia there, plus a few rhododendron bushes. These plantings had achieved great height and breadth, encircling and almost engulfing the small patch of lawn. It looked like a wild place, which pleased her. Raccoons who lived in the woods behind sometimes visited, and she had seen an occasional skunk, too. And of course there were plenty of squirrels, and birds. She decided to put a birdbath down there, in the middle of the rough circle of tall grass.

Olive, shivering, admitted that today was a winter day that, despite the erratic sunshine, offered no sign of spring. She would wait another week, maybe two, and then cut some forsythia branches to bring indoors, where their buds would slowly open, offering her bright, sunshiny flowers.

She went back inside, clasping her robe tight around her, closing the door firmly and shooting the lock.

Olive wandered restlessly through her house. She was troubled this morning, and she didn't know why. It was time to revisit the thought of taking a trip somewhere, she decided. She would consult with someone at the travel agency in the village. But not today. Today she didn't feel like going out.

Here it was, almost noon, and she was still in her housecoat.

"What the hell," said Olive, standing in her downstairs hall.

A sick, cold sensation enveloped her. She found it difficult for a moment to catch her breath. It was as if something or someone were trying to smother her. She pressed her hand on her chest, hard, and breathed deeply, slowly in, and slowly out. She did this several times, until she began to feel dizzy and had to sit down on the stairs.

"It is essential that I go out today," she said to her empty house.

She stood and made her way upstairs, clinging to the banister. She hadn't eaten yet. She hadn't even had her morning coffee. She thought she had taken her vitamins, because this had become automatic. She would lean against the kitchen counter looking absently through the window as she swallowed them, one at a time, all eight of them, with a glass of orange juice. She didn't actually recall having done this today, but then she wouldn't, would she?

Over-dramatizing events in one's life could create all kinds of problems. Getting panicky because she occasionally forgot things was foolish and unproductive. Everyone forgot things. But she resolved to increase her intake of ginkgo biloba, all the same.

And certainly, Olive told herself, critically inspecting the contents of her clothes closet, she must make sure she continued to get out and about. There was a rummage sale at the seniors' place, today. . . . Oh god. She couldn't go back to the seniors' place. She couldn't.

It had happened just before dinner was served. Olive had been understandably nervous, attending a New Year's Eve function with people she hadn't yet come to know well. She was a tiny bit tense. A wee bit on edge. Anxious to appear relaxed and charming, to seem genuinely interested in her companions. Let's face it, she thought: I was looking for friends.

She may even have been flirting, she admitted to herself, though in the subtlest possible way, with a particular person who seemed as interested in her as she was in him. He had twice asked her to dance. Olive had known for a while, that evening, that it was possible for a rapidly aging woman to feel once again like a teenager.

They had found themselves next to one another in the buffet lineup. Olive had begun to wish that she hadn't driven herself to this function. Her heart was light; she felt that she possessed an ethereal beauty. While he waited for her, his plate already laden, she selected a slice of turkey, a spoonful of mashed potato, a scoop of gravy, each small gesture full of grace. Then. . . .

"Charlie! There you are!" It was a woman Olive knew to be married; nonetheless, she cast an icy glance at Olive as she clamped her hand on Charlie's arm. "Susannah has come after all. She's over there." She turned Charlie around and pointed. "Saving you a chair."

Olive had waited an endless moment, blindly surveying the bowls of vegetables, the platters of meats, the dishes of pickles that jostled one another on the buffet table. She was aware of Charlie glancing at her, hesitating. She thought he murmured something in her direction before he was whisked away. But she couldn't hear what it was.

Olive sat down on the edge of her unmade bed. She would find other groups to join. Classes to take.

She pulled on a pair of slacks and a turtleneck sweater, brushed her hair vigorously, smoothed her eyebrows, applied lipstick. She would have lunch out. Whatever she felt like eating, she would eat. She briefly considered taking the ferry to Horseshoe Bay and spending the afternoon in Vancouver, but decided against it. She would pay a visit to the travel agent, and the bookstore, and have lunch at that café that overlooked the water, which served excellent halibut and chips. And this evening she would start planning a trip. And her spirits did begin to lift, as she thought about this.

He hadn't been immediately aware of Rebecca when she entered his space. She'd got close, so close, without him knowing it. He'd heard a light-footed somebody approaching, but hadn't had a clue that it was Rebecca sliding into his company — like sunshine through a crack in the wall, he thought, or the scent of flowers carried on a spring breeze. A footstep, the swish of her skirt,

maybe just the altered character of the atmosphere as it
expanded to admit her — something should have told
him she was there. But he hadn't known it, not until she
spoke. And this floored him.

He couldn't even remember what she'd said to him.
Only the timbre of her voice. And because she'd startled
him, he hadn't been able to respond appropriately.

Surely he must have said *something*. But if he had, he
couldn't remember what.

He'd watched helplessly as she left. It was as if the
room had emptied completely when she left. He'd felt
like the single, lonely inhabitant of a collapsing balloon.

She'd probably said, "Good morning." And she'd
probably smiled at him, too. He would have said "Good
morning" back to her, if he'd been alert, if he hadn't
been frozen in shock at the sight of her.

"Good morning, Rebecca," he would have said —
should have said. And he should have turned to her, smiling. "Happy New Year."

And she might have moved her head, then, in that
bold, inviting way she had. "Happy New Year to you,
too," she would've said.

It was over. He knew it. Yet . . . there was such warmth
in that imagined greeting, such allure, that he felt it on
the skin of his face and neck, like a shudder, just beneath
the surface.

Rebecca stood at the edge of the flowerbed staring
down at the rock, which she hadn't yet moved, because
she so hated the thought of it resting in his pocket, the
key to her house in some damn creep's pocket.

Suddenly she thought: What if he's watching me?
Right now? This minute?

She looked over her shoulder, feeling like a fool, and
saw nobody except the mailman across the street stuff-
ing envelopes into her neighbours' box. When he turned

around, he saw Rebecca and waved at her, and she waved back. But she was surprised. She hardly ever saw the mailman, hadn't had an opportunity to develop any kind of relationship with him, so what was he doing waving at her? She watched him move on down the street and up the next walk. Maybe it was him, the mailman, who had prowled around her house on New Year's Eve.

"Don't be an idiot," Rebecca muttered, and knelt to look under the rock.

It wasn't there, of course.

"Goddamn it," said Rebecca to the rock. She stood up and fished in her pocket for her key ring and let herself into her house, where she called a locksmith, who agreed to change her locks that evening.

She had had the presence of mind to bring the Jacksons' file with her so she could go straight there for her one o'clock appointment, wouldn't have to go back to the office first. She took off her coat and flung it over the back of a chair just as the cat appeared in the doorway from the bedroom, stretching. He sat down and regarded her solemnly.

"So who was it, Tommy?" said Rebecca, slumping onto the sofa. "Who was it in our house the other night, throwing my underwear around?"

She hadn't mentioned the incident to her parents when they had called from Edmonton on New Year's Day. They would have been upset, and worried. Her dad, he would have been enraged. Rebecca smiled a little, soothed by the thought of his concern.

She should get something to eat. Never mind that she was having a late lunch with Corinne, she was hungry now. But she didn't want to move. She was very tired. She was exhausted, in fact. It was the damn intruder, disturbing her sleep, screwing up her thought processes.

Somebody she knew. It had to be somebody she knew. The sergeant was right.

But Rebecca found this extremely hard to accept.

She hadn't realized at first what had happened. She had unlocked the front door and walked into her house not the least bit unsteadily, although it was almost five in the morning and she'd had her fair share of champagne. But Corinne and Rick had served chili, toast, and coffee before everyone left the party, so Rebecca was totally sober and feeling very good indeed, drowsy but content, as she slipped through her front door. She had hung up her coat, kicked off her shoes and carried them into the kitchen, where she poured a glass of apple juice, drank half of it, refilled the glass, and went into her bedroom, turning on the overhead light as she entered. She put the juice on her night table and headed for the closet, shoes in hand. As she approached she saw that she had left the closet door open, had apparently left shoes and clothes piled in a muddle on the floor; then she turned her head and for the first time became aware of the nightgowns and underwear spread upon her rumpled bed.

And that the cat was nowhere in sight. She could see where he had been lying, in his usual place, between the pillows; there was a hollow there.

In the space of an instant, Rebecca had become terrified. She stood completely still, not breathing, only listening. The purring of the refrigerator stopped, and the silence was profound. There could not be another person in the house. She would know it, feel it. But outside — outside — he could be outside. Lurking. Hiding. Waiting for her to come home?

Had she locked the door? Had she locked the door behind her? She could not move, could not go out there and try the door.

There is nobody here, Rebecca thought. Nobody in this room, in the house, but me. I know this. But still she could not move. She didn't want to move. Didn't want to find the cat. Not if he was dead.

Don't be such a bloody wimp, she told herself, furious. And moved.

Walked to the door, and through it, into the kitchen. Looked through the window at the yachts in the marina that were rocking gently, outlined with Christmas lights. There was nothing between her house and the water except a raggedy patch of lawn and, over to the left, a large willow tree. Rebecca liked to think it was the mate of the one in the front yard. They were estranged, had been estranged for years. When it happened, the quarrel that had separated them, one of them had walked off in a huff. But not so far away that they couldn't still see each other over the roof of Rebecca's small house.

Nobody was hiding out there.

She turned the kitchen light on. Called the cat. Went to the living room, turned on all three lamps, and called again: "Tommy . . . kitty kitty kitty . . . Tommy, where are you?"

From somewhere in the house she heard him meow. Relief rushed through her, a torrent of it.

"Tommy! Kitty kitty kitty? Come on, Tom-Tom."

She reached the bedroom just in time to see him emerge from under the bed. She picked him up and discovered that she was crying. She was suddenly so weak that she had to sit down on the edge of the bed, still clutching Tommy. He suffered this for a while before struggling to free himself. Then he sat on the floor at her feet, washing himself, while Rebecca wept.

Soon, though, she was angry.

Furious, she scooped the clothes from her bed and the floor of her closet and dropped them on top of the washing machine. She lined up her shoes in their customary rows. She examined the bed carefully and decided that he hadn't been in it, hadn't even pulled back the covers. He had only sat on it, god knew why, while he thought about god knew what — probably jerking off

into one of my nighties, she thought grimly, hoping, if
this was true, that he had at least had the courtesy to take
the nightgown with him.

Eventually she went to bed. But she didn't sleep
much. The next day she washed all her clothes and
scrubbed every piece of furniture in the bedroom, and
the floor, too. She had inspected the whole house, every
inch of it, and found no trace of his presence anywhere.

But she had felt him there. She still felt him there.

Rebecca, sitting on her sofa, watched by the cat —
who looked like a small, black, green-eyed statue placed
just so, at the entrance to the living room — became
aware of a persistent sound. The wind, perhaps, rattling
something. Maybe the lid wasn't firmly sitting on top of
the garbage can. Or maybe it was the letter slot in the
front door, which Rebecca knew had come loose. Or
perhaps the backyard willow tree was brushing against
the house. Something had caught her attention, a noise
that she badly needed to identify. And as she tried to
work out what it was, she realized that she no longer
felt safe. It was as if the house suddenly had glass walls,
or no walls at all.

It didn't occur to her that the police could help her.
She didn't know why.

It was the front door. She could see the flap over the
letter box shuddering as the wind nudged it.

She had begun making a list in her head of all the
people she knew, but she soon stopped. It was depressing to think of her friends as possible intruders. Once
she had cast them, however briefly, in this role, would she
ever be able to feel the same about them again?

Maybe the sergeant was wrong, and Corinne, too.
Maybe it didn't have to be someone she knew. Maybe
somebody *had* seen her take the key out from under the
rock. She'd certainly had to do it often enough in the
past. When she bought the house last year her father had

given her a special leather case in which to keep the keys, and she was always leaving it behind somewhere. And so she'd put a spare key under the rock. But for several months now she'd kept the house keys on the ring with her car keys, so she hadn't had to use the spare for quite a while.

Rebecca was very proud of her house. She couldn't have afforded one if she'd stayed in Vancouver. Real estate was a lot cheaper on the Sunshine Coast, which was one of the reasons she'd taken the job in Gibsons two years earlier.

And so yes, maybe somebody had seen her. In fact somebody must have seen her; probably she'd been observed on more than one occasion, using the key that was housed under the rock. This was considerably more likely, in Rebecca's opinion, than her home having been intruded upon by someone she knew.

She felt better, having established this to her own satisfaction.

So it was a stranger — perhaps a neighbour, but nobody with whom she had more than a nodding acquaintance — who had entered her house on New Year's Eve.

But why?

She had to admit that she was stumped here. She couldn't even speculate that she had surprised him when she came home before he'd had a chance to steal anything; it had been almost morning when she got home, too close to dawn for a burglar to be still skulking around.

So his purpose had not been to rob her.

He hadn't torn up the place, so vandalism hadn't been his thing, either.

He'd gone through her drawers and her closet, hadn't taken anything, hadn't destroyed anything, had just thrown stuff onto her bed.

It didn't make any sense. Rebecca went over it again and again and couldn't make sense of it, couldn't find a purpose there — a *meaning*.

She got up and put on her coat. "Time to go, Tom-Tom," she said, stooping to stroke him before picking up her handbag and briefcase. She would get her mind back where it belonged, on her work, as she drove out to the Jacksons' house, and later, at lunch with Corinne, maybe the two of them could work out a plausible scenario for her plunderer.

For that's what he was, she thought, climbing into her car. He may not have stolen or vandalized, but he had plundered her house. Her *life*.

She wished he had at least put back the key.

THIRTEEN

"I've been looking for her for years," he typed. "Rebecca, her name is. That's why I just can't believe I could have gotten it wrong, that she hasn't been looking for me, too."

"Hmmm."

"Listen. It isn't that I haven't gotten it wrong before, of course I bloody have, and of course I bloody *knew* it. Maybe not right away. But eventually."

He picked up the bottle of beer that sat next to the computer and drank. When the sky had lightened to morning, it would be Valentine's Day.

"For instance?"

And so he told Jemima about Lorraine.

"She was the first girlfriend I had after the old lady died. She was — I guess the first grown-up relationship I had. I was working on the Prairies, in this flat, flat town. Spent a fair amount of time in the bar there." It was a place with wooden walls stained and made shiny by time, cigarette smoke, and thousands of conversations. He didn't know if they'd been shellacked or what, but something had created a liveness — a burnished mahogany colour — in those walls that reminded him of a certain kind of burgundy shellfish he used to find along the shore.

"It was winter. I was sitting there with a bunch of guys from the forest service, just shooting the shit," he told Jemima, hunched over the keyboard, wearing a T-shirt and a pair of Jockey shorts. He remembered that he had been enjoying one of those rare moments in which he was happy and aware of his happiness — aware, too, that his contentment stemmed from nothing in particular, but just from being alive. His friends had wandered off home, and he finished his beer, looking out the window into the pub's parking lot, which was bordered by snowdrifts six feet high. A couple of pick-ups vibrated gently, lazily emitting clouds of exhaust, their drivers having gone back inside to wait for the vehicles to warm up.

He was starting to think about going home. He felt like having a few slurps of apple juice and a good stretch and then falling directly into bed and diving immediately into sleep.

And then over at the entrance, a small dust-up began.

"What's going on?" he asked the barmaid, a large young woman with her dark hair in a ponytail, wearing jeans and a green sweatshirt.

"I think she got dumped," said the barmaid thoughtfully. "Suddenly she don't have a ride. Seems upset about it."

The person in question was struggling into a white winter jacket, her head averted. She pulled up her fur-trimmed hood, and the jacket's zipper, thrust her hands into mittens, and disappeared out the door.

"You want another?"

"No thanks, hon." He had dropped money on the table then and grabbed his coat.

He took another swig from the beer bottle. "You still there, Jemima?"

"I'm here, honey-bun."

"So I go outside and I see her half a block away, ploughing through the snow. I caught up with her and offered her a ride, and of course she said no at first but it was sonofabitching cold and more snow had begun to fall so finally she agreed.

"I drove her straight to her apartment, called her a day or two later, and we started seeing each other."

"So? Is this your story? Is this all there is?"

"So I eventually — the thing is, she was very attractive, really, but she could have been a lot more attractive."

"Oh Jesus."

"I know, I know, I know it was a mistake."

"What did you tell her, exactly, you poor misguided jerk?"

"That she could have lost a few pounds," he typed, doggedly. "And a shorter hair style would have suited her better. And she really could have used some kind of dye job, to brighten her up."

"And you suggested this to her, did you?"

"I cared about the bitch, okay? I cared about her. Wanted her to look her very best. What's wrong with that? And at first she was real enthusiastic." He drained the beer bottle.

"And then?"

"And then she wasn't."

"So you broke up with her?"

"Yeah." He squinted through the kitchen doorway at the window, but it remained dark; night was still supreme. "So I kinda laid low for a while. Trying to be patient. Anticipating problems." He rubbed his hands vigorously through his hair and thought about getting another beer. Jesus, it was touch and go, too. Waiting. Looking. It was almost like believing in fucking Santa Claus.

But then, yeah, he'd always been an optimist. It was what had led him to Rebecca — made him open to Rebecca, when he met her.

"Tell me, Hotshot Harry. Have *you* ever been dumped?"

He laughed out loud. "Of course I have. Who hasn't?"

"Tell me about it."

"I'll tell you about the time that made me maddest." First, though, he got another bottle from the fridge, twisted off its top and took a long drink. Then he peeked through the kitchen curtains and found that the sky to the east was definitely more grey than black. "Getting dumped wasn't something I ever got used to, but I took it philosophically enough. Told the guys about it, took the razzing, the slaps on the back — it was usually pretty good-natured. Except there was this one girl."

Irina.

She'd actually come to see him at work, which he'd told her was a definite no-no. And he was incredulous. Outraged. As she spoke to him, her face was transfigured. She turned into a warty old crone, with a voice that he expected would bring all electronic devices within a fifty-foot radius to a sudden, sputtery death. He watched her, listened to her, disbelieving.

"Your face is getting all red now," she'd scolded him. "You're about to blow your top, don't think I don't know it. Why do you think I've come *here* to break up with you? And the reason I am dumping you is very simple: we are not compatible — *we are not compatible* — and I want you to stay away from me," she said, raising her voice, leaning over the counter toward him, her knobbly hands splayed, the nails bitten to the quick. Ugly hands. He had shuddered at the thought of those hands on his body.

"I told her to get the hell out of there," he typed. "Her mouth snapped shut like a turtle's and she did, she got the hell out of there.

"I got into trouble at work that afternoon," he confessed to Jemima. "The only serious blotch on my record happened that afternoon, and it was because of her." There was, he thought, a little bit of light filtering through the kitchen curtain.

"Hmmm," appeared on the computer screen. "So she made you pretty mad, then, this Irina chick?"

"What the hell do you think?"

"Got you in trouble at work and all."

"Right."

"You sounded pretty mad at Rebecca, when you first started talking about her."

"It isn't the same."

"Did you get even with Irina?"

The skin on the back of his neck began to prickle. He even put a hand back there to make sure it wasn't some bug crawling on him.

He wished he could hear the tone of her voice.

He wished he could be absolutely sure that she was a woman. He'd lied to her about his name, about his job, about — lots of things. She had every right to be lying, too.

"That's none of your business." He sat back and took another swig of beer. Put the bottle down and folded his arms. There was a considerable pause before she wrote, "Harry? Whoa whoa whoa. Hold on there, Harry."

"Don't tell me to hold on."

"Okay. Fine."

He pressed the beer bottle hard against the back of his neck.

"So what happened, Harry?"

He stared at the computer screen.

"Come on, Harry. What did you do?"

The beer bottle was sweating. He drank some more, wiped his hand on his Jockey shorts. "Sorry," he typed. "Gotta go." He left the chat room, and the Web, and switched off the computer.

He stood up and stretched and rubbed his face. It was dawn. He made coffee and drank it, sitting at his kitchen table.

When daylight came he put on a hooded waterproof jacket and left his house. He climbed the ramp, crossed the street, and aimed the door opener at the garage. He got into the Lexus and rested his forehead against the steering wheel. After a while, he fired up the motor, let it warm up for a few minutes, then drove away, toward Sechelt.

Twenty minutes later he turned off the highway onto Redrooffs Road — driving, driving — and eventually he pulled over, got out, locked up and started walking. He walked on the left, on the narrow gravel shoulder, close to the trees that grew thickly there, crowding the roadside, so close that he could hear the rain spattering upon their bare branches.

He felt a bit better, having finally told someone about Rebecca. He had meant to ask Jemima's advice, as well, but then had chickened out. You couldn't ask advice of someone who was not much more than a figment of your imagination.

He couldn't get her out of his fucking head. He'd thought for a while that messing up her house, her bedroom, would somehow set him free. But it had only made things worse. He'd once seen this program on the Discovery Channel, about spiders. And now he felt like a fucking retarded spider who'd forgotten to weave those essential non-sticky strands that would have allowed him to safely cross his own web: like a big, bloated, bewildered fly, he crouched, helpless, a captive in his own bloody snare.

Everything seemed smaller now. His house. His workplace. Even the Lexus. It was as if he'd become larger, swollen with rage, clumsy with mortification. He was always bumping into things. Only outdoors did the world seem able to comfortably accommodate his presence.

Until recently he'd been reasonably relaxed at work. In fact work had been his salvation — work, and the chat room. At work he had to be concentrated and diligent, and he'd been able to do this, to put Rebecca into a far-off corner of his mind and turn almost all of his attention onto other things, work-related things. Most of the time. Like Jekyll and Hyde, he'd been able, with a little effort, to keep one foot securely in each of his two worlds. Of course, they'd collided at the meetings, but the meetings were infrequent and between them he'd functioned smoothly.

Until now. Now she refused to stay in that far-off corner of his brain. She wandered out of there whenever she damn well felt like it. He'd be at the computer, for instance, the computer at work, and suddenly instead of the form he'd been working on he'd find himself staring at the screensaver, with no notion of how long his mind had been wandering, absorbed in thoughts of Rebecca, images of Rebecca.

He crossed the road and stumbled down a narrow lane that wound down the hillside through thick woods that were a mixture of coniferous and deciduous trees. He could glimpse the ocean now. He trudged toward it, hands in his pockets, the hood of his jacket up, his shoulders hunched against the rain.

The rain fell hard for a while, then slowed to a trickle. Mist wound among the treetops, sometimes dipping to ground level. And he created more, exhaling erratic ribbons of fog.

He stopped and listened — to the rain rattling in the trees, to the trees creaking in the breeze from the sea, to the cry of a bird. The whole world seemed to be asleep. He felt a tremendous sadness, and struggled strenuously against it, afraid that if he succumbed, he would die.

He began walking again, purposefully, dispatching himself heedlessly into the future. He looked neither right nor left but only at the ground. Suddenly he ploughed through knee-high ferns to the nearest tree, clinging to its trunk, and he wiped from his face rain that might have been tears.

What the fuck is wrong with me?

But he knew what was wrong with him. He was afraid it was going to happen again.

He gripped the rough bark of the tree, a cedar that was perhaps three feet in diameter. Its lowest branches brushed his shoulders. He breathed in its scent hungrily. He stretched his arms around it in a fierce embrace, his cheek pressed against the trunk. He stayed there for several minutes.

The problem was — had been — that he hadn't been able to keep everything in hand that time, years ago but never forgotten. It had been like driving six horses and losing track of which reins led to which animal.

He had gone to her house calmly, knocked at her door calmly, asked calmly to speak to her. And he must have been genuinely calm because she let him in.

He knew that his tone had become lecturing. He'd seen it in her face — in the spasm of impatience that flickered there, in the distaste that quickly followed.

"You've gotta understand, you've gotta understand it from my point of view."

"Oh I understand your point of view alright," she'd said, sarcasm dripping poisonously from every word. "I just won't accept it, that's all."

"Accept what?" he'd said, triumphant. "Accept the fact that I love you? Care about you? Want to look after you, for the rest of your fucking life?"

"I don't want you!" she'd shouted at him, her eyes squeezed shut. She'd looked really ugly then, her face squidgied up, her hair a mess, her whole body in this stupid threatening crouch, as if she were about to hurl herself at him and beat him to death with her feeble little fists. "I don't need you! I *hate* you now, you arrogant sonofabitch!"

They'd been in her kitchen, he remembered, standing by the counter where the coffee pot sat. Maybe he'd expected her to offer him some coffee. That he couldn't remember.

He'd been so totally pissed off, so speechless with rage, he'd given her a backhanded slap across the face . . .

. . . and watched, astonished, as she flew into the air, flipped ass over tea kettle through the basement door, and vanished. He heard her — thump, thump, thump — hitting the stairs in a series of irregular thuds on her way down.

It had killed her, that fall.

And so he'd gone home. And waited. And, in due course, returned to work. And waited. He'd waited for days — weeks — months, for the phone to ring, for a knock on his door. They had never come, either of them, not the ring, not the knock.

He shuddered, remembering.

He did not want to go through that again.

He realized that the legs of his jeans were soaked, his cheek was stinging and his arms ached. He let his arms drop and lifted his head, turning so that his back was to the cedar tree. He leaned against it. The woods into which he gazed were so thick that he could see nothing but trees and ferns and fallen logs. But when he turned his head to the left, he saw the ocean, maybe half a mile away. He considered trying to find a trail that would lead down there but the prospect wearied him.

He'd go home. What else could he do?

Eddie spent a couple of hours working that Sunday afternoon. Just before leaving her office, she checked her e-mail. Among several messages was one from Alan McCurdy.

"I didn't want to spook you with a telephone call," it read, "but you ought to know that I'm getting married. Do you think we could get together so I can show you her picture, and exhibit in your presence my commitment to her, and you can be assured that you've seen the last of me? Seriously, Eddie, I'd like to apologize in person for bugging you, for refusing to take rejection like a man. I'll meet you anywhere you like, any time you say. How about it?"

Eddie printed out the message and slipped it into her journal, then deleted it from her computer. She wondered if he really was getting married or if this was another big lie. A trap.

If it was true . . . was she finally free of him, then?

When Olive arrived home, around dinnertime, she noticed that the days were definitely lengthening. And this warmed her heart and made her feel better about her futile trip to Vancouver. Her intention there had been to shop for her upcoming travels, but this had proven a dispiriting experience. The Bay must have reduced the size of its sales staff, she decided, for she could find no one with either the time or the inclination to discuss her needs and offer her assistance.

It was time, she admitted to herself on the ferry trip home, that she sought the assistance of her friend Susanna, who lived in West Vancouver and was an experienced traveler. Susanna tended to appropriate situations, and Olive had no wish to be commandeered before time into destination decisions, or important wardrobe or luggage purchases. Still, she would be ill-advised not to take advantage of Susanna's expertise. Olive would call her this very evening.

By the time she drove up next to her fence she had convinced herself that she ought to have called her long before now, as soon as she'd decided to take a trip, as a matter of fact. Susanna might even want to come along, thought Olive. But she would discourage that. She wanted this to be a solitary adventure, requiring some courage.

She climbed out of the car, closed the door and locked it, and went through the gate. The rain was no longer falling, but it was still dripping from the trees, and the grass was sodden. Olive squelched across the lawn and around to the side of the house. A sturdy half-barrel at the corner displayed blue and yellow crocuses and a cluster of snowdrops, and several daffodils had sprouted. Under the lilac tree, grape hyacinths and lilies-of-the-valley had broken through the earth. Soon the first iridescent greening of spring would flicker through the woods. Olive gave a little sigh of satisfaction and headed back toward the front door, keys in her hand.

She found the door unlocked again. This was happening far too often. Unless she stopped herself in the hall on her way out to gather her thoughts (Do I have my list? Should I bring a book? Are all the windows closed?), she was as likely to leave the door unlocked as to lock it. She muttered under her breath as she slipped inside, and immediately secured the door. She put her handbag on the table, then switched on the hall light and turned up the thermostat.

Her raincoat was slightly damp, she noticed, hanging it in the closet. She had wondered when she had left early that morning whether she ought to wear her heavier cloth coat but had decided against it. Now she saw that the cloth coat wasn't in the closet; had she forgotten that it was at the cleaner's?

She went upstairs, her knees throbbing, and used the bathroom. She would change clothes before fixing dinner. Get out of the skirt that had gotten too tight around her waist, extricate herself from her bra, put on a comfortable nightgown, a wraparound robe, and a pair of cozy moccasins. After dinner, she thought, reaching for the toilet paper, she would call Susanna. Who would be astonished to hear about Olive's plans.

The toilet-paper roll was empty. Olive reached around to open the nearest cabinet, where she kept the spare rolls, but her flailing hand encountered only air. Exasperated, she bounced up and down several times on the toilet seat, stood, pulled up her cotton panties and squatted in front of the cabinet to peer inside. Empty. Damn. In another cupboard she found an unopened box of facial tissue and slammed it down on top of the counter.

She changed clothes, made her way back downstairs into the kitchen, and wrote "TP" under "balsamic vinegar" and "margarine" and "soup" on the memo pad that was affixed to the refrigerator door with a magnet.

Olive had decided to have a scrambled-egg sandwich for dinner. She placed bread in the toaster, chopped a green onion very fine, pulled a small non-stick frypan from the cupboard, and opened the fridge to get out the eggs.

No eggs. She stared into the refrigerator. The container in the door that held fifteen eggs was empty, except for the BEST BY date notification that she had carefully torn from the paper carton. It sat in the centre depression in the back row, lonely and irrelevant. Olive wrote "eggs" under "TP" on the memo pad.

She sat down at the kitchen table. She was frightened, and she acknowledged this, as calmly as she could. After a few moments she stood up and wrote "ginkgo biloba" under "eggs."

She looked in the pantry, found spaghetti and a jar of tomato-basil sauce, and took them out.

She had put the water on to boil and dumped the sauce into a pan when the telephone rang. So loud was its clangor that she leapt into the air with a shriek. She grabbed for it, trying to pick it up before it could ring again, but it discharged one more blast before she got her hand wrapped around it.

"Hello!"

"Olive? Are you okay?"

"Yes Danny. Fine. Hold on a minute." Gingerly, she inspected the side of the telephone receiver. The volume control was set at the highest register instead of the lowest. She slid it back where it belonged and sat down; her legs were trembling.

"Olive? Olive!"

"Yes here I am, I'm fine, Danny."

"You sure didn't sound fine."

"Oh the phone thing was set wrong, too loud, it startled me, that's all." She took a deep breath. "How are you, dear?"

"Me? I'm good. I thought I'd maybe come over, occupy your guest room for a couple of nights. Would that be okay?"

"I'd love it, Danny," said Olive, smiling. "I'd be delighted. When would you like to come?"

"Whenever's good for you," said her nephew, and they spent a few minutes discussing this. It was decided that he would arrive the following Wednesday and stay until Saturday.

"I'm very happy about this," said Olive, "but curious, too. This will be the first time you've ever stayed overnight. What's the occasion?"

Danny hesitated for a moment. "Well, the thing is, Olive, I think I'm going to be moving."

"Moving?" She thought for the briefest of moments that he might be moving to Gibsons, to the Sunshine Coast, but the tone of his voice didn't suggest this.

"Yeah. To Toronto."

"Toronto," said Olive dully.

"It isn't certain yet," said Danny. "I want to talk to you about it. Get your opinion. Your advice."

Olive's eyes were on her kitchen window, but she hadn't actually been looking at it, not really; her concentration had been first on the telephone and then on her nephew's distressing news. Now she focused on it. And stood, phone in hand, still pressed against her ear, to move closer to the window. And as Danny continued to talk, assuring her that if he were to move to the other side of the country they would still be in touch . . .

"There's the telephone, Olive, and there's e-mail — I'm going to make sure you're launched on the World Wide Web before I leave."

Olive stretched out her hand in search of the curtains that she knew only that morning had formed a neat frame around her kitchen window.

She could have forgotten to lock the front door. (*Was* her cloth coat at the dry cleaner's?) She could have imprudently allowed her toilet-paper supply to run out. She could have failed to notice that she had eaten her last egg. She could have inadvertently slid the volume adjuster on her telephone all the way up the scale. But she could not have removed the curtains from her kitchen window and forgotten doing that.

"And of course, you'll visit me there, Olive. If I go. Right?"

She remembered pulling them open that very morning, to reveal outside the window the fitful falling of the rain, which she had clearly heard, then, spattering the patio.

"Olive? Are you there? Please don't be upset."

"I'm not upset, Danny. I'm quite calm, in fact." She sat down again. "I am very much looking forward to your visit. I have a lot to tell you."

FOURTEEN

On Thursday morning Eddie left her house early, picked up a take-away coffee, and drove down to Gibsons, running the day's schedule through her head and wishing it were time to come home again. At least the sun was shining. Any situation, no matter how perilous, perplexing, or pessimistic, was at least easier to bear in sunshine. It was an endorphin-manufacturer, sunshine, thought Eddie, pulling up front of the detachment. She pushed her bag onto the floor, locked the Mercedes, and hurried up to the main entrance.

"Beatrice," she said, as the door closed behind her, "I want to leave you a couple of numbers." She looked through the receptionist's window. "Beatrice?"

Beatrice was sitting straight-backed in her chair with her head bowed and her hands, in fists, placed on top of a handwritten letter that was lying on her desk. When she lifted her head, Eddie was shocked. Beatrice's pale skin appeared irreparably wrinkled, a disquieting contrast with her black hair, which Eddie had decided some time ago was probably a wig. Her lower lip was trembling and in her eyes rested unshed tears.

"Beatrice. What's wrong?"

It wasn't one of Howard's work days, so Beatrice was alone in the reception area. Eddie heard laughter from the main office, and a female voice raised in protest — Johnny Greig, she guessed, and probably Bev Brooks.

"I'm old," said Beatrice, her voice quivering. "And useless."

Eddie pushed through the gate, plucked a tissue from a box on Beatrice's desk, and handed it to her. "That's ridiculous," she said heartily. "Age hasn't got much to do with years, you ought to know that better than anyone. And you certainly aren't useless. I mean, what would we do without you around here, for example?"

"I've had a letter from my niece," said Beatrice. She removed her glasses and dabbed at her eyes, which had spilled over. "She's gotten married."

"Well, is that bad?"

"She didn't tell me she was going to get married."

"Maybe they eloped," said Eddie. "I feel ineffective here, Beatrice, not knowing your niece, or the nature of your relationship with her." She stood up, glancing at her watch.

"They didn't elope," said Beatrice, thrusting her glasses back on. "They don't confide in me," she said bitterly. "None of them. I'm a useless old woman to them, that's all." She waved a dismissive hand in Eddie's direction. "Oh, you go on, get going, I know you're in Vancouver today."

Eddie handed her a slip of paper. "I've got my cell, but just in case, here's a number where I'll be later this morning. And Beatrice," she added gravely, "I depart confident that the detachment couldn't be left in more capable hands."

Beatrice shot her a glance. Her mouth was twisted in a sneer, but her eyes were bleak. "You're leaving it in Buster Sheffield's hands."

"Ah, the *law* side of things, yes. Sure." She leaned toward Beatrice, hands on her thighs. "But the rest of it. The civilians. The organization of this place — the *order* part — that's your responsibility." She stood straight. "You've never failed us yet, Beatrice. I know I can count on you."

"Oh, you can," said Beatrice, resigned. She smoothed the letter with the palm of her hand, picked it up, and slid it into one of her desk drawers. "You can."

"Send them a nice gift," said Eddie confidentially, as she slipped through the gate. "You'll feel a lot better. I promise."

The lineup at the ferry cafeteria wasn't a long one that Thursday morning, and since Eddie hadn't eaten yet, she ordered the Sunshine Breakfast. This consisted of a scoop of scrambled eggs, two slices of bacon, and two limp pieces of brown toast. She also got a glass of orange juice and a mug of coffee before paying for the meal.

She took her tray over to a table in the corner. She had bought a copy of the *Province* newspaper from the newsstand and read while she ate, eventually turning to the classified section, where she scanned the Pets for Sale column. She had a three-thirty appointment with a member of the RCMP dog squad. Dreading this day, Eddie had also scheduled dog research and a visit to Marjorie in it as rewards. Like her mother had rewarded her with an ice cream cone and a visit to the library on the days when she'd had allergy shots.

Eddie's allergies had disappeared when she left home. She had always found this deeply significant.

She ate only half of her breakfast. The eggs didn't taste like eggs, the bacon was brittle rather than crisp, the limp toast was clammy. It could be me, though, she thought. It could be that her taste buds had withered at the very thought of living through this day.

She sipped her coffee and thought about Beatrice and, for a while, entertained herself by imagining the woman's family, a far-flung group of warm, friendly people who, Eddie decided, would have been trying for years to haul Beatrice within their collective embrace and who were now beginning to give up. At least the

letter would be safe, she thought, and allowed herself a
moment of self-congratulation.

It had been a Wednesday, she remembered. She'd
been in the new job for about a month, and was slav-
ing away over the paperwork she wasn't yet used to.
She had begun shortly after eight in the morning and
it was now almost one o'clock. It was the sound of her
stomach crossly rumbling that had finally broken her
concentration. She sat back in her chair, stretching, and
glanced with satisfaction at her IN and OUT boxes.
She reached for the phone to buzz Beatrice in, then
changed her mind. She put on her jacket, tucked her
cap under her arm, and picked up the contents of the
OUT box. Both boxes were empty, and she observed
this wistfully, knowing it was a wholly temporary state
of affairs.

It was unusually quiet in the detachment. She walked
silently along the hall, through the central office and into
the reception area, passing Howie Peck beavering away
at his computer and Beverly Brooks murmuring so confidentially into her phone that Eddie assumed she was
talking to Jim Partridge, who was off duty.

When she entered the reception area she saw that
Beatrice wasn't at her desk. William Kirkpatrick was
crouched in Beatrice's chair, rummaging through her
desk drawers. Eddie stopped, and watched. He didn't
appear to be looking for anything in particular. He'd dig
around, pull something out, hold it up to the light, and
peer at it intently — a greeting card, a small spray bottle
of eyeglass cleaner, a letter — then put it back, poke
around some more, hold up something else — a vial of
painkillers, an extra pair of glasses. . . .

"What're you doing, William?" she said curiously.

He slammed the drawer shut and shot to his feet.
"Nothing." His face reddened. His arms hung awkwardly from his shoulders and Eddie noticed that his hands

were unusually large. "Thought I just might have — I wanted to borrow an aspirin."

Eddie deposited the pile from her OUT basket on the desk and took a piece of scrap paper from a small plastic box and a pen from a matching pen-and-pencil holder.

"She's out for lunch," said William.

"Done!" wrote Eddie on the scrap paper, and signed the note with her initials. She smiled at William. "Me, too," she said.

Before Beatrice left that day, Eddie called her into her office. "Does your desk lock?"

"It's got a key," said Beatrice. "But I never bother to lock it."

"You do now," Eddie had told her.

And a good thing, too, she thought now. She left the cafeteria and made her way to the bow of the ship, where she found two empty seats facing each other, next to the window. She sat on one and put her feet up on the other.

She was wearing jeans, a sweatshirt, a denim jacket, and boots, and she carried a small black backpack. Her hair was pulled back in a rather severe bun and anchored to her head with combs. She had put on no makeup. None.

Eddie looked out the window at the ocean and the lumbering mountains and the sky, which was mostly blue today for a change. She rubbed her hands together and took several deep breaths, missing the uniform, missing the weight around her waist of her cop paraphernalia, her handgun.

Marjorie was up and dressed, but the aroma of toast and peanut butter lingered in the air of her fourteenth-floor apartment when Eddie got there in mid-morning.

"You want some?" she asked when Eddie commented on this.

"I ate on the ferry."

"Then you really *do* want some."

"No. Really. Thanks."

"Just some coffee, then."

"Yeah. Coffee would be good."

Marjorie poured two cups and set them down on the kitchen table, under a bay window that looked fourteen stories down at Central Park. "Cream? Sugar?"

"Neither, thanks."

"Come on, Eddie, sit down. And tell me whatever it is you wanted to tell me."

Eddie slid her backpack off her shoulders and put it on the floor, then sat down opposite Marjorie. She looked around the kitchen, at the appliances lined up on the counter: a food processor, a juicer, a toaster oven, a blender. She wondered if Marjorie regularly used all or any of these things, or if she just enjoyed knowing she could shred a salad, chomp up an orange, warm a muffin, or concoct a milkshake if she wanted to.

"Alan's asked me to see him. And I said I would. I'm meeting him at one o'clock."

Marjorie looked at her in silence for a moment. Then, "Wow," she said. "How come?"

"He says he's engaged." Eddie tilted her head, squinting at her friend. "Have you heard anything about that?"

Marjorie shrugged. "I'm not exactly close to the guy."

"How will I know if it's true?"

"I'll find out for you." The buzzer in the lobby sounded and Marjorie got up to pick up the intercom phone. "Hiya. Yeah, bring him up." She replaced the receiver. "I'm babysitting today," she said to Eddie. "As soon as he's up here, I'll make a couple of calls. Where are you supposed to meet the bastard?"

"That place on Kingsway. By Willingdon."

"Well, I don't want you to do it, if we find out he's got no bloody fiancée."

Her doorbell rang and she went off to answer it. Eddie
heard muffled conversation but couldn't distinguish words.

A moment later, a dog bounded into the kitchen, a
large, blond, woolly dog with long ears, a long nose, and
brown eyes. The dog planted himself in front of Eddie,
his tail wagging. He stretched his head toward her and
sniffed, delicately but thoroughly, starting with her
denim-clad knee, making his way down her calf to her
booted foot. She put out her hand and he sniffed that,
too, and gave it a casual swipe with his tongue.

"His name is Andrew," said Marjorie, coming into the
kitchen. "He belongs to a guy at work, but he's gotta find
him a new home, I forget why."

"What kind of a dog is he?" said Eddie.

"A standard poodle." Marjorie filled a pan with water
and set it on the floor. The dog immediately began to
drink. "I hate it when people decide to give away their
animals," she said passionately. "There was a dog here in
Burnaby — a beagle, I think it was — a couple of hotshot
dot-commers had him. They decided to move to L.A. or
some damn place, and they just left the dog behind, in the
empty apartment, if you can imagine. Just abandoned him.
At least that won't happen to this guy. Steve's very respon-
sible. He'll find him a good home." She rubbed Andrew
behind the ears. His tail wagged politely, but he didn't stop
lapping up the water. "Okay, I'm going to make a couple
of calls," said Marjorie. "The phone's in the living room.
I've only got the one, believe it or not. Plus my cell, of
course. Help yourself to more coffee." She left the room.

Eddie sipped her coffee.

The dog eventually stopped drinking. He looked
around, as if wondering where Marjorie had gone,
then wagged his tail at Eddie and dropped to the floor
at her feet.

She reached down to pet him. "You feel like a sheep,
you," she said.

Andrew twisted around to lick her hand, and looked at her intently.

"My name's Eddie."

The dog continued to look at her.

"And you're Andrew, right?"

His gaze was steady and watchful. Eddie thought.

"I'm very pleased to meet you," she said.

Finally, the dog sighed and rested his head on his paws. He was lying partially on Eddie's left foot. By the time Marjorie returned, her foot had started to tingle.

"She's gonna call me back in five," said Marjorie. "She knows everything about everything, this gal." She sat at the kitchen table with Eddie and reached over to scratch Andrew's head. The dog shifted on the floor, removing himself from Eddie's foot. "So tell me," said Marjorie with a grin, "what's life like behind that big old desk on the Sunshine Coast?"

"I'm still getting to know the ropes," said Eddie, rubbing the top of Andrew's woolly head.

"But what do you *do* there? I mean, what kind of crime do the denizens of Gibsons get up to?"

"The usual, Marjorie," said Eddie with dignity. "Same as anyplace else. Alcohol. Drugs. Robbery. Vandalism." She sat back and the dog looked up at her expectantly. "There's even a stalking going on. It looks like it was a one-shot deal, some guy got drunk on New Year's Eve and let himself into a woman's house and fingered her undies. Déjà vu, except Alan never got into my apartment, the sonofabitch."

"Doesn't sound like this guy's in Alan's league."

"No, thank god." The dog was nudging her knee with his head. "What does he want?"

"He wants you to pet him some more. You've made a friend, Eddie. There she is," she said, getting up to answer the phone.

———

Olive awoke early that morning, as usual, and got dressed, moving quietly so as not to disturb Danny in the guest room across the hall. Quickly and efficiently she made her bed, washed her face, fluffed up her hair and brushed her teeth.

He had arrived the previous evening, Wednesday, as they had agreed. He looked sheepish, standing on her doorstep. This, she knew, was because he was moving to Toronto and felt guilty about abandoning his old aunt.

It was amazing how much she still missed her brother, Horace. It wasn't as if they had ever been particularly close. As children, there had been too many years between them; she was seven years older. As adults, they had always been polite and affectionate toward one another, but nothing more.

Olive recalled a moment shortly after the death of their father, six years earlier. She and Horace and Danny and Danny's now ex-wife Gwen had visited his grave together and then they had repaired to Horace's house for dinner.

Their father had lived with Horace for the last two years of his life. Horace was a good-natured man, even-tempered, tolerant. He had always sworn that he hadn't minded looking after their father; in fact, he had insisted that he actually enjoyed the old man's company. Olive was skeptical. Their father had been irascible all his life, and miserably crotchety toward the end.

Anyway, he had eventually died, and on this day shortly after the funeral they were gathered, the four of them, in Horace's house. Olive's brother had drunk considerably more wine with dinner than was his habit. Suddenly he threw his arm around Olive's shoulder and walked her across the living room, through the sliding doors, and onto the patio.

"My god, big sister, do you realize — we're orphans?"

He said this in a voice that broke, and his eyes were shiny
with tears.

Olive hadn't been able to think of anything to say that
would make him feel better, so she had just hugged him
and patted him comfortingly on the back.

She was — she might as well face it — she was deeply
hurt that Danny had taken it into his head to move to
Toronto. She knew how ridiculous this was. She was
only the boy's aunt. And he wasn't exactly a boy anymore. He was a man of thirty-seven whose fair hair was
fast disappearing, and whose substantial bulk was threatening to convert itself from mostly muscle to mostly fat.
But the fact remained that he was Olive's only living rel-
ative, or at least the only one she knew about, and she
was completely disheartened by his impending absence
from her life.

"Get a grip, woman," she muttered on her way downstairs, reminding herself of resolutions she had made, not
on New Year's Day, but more recently, which made them
in Olive's opinion more substantive.

She had resolved to start attending activities at the
seniors' hall again. It was ridiculous to deprive herself of
whatever entertainments might be available there just
because of one embarrassing incident . . . although she
did hope never to lay eyes upon that man again.

And there was her upcoming trip to Europe, which
she would organize to take place in the fall.

Sunlight was streaming through the curtainless window above the kitchen sink. Olive put on the coffee and
set the kitchen table for two, and by the time the coffee
was ready, Danny had come downstairs.

Olive hoped the bright day would dissipate the awk-
wardness of the previous evening, and in fact it did. The
sunshine was the first thing Danny remarked upon as he
entered the kitchen, and they smiled at one another, he
and Olive, as they said their good mornings.

"How about bacon and eggs for breakfast?" Olive suggested, and Danny promptly agreed.

"While I cook," said Olive, "tell me about this new job of yours." Her tone, she knew, was relaxed and agreeable, and unmistakably (she was pretty sure) interested.

Shortly before one o'clock, Eddie was sitting at a table in the restaurant on Kingsway. Her back was to the wall; the entrance was straight ahead; the large window that looked out onto the street was on her right. She was turning her wine glass with her fingertips, slowly, waiting for him.

He showed up precisely on time. She noticed the way he moved, a prowling, ranging, roving but purposeful stride that she had once found inordinately sexy, and she thought about Rebecca Wilson's stalker, envying her, briefly, because Rebecca didn't know whom to fear. But she knew that was even worse. To be looking at the men passing through your life and wondering, Is it him? Or him? Or maybe him? Yeah, that would certainly be worse.

There wasn't one specific type of man who behaved this way, she thought, watching Alan approach. But the men who stalked shared certain characteristics. They were often good-looking. Sexy. Sure of themselves, in a way that appealed, at first. Intelligent. Confident.

No, it was more than confidence. It was arrogance, she thought, her eyes fixed on Alan McCurdy.

As he drew closer, Eddie observed him as if through the wrong end of a telescope. She saw him spot her — recognize her — hurry in her direction — and she wondered if she would be able to hear him when he spoke, so far away he seemed, so small, so distant.

But then he said, "Hi, Eddie, good to see you," and this brought him swiftly near. The background was re-established — the restaurant; she heard again the clinking of cutlery against china, the babble of conversation.

He bent toward her, to kiss her cheek, but something in her face dissuaded him. Instead, he held out his hand. She shook it and, with a shock of relief, experienced nothing when their palms met.

"Hello, Alan," she said.

He was as good-looking as ever. Probably even more so. He had some lines and wrinkles now. He was less bland, less picture-perfect, a little rougher around the edges, and therefore more appealing. But still she felt nothing.

She was experiencing a certain amount of light-headedness that she realized she couldn't let him know about.

"I'm not late, am I?" he said, sounding concerned.

"No. I was early."

He waved a waitress to the table and asked for a glass of "whatever my friend is having." He smiled at Eddie, but she didn't think he meant it.

He made small talk, and she let him. She had begun to look upon this meeting as research. She remembered his persuasive murmurings as he tried to woo her back. The coldness in his eyes when she refused to give in. It was as if rejection were both expected and inconceivable.

The thing about Rebecca Wilson's guy, though, was that she didn't even *see* him. He didn't exist for her, even though he had to occupy some small place in her life. Eddie, studying Alan across the restaurant table, tried to imagine the dimensions of this unknown guy's humiliation, tried to imagine how Alan might have reacted if she had been unaware of his continuing passion for her.

"So are you enjoying being the boss?" he said, and behind the counterfeit warmth she heard a sneer.

She answered, though, politely — but she was distracted. Becoming uneasy. Maybe the guy's moved away, she thought hopefully. It could have happened. Otherwise, he'd surely have done more, done something else to Rebecca Wilson, after New Year's Eve.

Unless of course he was a wimpy guy whose hurt feelings had been entirely assuaged by one evening roaming about in her house without her permission. That was possible, she told herself. Sure.

She gave Alan McCurdy her full attention. "So show me her picture," she said.

He pulled out his wallet and extracted a photo of a dark-haired woman who was wearing a lilac-coloured V-neck sweater. Her hands were behind her back. Her head was pitched to the right, and her expression was curious but patient.

"What's her name?"

"Amanda. Amanda Stewart." He was still smiling, watching her fixedly.

Eddie handed back the photo. "And when's the big day?"

"We haven't decided yet," said Alan, tucking the picture back in his wallet. He leaned to one side as he slipped the wallet into a back pocket. He was wearing casual pants, an open-necked shirt, and a dark blue cardigan. "In about a year. Next spring, probably."

"She's not a cop," said Eddie.

"No. She's a legal secretary."

"Here in Burnaby?"

"Vancouver."

"Are you two living together?"

"No. Eddie, why all the questions?"

She lifted her eyebrows at him. "She's the reason we're having this meeting, Alan. I'm very interested in her. As you might imagine."

"Okay. Fine. What else do you want to know?"

She sat back and blew an exasperated breath through her teeth. She picked up her backpack from the floor

and put it in her lap. "How come nobody knows about
this engagement?"

"What are you talking about?"

"Nobody you work with even knows you're dating
this woman."

Alan had red hair and the fair complexion that usually goes with it. His face darkened when he was agitated
or distressed. Eddie watched it darken now.

"I'm a private person, Eddie," he said. "You ought to
know that." He was struggling to remain calm. "Would
you like to meet her?"

"Sure."

"Well, I could arrange it."

"Good. I'd like that." She leaned across the table.
"But Alan. I really don't give a shit in hell whether
you've got a fiancée or not. All I want is never to hear
from you again." Looking into his eyes, Eddie thought
of storms at sea — thunderclouds — lightning bolts —
the tornado that blasted Dorothy out of Kansas and into
the land of Oz. "No e-mail," she told him. "No phone
calls. No letters."

"Or else what," he said, flat and cold.

Eddie sat back. "There was a piece in the paper
recently," she said, "about this cop — RCMP he was, too
— he was charged with criminal harassment and making a harassing telephone call. Did you happen to see it?
No? Well, the guy lost his job, Alan. They made him
resign." She stood up. "Have a nice day."

She forced herself to walk away slowly. She knew his
eyes were focused on her back. Her skin slid and puck-
ered and shuddered until she was out the door and on
the sidewalk.

The sun was still shining that afternoon when Olive and
Danny drove up the coast in Olive's car, with Olive at
the wheel. She related what local history she knew,

while Danny admired the scenery. Then they were each of them quiet for a while, enjoying the sunlight flashing among the bare tree branches and the knowledge that spring was only a heartbeat away.

Then Danny said, "So what did you mean on the phone? You said you had a lot to tell me."

"Somebody got into my house while I was out," she said. "And they took things. And moved things around." She enumerated them for him: the unlocked door, the coat that wasn't at the cleaners, the toilet paper she had stocked up on just the previous week, the disappearing eggs, the volume adjuster on the telephone, the missing curtain. "I found the curtain a couple of days later," she told him, "stuffed in behind some canned goods in the pantry."

But spoken aloud, the list sounded foolish. "I swear to you, Danny," she said, "I am not imagining things."

"Oh, I don't think you are," he said. "I don't think you imagined the stolen books, either."

Olive frowned at the road ahead, unease twisting through her stomach. "You're connecting these things?"

He turned so that he was facing her. "Sure, I'm connecting them. I think you should report this, too," Danny said quietly. "It could be somebody's trying to harass you, Olive."

Olive drove in silence, inadvertently speeding up so that the woods crowding to the edge of the highway became a streaky blur. She'd never told Danny about the car that had almost killed her. Would he connect that event to the others? Should *she* connect them? Tension had invaded her body, causing her heart to thud and her armpits to sweat: stress had taken over, like an occupying army. "Will you come with me?" she asked her nephew, sounding deceptively calm.

"Of course," said Danny. He put a big, clumsy hand on her shoulder and gave it a pat.

"We'll do it tomorrow, then," said Olive. "First thing."

———

That evening, back at home, Eddie called Marjorie.

"You did it, didn't you?" Marjorie cried. "You went and met the bastard, didn't you?"

"Yeah. Marj, it's okay, he knows I'll charge him if he starts up again. Listen. About Andrew."

"Andrew?"

"Yeah. I'd like to adopt him."

FIFTEEN

He reported to work Friday morning and lived the day and did the work as best he could. But he looked at his watch more often than usual. He sweated a lot more than usual. He found the people he encountered fiercely irritating and himself completely lacking in patience. He ground his teeth and clenched his hands so frequently that he got some curious glances — and finally, an exasperated reprimand.

"Lighten up, for godsake. Relax. If that precious car of yours was wound up that tight you'd have it in for servicing."

This scared the hell out of him. He managed to grin. He managed to pretend to relax. And he looked again at his watch and saw that it wasn't even noon yet. But at least he didn't have to spend the rest of the day in here. He'd just finish this up, then . . . he squinted at the computer screen, concentrating.

It was early afternoon when Olive Parfit and her nephew presented themselves at the RCMP detachment and Olive asked to speak with Sergeant Henderson.

"Sergeant, I'd like you to meet my nephew, Danny Parfit," she said, once they were in Eddie's office. "Danny, this is Sergeant Henderson."

"Why don't we talk over here," said Eddie, wheeling

her desk chair to the table in the corner. "Sit down, please. How can I help you?"

Olive glanced at Danny. "My nephew thinks someone is harassing me. What with the books being stolen and then turning up in the bookstore. And now this."

"Now what, Ms. Parfit?"

"Somebody entered my house while I was out," said Olive. She gave Eddie a detailed report. "I do feel like an idiot, telling you about it. I wouldn't be here, I assure you, if Danny hadn't insisted."

"It's too much of a coincidence," said Danny. "In my opinion." He was a large man with fair hair and a pale complexion. He had a steady, curious gaze, and there was weight in his voice that compelled attention.

"There was no sign of a break-in?" said Eddie.

Olive stiffened with embarrassment. "I have to admit to you, Sergeant, that I am not entirely certain I locked my door that morning."

"Well, that's a mistake I hope you won't make again," said Eddie with a smile. "But it's still a crime, even if he entered through an unlocked door, for someone to go into your house, and move stuff around, and steal things. He might have taken only toilet paper, eggs, and a coat from your closet, but it's still theft."

"You believe me, then. You believe that someone did that."

"Why wouldn't I believe you? I just don't know what we can do about it. Except suggest that you stick a note on your front door reminding you to lock it every time you go out."

"If somebody's been deliberately harassing her," said Danny, "he's not going to stop now, is he?" He turned to Olive. "I'm sorry, Aunt Olive, but we have to consider it."

"It's possible, maybe even likely," said Eddie, "that the two events aren't related, that one person stole the books and a different person went into your aunt's house. If that's the case, I doubt very much that anything else will happen."

"But what if . . . ?"

"Danny," said Olive. "Enough."

"I'll make sure all the Members know to keep an eye on the house," said Eddie. "Keep your door locked," she said to Olive, getting to her feet. "And if anything else happens, anything that's at all unusual, call me. Okay?"

"Okay," said Olive. "Thank you, Sergeant."

She and Danny shook Eddie's hand as they left. But Eddie knew that Olive's nephew wasn't satisfied.

She wheeled her chair back behind her desk, frustrated but truculent. They couldn't be everywhere. They couldn't do everything.

He hurried home from work, changed, drove to a place several blocks from Rebecca's house where he'd never parked before, and left the Lexus. He knew his vehicle was instantly recognizable to anybody who knew even apeshit about cars. He knew this ought to scare him.

It did scare him.

He got out of the car and looked around, casually, seeing no one on the street. He'd parked in front of a modest, white-shingled house separated from the sidewalk by a thick hedge about three feet high.

The day was cool and damp. He could smell the sea, and he heard the cawing of a crow. He patted the pockets of his jacket and the cargo pockets in his khaki pants, checking. He was surprised to notice that his lips were moving, as if he were praying, which he wasn't.

He walked along the street toward her house. Two cars passed, but no pedestrians. People were either at work or busy doing whatever behind their closed doors.

He passed a house with a front porch that looked to be falling apart. No curtains on the windows. Paint peeling from the walls. Inside, the blue-grey glow of a television set. He imagined an old guy huddled in a frayed easy chair, drinking beer, not so much absorbed in the TV program as accompanied by it.

The next house was constructed on two levels, its windows bracketed by bright green shutters. No lights shone inside. It looked empty, except for the dog in the window. A black Labrador retriever, its head draped over the back of a sofa, gazing out onto the street.

Farther along the block, he ran his hands along the top of a stone wall maybe four feet high, oddly comforted by its roughness, by the threat of scrapes and grazes, of mild bloodletting.

He was taking action — but action that was planned, that offered no opportunity for the kind of disaster he'd encountered with the other bitch. And so he was — for the moment, anyway — free of anger, filled with purpose. This stroll along her sidewalk was completely different from his appearance there on New Year's Eve. Today, he wasn't just wandering, he was there by design. He wasn't going to stand under her goddamn willow tree staring wistfully at her darkened house, feeling furtive and guilty, even though he had not one damn thing to feel guilty about. Today, he was walking tall and obvious, as if in bright sunshine. The sky was overcast, true; but he felt the sun behind the clouds, felt its warmth on his shoulders encouraging him, urging him on.

As he approached her house he kept himself loose, turning into the driveway, his mouth pursed in a silent whistle. His back was burning — from the sun? Or was a neighbour eyeing him with a curiosity hot enough for him to feel? Too late now. He fumbled for a while at the front door, the hot spot on his back aflame. And then he was inside.

Again, her fragrance hung in the air.

He walked slowly through the rooms of her house, nostalgia flooding his chest and tightening his throat. He

stroked her bedspread and fingered the clothes in her
closet with a sadness approaching grief. What a waste.
What a deplorable, immoral *waste*. It was criminal, that
she could have rejected so carelessly the future that could
have been theirs.

He didn't know exactly when she was likely to get
home from work, but he was pretty sure he had at least half
an hour. It didn't feel like that was going to be enough.

They hadn't caught the guy, of course. Rebecca wasn't surprised. But she was indignant. What were the police for, for
heaven's sake? They were supposed to hunt these people
down and make sure they got punished. Another part of
her did know what an impossible task it was, because there
were no clues, no clues at all, and because she hadn't been
able to help them by coming up with suspects.

She didn't think about it nearly as much anymore.
Weeks had passed, and even though the guy was still out
there somewhere, she felt that she no longer had his
attention.

As she drove home from work that Friday, she was
thinking about it again only because Corinne had asked
if there'd been any news. And she'd had to say, "Not that
I know of."

And Corinne had said, "Maybe it's time you gave
them another call." She meant the police. But Rebecca
just groaned.

She and Corinne had made an extensive list of people Rebecca knew: relatives, friends, colleagues, fellow
students from high school and university, men who had
repaired her appliances and laid her carpets and worked
on her car. But she had ended up scratching out almost
all of them.

"You know what?" she'd said to Corinne. "I've had
the locks changed, now I'm just going to forget the
whole damn thing."

And that's what she'd tried to do.

She was rounding the marina now, turning into her street, and when she was still blocks away from her house she became aware of a rhythmic, pounding noise; and the closer she got to home the louder the noise grew. She eventually recognized it as music. "What the hell . . . " said Rebecca, under her breath.

It was coming from inside her home. Her next-door neighbour was standing on the lawn staring at Rebecca's front door, her hands clapped over her ears. People had emerged onto their porches or into their yards to peer in the direction of Rebecca's small, tortured house, their shoulders hunched against the onslaught.

Rebecca stomped on the accelerator and drove in a frenzy to the detachment. Inside, she banged the flat of her hand hard on the receptionist's counter, causing William Kirkpatrick to turn, startled, from the filing cabinets. Rebecca, despite her distress, thought to wonder if he was still trying to find homes for the same troubled documents he'd been ministering to the last time she was there.

"I need to see Sergeant Henderson." The pitch of her voice was alarmingly high, and this increased her anxiety.

The detachment seemed deserted except for William, who was apparently transfixed, staring at her, one arm abandoned in an upright position, the other hand clutching a file folder against his chest. His eyes were wide and his mouth was slightly open. Rebecca felt that he ought to be better prepared for crises. Don't they *train* people around here? she thought indignantly, and banged the counter again.

Beatrice emerged from somewhere in the back of the building.

"I need to see the sergeant," said Rebecca. "It's an emergency." Where *was* everyone, for heaven's sake? The place had been teeming with cops the last time she was here. It occurred to her that there might have been some kind of emergency. A five-car pileup on the highway. Possibly an earthquake. And they were all out attending to it.

Beatrice picked up the phone and murmured into it, listened, nodded, put the phone down. "She'll be right out. Take a seat."

Rebecca turned around. Her hands were shaking. She thrust them into her pockets and made them into fists, her fingernails pressing sharply into her palms. She heard footsteps and turned quickly to see Sergeant Henderson approaching.

Eddie looked, to Rebecca, very reassuring. Tall and strong and confident and beautiful, with a yellow braid and sympathetic blue eyes. An able and undoubtedly a courageous woman. With a gun.

"Miss Wilson. What's the problem?"

Rebecca scrabbled at Eddie's arm. "Please come."

Eddie saw a woman teetering on the edge of hysteria. Her eyes were huge. There was oily sweat on her forehead. Blood pulsed frantically in her throat.

Music thundered from the house — earsplitting heavy metal, so distorted it couldn't have been identified by its creators. It was easy for Eddie to imagine that the roof was loosening and would soon be blasted into space.

"What the hell's going on, Rebecca?" shouted one of the neighbours, a woman in her fifties wearing a dark blue suit and tailored grey hair.

"We don't know yet, ma'am," said Eddie, climbing out of the patrol car onto Rebecca Wilson's driveway. She unfastened her holster. "Let me have your keys," she said to Rebecca, who handed them over. "Please go home, ma'am," she said loudly to the neighbour, who reluctantly withdrew across the grass to what Eddie assumed was her own front door. "You stay here by the car, Miss Wilson."

"I will."

Eddie tried the door, which was unlocked. With one hand hovering near her weapon, she pushed the door all the way open. The music blasted out with a force she felt as heat on her face, so corrupted by volume that it had dissolved into toxic racket. Eddie tried to ignore it as she checked out the house. When she was certain it was empty, she turned off the CD player.

The silence was sudden and complete, but filled with echoes that collided clumsily, like aural bumper cars. As these faded, the house seemed to sigh and shudder. For a moment, Eddie thought it might collapse, mortally weakened by the onslaught of noise.

Rebecca sidled through the door. "My god," she whispered. "Oh my god."

Eddie had seen worse. Rebecca hadn't.

Cushions had been slashed, the coffee table and piano gouged, boxes of cereal and bags of flour upended all over the furniture and the floor along with bottles of various liquids. Eddie smelled salad dressing and maple syrup.

Rebecca clapped her hands over her face, tears spilling between her fingers. "Tom-Tom." She called out to him, but didn't move. She remained standing in the middle of the room, in the middle of the chaos, as if rooted there. "Tom-Tom. Tom!"

Eddie put her arm around Rebecca's shoulders and moved her back to the front door. "Stay here."

"It's my cat," said Rebecca. "Tom-Tom."

"I'll look for him," said Eddie. "You stay put."

In the bedroom she found a butchered bed, a slaughtered wardrobe, but no cat. In the kitchen, spray-can graffiti on the walls and cupboards and the remainder of Rebecca's provisions on the floor — gleaming drifts of flour, golden puddles of honey, a small vermilion mound that Eddie figured was strawberry jam. It could almost have been a composition, carefully positioned elements of a still-life painting. But no Tom-Tom. In the store-room/office, papers torn and scattered, a filing cabinet emptied upon the floor — but no cat.

Eddie returned to Rebecca, who hadn't moved except to wrap her arms around herself. "He's not here. He probably ran out when the guy opened the door to leave."

Rebecca dropped her head, moaning.

"This is a crime scene, Miss Wilson," Eddie said gently. "You're going to have to stay somewhere else for a couple of days."

The last thing he'd done was to put on the player the CD he'd brought with him and to crank the volume up as high as it would go. The blast of sound damn near deafened him, and it brought the cat out of hiding. When he opened the door and slipped out onto the deck, the cat shot past him, a shiny black projectile, and raced away along the rocky beach. He followed quickly, trying not to stumble. The music shrieked behind him, so loud that it caused his brain to rattle inside his skull. When he had passed several houses, he swerved up from the beach and emerged onto the road.

At his car, he could still hear the music.

He'd climbed behind the wheel of the Lexus and started the engine when he saw her car approaching, Rebecca at the wheel. He ducked and turned away.

But a moment later he had to will himself not to follow her, so intense was his longing to come to her rescue, to help and comfort her. . . . Oh jesus it was hard not to do that.

And all the way home he wondered if in fact maybe he should've done it. Gotten out of his car. Run to her

house. Rushed inside to turn off the noise. Held her —
soothed her when she surveyed the shambles her home
had become. Wouldn't it have finally, irrevocably, put
everything right between them, if he'd been there when
she most needed his support and consolation?

But how would he have explained his presence in her
neighbourhood?

And besides. It was too late for reconciliation.

Driving home, he was exhilarated. He was pumped.
He banged the steering wheel with his fist and hooted
out loud. Jesus he felt so good so goddamn *good*.

SIXTEEN

Eddie and Rebecca Wilson were sitting in the front seat of Eddie's patrol car. Two more cars were parked across the street.

"I've got no idea, my god, who could have done this," said Rebecca, weeping. "I've got no idea, my god, *no idea*. My god, *who could have done this!*" She was bent over as if with a stomachache. And shivering, despite the fact that Eddie had turned on the engine and the heater.

"The guy who emptied your underwear drawer is who did it," said Eddie, flipping open her notebook.

Rebecca's house and yard had been cordoned off. Eddie had assigned the investigation to Buster Sheffield, who was inside videotaping the crime scene while Beverly Brooks sketched the rooms, taking notes. Bert Chapman was videotaping the exterior of the house and its immediate surroundings, and examining the ground for evidence. Up and down the street Johnny Greig, Nick Orsato and Marlise Beyer were knocking on doors, talking to the neighbours.

"This is a very serious escalation," said Eddie. "Are you sure you haven't had problems with anybody at work? Parents of kids taken into care, maybe," she said, recalling the child Elizabeth. "Anything at all — an argument, a disagreement, somebody pissed off about something, even something that seems insignificant."

Rebecca was shaking her head. "No. Nobody. My god, do you think I wouldn't have *noticed*, if somebody was mad enough at me to do *this?*"

"What about little things — any strange e-mail, for instance, or telephone hang-ups?"

"No."

"Deliveries? Pizza, whatever — stuff that came, but you didn't order it?"

"No."

"Any cancelled appointments?"

"No more than usual. And nothing that didn't turn out to be just what it seemed."

"Unusual behaviour among your friends?" Eddie went on doggedly. "Someone suddenly cool to you?"

"No. I'm sorry, Sergeant." The handful of damp tissue she'd used was now in shreds. She looked around for a wastebasket, didn't see one, and wrapped her hand more tightly around the mess.

Eddie saw Bert appear from the direction of the marina, training the video camera on the side of the house, then on the door. He would be aware of the fading light, trying to hurry without rushing, trying not to miss anything.

"You were going to make a list for me, after the first time," said Eddie. "Have you done that?"

"No." Rebecca shook her head. "Oh god. I'm sorry."

"I need it. Now. We'll do it here and now. Everyone you know. Every man and boy."

Through the window she saw Buster Sheffield stooping, then standing upright again, moving slowly across the living room, his eyes on the floor.

"I can't do this. I can't." Rebecca moaned and clutched herself, still shivering.

"You've got to do it," said Eddie grimly.

"Tom-Tom. My cat. What if he did something to my cat?"

"Your cat got scared and ran away. He'll be back. Let's go, Miss Wilson. I'm sitting here with my pen poised. Start with the people in your office."

Through the windshield she saw Johnny Greig standing on the porch of a house halfway up the block. The front door was open and someone was leaning against the jamb while Johnny scribbled in his notebook. While Eddie watched, he snapped the notebook closed and gave the person in the doorway a two-fingered salute, then walked quickly down the steps and along the walk to the next house. She hoped to god he was getting some good information.

"Oh god," said Rebecca. She turned suddenly to Eddie. "How am I going to clean up that mess?" Tears spurted into her eyes and spilled down her cheeks.

"Don't think about it now. You won't be able to get in there until we're done with the place anyway," said Eddie. She put her hand on Rebecca's arm. "You're going to want to call someone. Somebody you can stay with for a few days."

"I know. I will."

"Miss Wilson. Rebecca." Eddie waited until Rebecca had raised her head and met her eyes. The woman looked dazed.

"Yes? What?" she said.

"That 'mess' in there is something truly savage. Do you understand me? Somebody has committed an extremely violent act. And he's done it to you."

"To my *things!*" said Rebecca, banging her fist on her knee. "To my *stuff*. Not to *me!*"

Eddie sat back, frustrated, wondering if another Member would be more successful in getting her to cooperate. She looked through the back window and saw Marlise Beyer approaching the front door of a small weatherbeaten house with a large Japanese maple tree in the yard. Maybe she ought to do the house-to-house and let Marlise try her luck with Rebecca Wilson.

"Sergeant."

Eddie turned back to her.

"It can't be anybody I know. It just can't be."

"Miss Wilson," said Eddie quietly, "it can't be anybody else."

"Something random," Rebecca said stubbornly, her eyes wild. "A random act of violence. They happen all the time."

"Once, maybe," said Eddie. "But not twice. This guy has gotten into your house twice. This is not random. This is personal." She shook her head. "The next time . . . well, we can't let a next time happen. So let's get started on that list."

Several hours later, Eddie was entering her notes into a computer file when Buster tapped on her office door.

"I'm ready to bring you up to speed," he said.

"Come on in."

He was followed into her office by Beatrice, who was bearing a tray.

"Beatrice, how come you're still here?" said Eddie.

"I thought you might want something to eat," said Beatrice. "And so I ordered a pizza. Paid for it with petty cash." She put the tray and a handful of paper napkins down on Eddie's desk.

"Ahhh," said Eddie, sniffing the air. "That smells wonderful. My mouth's watering. I forgot I was hungry."

"I'll let you help yourselves," said Beatrice, brushing her hands together. "And I'll get on home now."

"Beatrice," said Eddie. "Thank you so much."

"There's a fresh pot of coffee, too."

"You're a treasure," said Buster. "You want a piece before you go?"

Beatrice shook her head. "No thanks. See you tomorrow."

"I'll serve this if you get the coffee," said Buster to Eddie. When Eddie got back with the coffee, he was holding a slice of pizza high in the air. He waited patiently until the strands of cheese holding it to the container snapped. He set it on a plate, did the same thing again, and handed one of the plates to Eddie. Then he settled in the diner chair.

For several minutes, neither of them spoke; they just ate.

"I had no idea," said Eddie, her mouth full, "that I was so damn hungry."

Buster groaned in agreement.

Finally, they stacked the plates on the tray with the empty pizza box and Buster put the tray on the small table in the corner of the office. When he returned to the diner chair, he pulled out his notebook. "What did you get out of the victim?" he asked, and took a slurp of his coffee.

"Very little," said Eddie grimly. She wiped her mouth with a paper napkin and chucked it into her wastebasket. "She still doesn't want to think she knows the guy. Can't believe this is happening to her."

"Denial. Yeah," he said.

"We made up a list of some of the men in her life," said Eddie, turning pages in her notebook. "She's absolutely adamant — she doesn't have a clue who did it — there's nobody in her life who's capable of doing it."

"How long is this list?"

"Not long enough. I had to drag it out of her, name by name. There are two people in her office, but they were at work all afternoon. She didn't want to tell me about any of her clients at first, but I persuaded her, so that's another half-dozen or so. She also gave me some people who've done work around her house. All in all, there are — let's see — twenty names." She tore the page from her notebook and handed it across the desk to Buster. "I'm going to talk to her again, get some more."

"Yeah, because twenty people, there's got to be more than twenty men in her life. What about dates? Friends?"

"They're in there. I know, you're right, she knows a lot more than twenty men. But she was pretty shaken up. She'll be calmer tomorrow. Especially if her cat turns up."

"Well, we got diddly-squat from the neighbours, apparently," said Buster, flicking a contemptuous finger at his open notebook. "I'm gonna give you a précis, here, of what the guys found out. Most people were at work. There's a couple across the street and the woman who lives next door, they were home when the music started. Scared the piss out of them. 'I just froze there in my chair, couldn't move a muscle at first,' says the lady next door. Meanwhile, of course, while she's frozen in her chair the perp's hightailing it off down the beach."

"Do you know that for a fact?" Eddie drank some coffee, put the mug back down on her desk.

"I deduced it," said Buster, winking at her. "The people across the street, they heard this music blaring away and they ran to their living-room window, looked up and down the street, saw nothing and no one." He shrugged. "So if the guy didn't go down the road, he must've gone down the beach. Because turning up the music, that must've been the very last thing he did."

"And that's it?" said Eddie. "From the neighbours?"

"That's it. The guys also asked about unfamiliar cars, strangers walking around. Nothing."

"What about physical evidence?"

"Well, there's the CD. You said it doesn't belong to the vic, right?"

"Right."

"We'll print it, just in case. And Bert had a look along the beach; he's gonna go back down there tomorrow. I doubt he'll find anything. And hairs in that gooey mess all over the goddamn floor, yeah, there were some, I bagged 'em." His lip curled in distaste, such an incongruous expression on his craggy face that Eddie laughed. "They're probably cat hairs," he said, ignoring her.

Eddie pulled her shoulders back and lifted her arms, elbows high, stretching.

Buster closed his notebook and dropped it onto the desk with a sigh.

Eddie said, looking out the window into the rainy night, "What worries me . . ."

"Yeah," said Buster. "Me too. This is one angry dude. He's not gonna stop here."

"Also, he's got a certain amount of skill."

"Yeah. Jimmied that door open, slid into that house like shit through a goose. Not all that easy to do — that new lock, it's a good one." He looked vaguely upward. "I knew a guy. Taught me. Once. . . ."

"Bet he wasn't from around here."

"You got that right."

"He wrecked the place, but he didn't go berserk," said Eddie. "Kept quiet. A cold sonofabitch. Didn't make a lot of noise, until he put on the CD." She looked at Buster. "What do you know about the music? Is there something significant about that CD?"

He shrugged. "It's about as loud as that stuff gets. I think that's what's significant."

"So what else?" asked Eddie. She opened a desk drawer and propped her feet on it. "What else, Buster?" she said impatiently. "There's gotta be something we're missing."

He sighed. "Nothing stolen. At least, not that she can tell so far."

"Right. Okay. Go on."

"He's gotta be an ordinary-looking type of individual, nothing particularly noticeable about him."

"Well, nothing deformed or repulsive, anyway," said Eddie.

"Could be he's invisible, you know? The guy who delivers milk. A Federal Express driver. A kid with a pizza truck."

Eddie linked her hands behind her head. "Plus he's audacious. Reckless. Smart." She frowned at the ceiling. "So he knows what he's doing. Is he somebody we oughta know, then?" She looked at Buster. "A perp?"

Buster was shaking his head. "I know them all. You pretty well know them all by now too. There's nobody fits the bill, Sarge." He drained his coffee mug.

"It's hard to believe somebody like that can be in her life and she doesn't know who he is."

"We've gotta get it out of her somehow, Eddie. I mean, she knows the guy. So we've gotta just keep at her until she's given us every single man she's ever had anything to do with."

"I'll talk to her again tomorrow. If I don't get anywhere, I'm going to hand her over to Marlise." She glanced at her watch. "And now, let's you and I pack it in."

"Sounds good."

"Did I tell you," said Eddie, grabbing her cap and her jacket from the coat rack, "about the dog I'm getting?"

Almost a week later, Eddie was at her desk, doodling in her journal, searching her brain for inspiration. She had got nowhere with Rebecca Wilson over the last several days, and neither had Marlise Beyer. The woman couldn't — or wouldn't — remember any occasion on which she had offended anybody.

Eddie sighed, pushing her journal to one side. That wasn't strictly true, she admitted. Rebecca had come up with several incidents, and they'd all been checked out. Each had involved people she didn't know at all, or with whom she had only a nodding acquaintance: a telemarketer she'd told off on the phone, a neighbour complaining that her cat peed in his rhododendrons, the receptionist at her work who'd burst into tears when Rebecca snapped at her for losing a telephone message, the newspaper carrier whom she'd forgotten to pay.

The first time, she thought, that would've been easy pickings. It was New Year's Eve. Anybody could have sauntered in and out of that house and nobody would have noticed — certainly nobody would have remembered seeing anything the next day. The guy gets himself in, using her key. . . .

Eddie was for a moment distracted by remembering yet another useless conversation with Rebecca: Who knew about that key under the rock? she'd asked her. To hear the woman talk, the whole damn town knew, or could have known about that damn key. Including, Rebecca was convinced, a bunch of nameless, faceless perpetrators of "random violence."

Okay, so he was one of the dozens of people who know about the key. He gets in. Maybe on a whim, maybe he was just passing by, on his way to a party, or the ferry. He does no damage. Wanders through the house. . . .

She wondered how long he'd been there, whether he'd sat on her sofa, looked out the windows at the boats in the marina, played her piano, maybe got himself a drink of water, carefully washing and drying the glass afterwards and putting it away.

And he ends up in her bedroom, where he strips her hangers bare, dropping the clothes on the floor, and empties her dresser drawers onto the bed. Did he bury his face in her underwear? Rub himself with one of her nightgowns? Ejaculate into her pantyhose? If he did, he left no sign of it.

He didn't care that she'd know he'd been there, though. In fact, he wanted her to know he'd been there.

And so, sometime in the days following New Year's Eve, had he been present when she talked about the break-in? Had he been a sympathetic listener while she complained about the violation and expressed her fears?

Eddie got up and stuck her finger in the soil of her two plants, but decided they didn't need watering.

Six weeks had passed. Who the hell knew what was going on, either in Rebecca's life or in this pissant's head, to build up that kind of pressure? But something did, and six weeks later, it blew.

Eddie dropped back into her desk chair and thought, It's somebody like Alan. A stubborn s.o.b. with hurt feelings.

Like Alan.

The second time was different. This time was definitely planned. He popped the new front-door lock. He brought tools with him: a knife with a wide six-inch blade, cans of spray paint, a Marilyn Manson CD; he wore gloves; he arrived in the late afternoon, did what he had to do, and slipped out through the back door and along the beach.

What kind of a guy was this?

Rebecca had given her twenty names. Why wasn't he there? Of course, she'd probably left out some she thought were beyond suspicion. Eddie needed them all, dammit.

What would my own list of acquaintances look like, she thought. Who would she leave out on the first round? Her father. Her doctor. If she'd gone to church, she'd probably leave out the minister. And of course her colleagues.

Except for Alan.

Eddie sat down. She spread her hands on top of the desk.

Rebecca would rule out a cop too, she thought. Most people would. They would automatically rule out a cop.

Several days later, returning home from a drive up the coast, sailing in the Lexus around a corner on the outskirts of Gibsons, he noticed a late-model Camry parked by the side of the road with the hood up.

He slowed, pulled over, and got out of the Lexus. A young woman was staring into the engine compartment with a packaged fan belt clutched in her hand.

"Maybe I could give you a hand," he said with a smile.

She was medium height, no more than thirty years old, with a long brown ponytail and dark green eyes.

He introduced himself.

She hesitated. "I'm Rhoda," she said finally.

She was somewhat heavier than he would have liked. But beneath her sweatsuit, she looked to be well-muscled rather than fat.

She told him that she lived in Sechelt.

"Would you like me to do that for you?" he asked, nodding at the fan belt.

She laughed. "Sure." She held it out to him.

"It's a pleasure." He got the thing installed in a jiffy, of course. "There."

She shook her head admiringly. "I could never have done that. Thanks. Thanks a lot." She looked at him appraisingly. "I'm heading into Gibsons. Can I buy you a coffee?"

Eddie was closeted in her office again that evening. She thought again of Alan, and of the handcuffs glinting at her from the shadows in the lobby of her apartment building. . . .

Slowly she pushed her chair away from the desk and stood up. She walked to the window and looked out at the parking lot. On one side, RCMP vehicles; personal transportation on the other. And there was her Mercedes, in the spot right next to the door. A perk, she observed with one part of her mind, admiring once again the fact that a mind could so effortlessly divide

itself up, applying a few million cells to this subject and
a different few million to another.

Let's not get ahead of ourselves here, she thought.

Of course the woman knew some cops. She knew
Eddie. She knew Nick Orsato. She probably knew most
of the detachment. Jesus Christ.

Eddie looked up, blindly. *Is there any justification for
pursuing the investigation into this area?* The thought rang
in her head, a bland, dispassionate, but persistent inquiry.

She'd start with her own detachment. Figure out, first,
who it couldn't have been: who was on duty both New
Year's Eve and February 18th. Then, of those who were
left, who couldn't have done it for reasons equally obvious.

When he awoke the next morning he knew that his life
had changed. He had a future. A new focus.

He showered, shaved, and dressed carefully. He would
make up a reason to drive to Sechelt today. She'd told
him she worked in a bank there. He'd give her a little
thrill, let her show him off to her friends.

He smiled to himself, pulling on the navy trousers
with the gold stripe down the side. He knew how good
he looked in his uniform.

SEVENTEEN

Rebecca slept fitfully, reluctant to use the sleeping pills her doctor had prescribed in case her persecutor should return in the middle of the night. She ate little and had lost weight. She had difficulty concentrating.

Her colleagues had been, and continued to be, solicitous. Peter had offered to reduce her workload, but Rebecca knew that would just mean more for Corinne to do. Besides, she needed the distraction of work, and she had told Peter so.

Every male person she encountered she suspected.

She hated living this way.

On the first Thursday in March she looked up from her desk to see her father coming through the glass door. And instantly she knew that she'd been expecting him.

She had tried not to tell her parents about the trashing of her house and in fact had managed at first not to do so. But finally, four nights ago, when they called, as they did every Sunday, she couldn't help it, she'd just blurted it out. And then had insisted that she was fine, fine, coping well. . . .

An expression of grim determination was fixed upon her dad's face as he approached the receptionist's desk. But before he got there, Rebecca was on her feet, flying across the office. She flapped through the gate and flung her arms around him.

"I'm a big girl, Dad," she whispered. "You shouldn't have come. I can take care of myself."

"I am not leaving this town," said her father, embracing her, "until that bastard's caught."

"Good," said Rebecca.

He purred up the highway toward Sechelt, on patrol. He was keeping a lid on it, keeping his speed down, keeping his mind on the job — keeping himself in the here and now. The here and now, it was a good place to be, after all. Jesus, he'd done some weird and shitty stuff lately. But those days were over, thanks to the new woman in his life — thanks to Rhoda, who was gonna wipe Rebecca right out of his head.

He was proud of himself because he'd taken his frustrations out on her house, trashing her belongings instead of slapping her around. And he'd gotten away with it. He'd avoided disaster and gotten away with it.

His hands were gripping the wheel so tightly he could feel it all the way up his arms, so he flexed them, one at a time, easing the strain in his muscles. It was hot in the car, although he hadn't turned the heater on, and he opened the window, turning his face into the cold air.

The patrol car rounded a corner, and the highway now paralleled the shore. As he drove up the long hill that led into Sechelt, he remembered his mother's death and how it was supposed to set him free. She had wanted the whole nine yards, and she'd gotten it. There was a funeral ceremony in the United Church that she and his father had attended three or four times a year. He wondered if his father would keep on going, now that he was on his own, and it occurred to him again, shamefacedly, how little he knew about this man, how little curiosity he had felt about him throughout his life. Was this going to change now? (He'd never know, as it happened, since his father

would die in a car crash before the summer sun
returned to Nova Scotia.)

She died of a heart attack. He found this utterly
bewildering. He hadn't yet reached that point in a young
man's life when the death of his mother becomes a
believable concept even in the far-distant, unimaginable
future — although the possibility of existence without
his father had for years in his mind been a real and
acceptable one.

He felt at risk, threatened. Yet this was accompanied
by a tenuous, unarticulated relief. He stood next to his
father at the burial site patting his shoulder ineffectually
and gazing into the hole that contained his mother's cas-
ket, which was a huge, massive, gleaming thing large
enough, he was sure, to hold at least two of her.

Throughout that afternoon, the dry November winds
brushed the last bronze and gold and burgundy leaves
from the trees, and the winter sun squinted his eyes but
left his skin cold, and friends and neighbours and the few
remaining relatives still clinging to his mother's family
tree gathered to pay their respects and then repaired to
his parents' home to clink teacups and eat pound cake
and murmur among themselves.

He rested the palm of his hand against the fireplace
mantel and gazed intently at the floor, at the rectangle of
black tiles on which the fireplace screen sat, and he tried
to empty his mind of memory, and contemplate his freedom. These went together, chucking bad memories and
reaching out to the future. But what if he couldn't do it?

He remembered his father's persistent reproach that
day: "Why didn't you wear your uniform? I wish you'd
worn your uniform. She'd have been so proud."

Now, looking back, he seemed to have been fated to
devote himself to shallow, pointless women who weren't
able to appreciate, let alone return, the kind of love he
offered. What kind of freedom was that?

But maybe there was some purpose to all this, he thought, signalling a left turn at Sechelt's only traffic light. Maybe they were better people when he'd finished with them. Maybe they learned something from the experience, if only that their actions had *consequences*, goddamnit, and that if they offended, they were damn well going to be offended in return.

He drove slowly up the street, looking for the bank she'd mentioned.

He pulled from memory the sight of Rebecca's living room just before he'd cranked up the CD player. In the chaos he had created there he'd seen elegance and a savage kind of grace.

And then, when the music struck, the wreckage had appeared to spring to life. The gaping wounds in the sofa and chair stretched their mouths wide; the gashes in the top of the piano began to throb; cereal and flour and salad dressing and maple syrup pooled and puddled on the floor, their separate scents clashing in the air. He remembered the bedroom, too — the damaged bed, the upturned chest of drawers. And the kitchen — he'd gotten a special thrill out of spray-painting BITCH and WHORE on the cabinets, even though the word "banal" had repeated itself in his head while he did it.

But it was the living room that stuck in his mind, because he knew it was the first thing she'd see, and because of how the sudden blast of music had kindled it into life. That had been amazing. He had wanted to stay, to see if the enlivening he'd perceived was real, and if it would escalate into something truly uncanny — he couldn't imagine what.

He parked the patrol car, got out, locked up, and tugged at his jacket. Not nervously. Fastidiously. He strode to the bank, glimpsing himself in the window, watching his hand reach for the door handle.

Inside, he cast a comprehensive glance around. It was a small bank, with potted plants at either end of the counter and another large one by the door. There were three tellers. To the left, outside what he took to be the manager's office, a young couple sat on a bench. The woman held a file folder on her lap and kept stroking it, as if reassuring herself of the validity of its contents. The man was leaning forward, arms on his thighs, studying the floor.

Rhoda stood at the till that was farthest from the door. Her head was down as she counted out bills for an old woman who was wearing a plaid jacket, baggy jeans, and a worn felt hat with a wide brim.

His gaze was riveted upon Rhoda's face as he waited for her to notice him. And when she did, he wasn't disappointed.

There was a place in the centre of him where pain lived. It was a cold, dark place. But Rhoda's delight at seeing him directed a beam of warmth and light into that place. Her eyes brightened; her smile was quick and shy and genuine. His heart stumbled, and he felt the quickening of tears.

"I keep telling you, the sofa's just fine."

"It might be fine with you, but it isn't fine with me," Rebecca called out from the storeroom.

It was evening now. Rebecca had left work when her father arrived. Over his protests, they had borrowed a bed from Corinne and Rick.

Grudgingly, he had helped Rebecca push her desk and filing cabinet against the wall, making room for the bed, which now filled up most of the room. Into the storeroom Rebecca moved the coat rack that usually stood by the front door so he would have something to hang his clothes on; she wheeled the desk chair over next to the bed, to serve as a night table, and put the small halogen desk lamp on top of it.

"There," she said now. "See, Dad, what if I want to bring someone home one night? I can't have you dozing on the sofa, right out there in plain view."

"Ha ha ha," said her dad. "How much of your stuff did you have to replace?"

Rebecca sat down, suddenly exhausted. She felt like she'd been exerting herself for hours, beyond her physical capacity. "I'm so glad you're here, Dad."

He was sitting on her new sofa, cradling his belly and Tom-Tom on his lap. He nodded. "Good. I thought you might resent it. This is why I didn't call first."

"You must be hungry. Let's go out to eat."

"You haven't answered my question," said her dad. "How much of all this is new?" He gestured at her living-room furniture.

"The coffee table," Rebecca said wearily. "I had a big glass one. The sofa. It was slashed all to hell." She looked around, as if trying to remember. She still wasn't used to the new stuff. It hadn't settled into place yet. Her home felt like a display area in a furniture store. "It's so depressing, Dad. And I — well, you know me. I don't *get* depressed."

"And don't be depressed now. Be angry. Be enraged." His face was red with indignation.

Rebecca smiled. "I don't have to get angry. Not with you around to do it for me." She looked at Tom-Tom, dozing on her father's lap. "I'm just so damn grateful that he didn't get hurt. And that he came back. I drove over here the morning after, from Corinne's place, on my way to work, and there he was, meowing at the front door."

"What else got wrecked? A coffee table, a sofa — what else?"

"A big chair that sort of went with the sofa. My bed. And he made big gouges in the desk and the top of the piano."

Her father glanced over his shoulder at the piano. "Does it still work? The piano?"

"Yeah. It still works."

"Okay then."

"And I had another carpet here. There was honey and flour and feathers from one of my pillows all over it. We just rolled it up and chucked it. A bunch of people helped me clean up. Friends." She put a hand over her eyes. "Oh god, I'm shaking again. I've never seen anything like it, Dad. I was terrified — I thought for sure I was going to find Tom-Tom dead in the middle of it all."

William put the cat down on the floor and crossed the room to crouch next to his daughter. He hugged her close, and Rebecca allowed herself to weep for a while.

When she was finished, they went out to eat.

In the café Rebecca felt weak and pale, like a person just released from hospital, recovering from a bout of pneumonia, perhaps, or from injuries suffered in a car crash. And in fact she *was* convalescent, struggling to reclaim herself not from disease or accident, but from psychological damage.

"I need red meat today," she said, scanning the menu.

"Steak sandwich, maybe," said Earl. His huge apron had two large pockets. In one he kept an order pad and a pen. In the other, a thick pot holder. This was mere decoration, however. Earl didn't need either. He had a prodigious memory and asbestos hands.

"Or a burger," Earl offered. "A burger's red meat, too."

"A burger. Good idea."

"And Rebecca's dad?"

"How do you know I'm her dad? How do you know I'm not her boyfriend?"

Earl grinned. "Family resemblance. Otherwise — sure. Could be boyfriend." He chuckled and winked at

Rebecca before hurrying off to deliver their orders to the kitchen.

"So. Have the police made any headway?"

Rebecca shook her head.

"No clues at all?"

"None."

"None of your neighbours saw anything?"

"Nope."

He regarded her with exasperation. "Well, somebody must have seen something." Earl returned with two cups of coffee and a small metal jug containing cream. A glass sugar canister was already on the table.

"Nobody did, Dad," said Rebecca. "Not only did the cops go up and down the street talking to people, so did I."

"And nobody saw a damn thing either time?" He shook his head. "The first time, I can understand that," he said, stirring cream into his coffee. "It was night, it was New Year's Eve. But the second time, that was in broad daylight."

"Yeah, but it was during working hours, you know? And there are only two houses on the block where people weren't away at the office. And nobody there saw anything."

"What about fingerprints, footprints — I don't know, some kind of clues found at the scene?"

"None," said Rebecca.

"Okay. No witnesses. No clues. Then the only thing we've got to go on," he said, "is that this person is somebody you know."

Rebecca's head ached. Her muscles ached. Her bones ached. She would never be able to sleep long enough to make all of her aches go away. "I've been through this, Dad," she said patiently. "First with Corinne. Then with the cops, with Sergeant Henderson. I have made mental lists, I have made written lists. I've listed every single person in my life with whom I've ever had any kind of trouble, the smallest kind of trouble."

"Sure," said her father. "But what about people you haven't had trouble with?"

"Two burgers with fries," said Earl, setting plates down in front of them.

Rebecca's mouth watered. "This smells so good."

"Why do you sound surprised?" said Earl indignantly. "My food always smells good."

"I just didn't expect to feel like eating tonight," said Rebecca meekly.

"You want ketchup? Vinegar?"

"Vinegar, please," said Rebecca's dad.

"Ketchup, please," said Rebecca.

Earl snatched them from a neighbouring table. "Enjoy."

"We need a piece of paper," said Rebecca's father, when Earl had moved away.

"Dad. Please. Eat."

And for a while, in silence, they did.

"This is very good," said her father. "This is one of the best hamburgers I've ever had." He sounded astonished.

A few minutes later, Earl came around with the coffee pot.

"This is very good," said Rebecca's dad, waving what was left of his hamburger in the air. "And the fries, too. Excellent. Really."

"I know," said Earl amicably, topping up their coffee.

Rebecca was still eating when her father pushed his plate away. "Do you have some kind of notebook in that purse of yours?"

She stared at him reproachfully.

"I'm here to help, Rebecca. I'm here to watch out for you, sure. But I'm not going to just sit on my hands and wait for the police to catch this guy." He leaned across the table toward her. "Another pair of hands, it can't do

any harm, right? A new perspective? A new kind of list?
How about it?"

With a groan, Rebecca dragged a notebook and a pen
from her shoulder bag and handed them over.

EIGHTEEN

Eddie had narrowed the field to Howard Peck, Glen Hammond, and Matt Tomlinson. Everyone else had either been on duty December 31st and/or February 18th or was off the hook for other reasons: Jim Partridge and Bev Brooks were out of town over the holidays, and Marlise Beyer was a newcomer and a woman, besides.

She got out the three files and went over them in excruciating detail, reading the words printed on the page and seeking out others she knew were hidden between the lines. She found nothing she hadn't read before.

There was an accusation of excessive force during an interrogation.

A reprimand following a high-speed chase.

An official inquiry, automatic whenever a weapon was fired in the line of duty.

Eddie sat back and supported her aching neck with her hands, seeking wisdom, or at least guidance, from the corner of the ceiling.

Think about Alan, she told herself. Who among these guys rings similar bells? Is this guy contemptuous of women, like Alan? Afraid of women, like Alan?

Not Matt Tomlinson, surely.

But why not? She didn't know the guy — not really.

She could believe that either Howie or Glen was contemptuous, arrogant, smart. But she could not believe either of them capable of doing what had been done to Rebecca Wilson's house.

Christ. She felt guilty just thinking about it, just considering the possibility.

She put the files away, made a few self-mocking notes in her journal, and sat behind her desk, brooding, her mind travelling in endless, futile circles.

A little while later Beatrice buzzed her, announcing Rebecca Wilson and her father.

Rebecca Wilson's father was short, fat, and balding, and Eddie liked him immediately. She thought this was probably because the man was the direct opposite of her own father. Eddie could imagine crying on this man's shoulder. He would pat her on the back and say, "There there," or "It's going to be fine, everything's going to be just fine," or "Don't you worry, I'll take care of it," and she would be comforted. It was embarrassing, she thought, shaking his hand, to admit that there were moments when she would like to hand over her life into the care of someone else — and who better than one's dad? She envied Rebecca. But smiled at her anyway.

"Drag one of those chairs over here, will you, Mr. Wilson?" she said, and he did, and held it for Rebecca while she sat down. He took the diner chair for himself, inspecting it curiously first.

"We've got a new list for you," said Rebecca's father, whose name, he had told her, was William.

Eddie looked at Rebecca expectantly.

"It's his idea," said Rebecca grimly. "It's a very long list," she said, digging it out of her handbag.

"It's a waste of time trying to get her to come up with people who'd want to hurt her," said William. "She doesn't believe anybody would want to hurt her. Certainly doesn't want to name anybody. That's like making an accusation. And Rebecca . . ."

"Oh, shut up, Dad," said Rebecca crossly, and he shrugged, giving Eddie a look that meant, See what I have to deal with? Rebecca slapped the list down on Eddie's desk. "Everybody I know is on it. Every person I know. This is just a *list*, Sergeant," she said sternly.

"I figured this is what you wanted in the first place," said her father.

"It is, actually," said Eddie.

"Because if this guy — if you could see in his face that he was capable of that kind of — of criminal activity, then Rebecca wouldn't have had anything to do with him in the first place."

"Right," said Eddie.

"And so he must be a perfectly ordinary guy," said William. "Somebody you wouldn't think in a million years could do that sort of thing, wrecking a person's house."

"Right," said Eddie again.

Rebecca was trying to sit straight and look calm, but suddenly tears began flowing down her face and she fumbled in her bag for a package of tissues. Her father put a protective hand on her shoulder. "I'm not leaving town until you catch him," he said.

"Oh god," said Rebecca, blotting her tears.

"Have you got pictures?" William asked Eddie.

"Oh Dad, for god's sake."

"Pictures of the damage?" said Eddie. "Of course."

"Can I see them?"

Eddie looked at Rebecca, who gave her cheeks a final swipe. "Let him see them, okay?"

"Okay. Sure." Eddie opened the file — she'd been studying it when they came in — and handed William the crime scene photographs that were inside. "Listen, I'm going to bring Corporal Sheffield in on this. I'll be right back."

When Eddie returned with Buster in tow, Rebecca was standing by the small high window, looking out into

the parking lot. William was studying the photographs.
Eddie said, "You know Corporal Sheffield, right?"

"Right," said Rebecca. "I remember. Nice to see you."

"I'm glad your father can be with you," said Buster.

"Yeah, me too." She gave a shaky laugh. "I think."

"Okay," said William. "Thank you." He put the stack
of photos face down on Eddie's desk.

"Mr. Wilson," said Eddie, "this is Corporal Sheffield.
I'd like you and Rebecca to go through the list with
him, okay? Tell him how Rebecca knows each person."

"It's not alphabetical or anything," said Rebecca. "It's
just as they came to me, as I thought of them. Dad would
say, what about deliveries? Or, how about the people in
the stores you go to? Or, who cuts your grass in the
summer and shovels your driveway in the winter? And
I'd think of people, and write down their names."

"Good," said Buster. "Why don't the two of you come
out here to my desk, I'll get you some coffee, you can
clue me in, and I'll divvy up the names among the men.
The officers."

Eddie's phone rang as they were leaving her office.

"Steve wants to keep him until the last minute,
Eddie," said Marjorie.

For a moment, Eddie's mind was blank.

"So it'll be sometime next week."

Andrew. "Right. Next week."

"I'll let you know when."

"Yeah, okay. Fine." She hesitated. "He sounded like a
nice guy, Steve, on the phone. He's going to miss him a
lot, isn't he."

"They're going to miss each other, I guess."

"Yeah. Of course."

Out in the main office, William Wilson tapped the
list of names lying on Buster Sheffield's desk. "There's

a couple of your guys on here," he said.

"You see, that's the kind of thing I mean," said Rebecca, exasperated. "There are perfectly innocent people named there."

"I know," said Buster. "They're probably all perfectly innocent. If we're lucky — all but one."

"Come on. We've only known each other five minutes," she said, but she laughed, and flicked her hair over her shoulder with a toss of her head.

"It's been longer than that," he said, touching her forehead with the back of his hand.

"Yeah, okay. But still not long enough."

"Not long enough for what?"

"For what you're suggesting."

"So how long do we have to know each other before we can go away for a weekend?" he said curiously.

"I'll tell you when we get there."

Rhoda had dark hair and large, dark eyes and olive skin. He knew she'd be devastatingly beautiful with a tan, and he wondered if they'd still be together in the summer.

They were sitting in his patrol car, which was parked behind the apartment building where she lived. The building was right on the ocean, but she'd told him that her apartment faced toward town.

She shifted in the seat next to him. "Thanks for the hamburger."

"You're welcome."

"You can come in, if you like. I've still got half an hour of my break left."

"Have we known each other long enough for that?" he said with mock solemnity, wanting her to laugh again. But she cocked her head and looked at him appraisingly instead.

"I think so," she said finally.

He knew that meant she was ready to have sex with him. He studied her for a moment, brushing a strand of shiny hair away from her forehead, imagining his mouth on her breast, his hands gripping her ass. He wondered what she'd say, and do, if he turned her down.

"Okay," he agreed. "Good. I think I will."

Late that afternoon, he came back from somewhere far away in his own head and found himself staring at a form on his computer screen. He couldn't remember what the hell he was supposed to be doing with it. He leaned closer, trying to concentrate.

Someone clapped him on the back and he nearly jumped out of his skin.

"Sorry, Bud. Didn't mean to spook you." Buster Sheffield rolled a chair over from the next carrel and straddled it, dropped a file on Glen's desk and rested his big hands on the chair back. They sat there, those hands, one on top of the other; he thought they looked complacent.

"Got some names I want you to check out," said Sheffield. "In connection with that Wilson woman's house getting wasted."

"Okay."

"She's finally come up with a comprehensive list — not just guys she figures don't like her for one reason or another, but every guy she's ever met, practically. So I've divided it up. I'm giving you ten."

"Okay. Good."

Buster grinned. "You're on it."

"On what?"

"On her big long list. Because of being on the Neighbourhood Watch thing with her." He winked. "So Marlise Beyer, she'll be checking *you* out."

He shrugged, managed a smile. "Fine. She knows where to find me."

Buster ambled away.

He pressed the space bar to get rid of the screen saver and stared again at the computer screen. Rage started to build, swirling and growing and ripening inside him. Soon he would feel it on his skin and in his bones and muscles, taking rough hold of him.

"The bitch. The bitch. Putting me on her fucking list."

He realized that he was whispering, speaking aloud, although softly, and quickly he cleared his throat and shook his head, struggling to dismiss her.

NINETEEN

It was almost time to go home when Glen Hammond knocked on Eddie's half-open door and stuck his head in. "Got a minute, Sarge?"

"Sure," said Eddie. "Come on in." She turned from her computer screen. "What can I do for you?"

"I was just wondering, what's happening with that vandalism file? The social worker's house. Any developments?"

Eddie was looking searchingly at the surface of her desk. She forced herself to meet his eyes: they were an extraordinarily compelling shade of blue. "Well, she's given us a new list. Buster's assigning names. You'll probably get some. Other than that, nothing." He was sitting on the edge of the red vinyl chair, hands linked between his knees, staring at her thoughtfully. "Why?"

He shrugged. "I don't know. She seems like a nice woman. I'm just curious."

"Do you know her?"

"No. Well, not really. Met her a few times, that's all."

"Oh?"

"Yeah. We're on this committee together."

"Oh yeah? One of ours?"

"Neighbourhood Watch. Plus — I guess we got to be friends. Casually."

"Uh huh."

He leaned back in the chair, legs spread, hands folded

in his lap. "I gave her a ride home a few times. She invited me in for coffee. You know."

Eddie's face shield had dropped into place moments earlier. She looked at him through the slits, hoping he couldn't see the colour of her eyes.

He shrugged and smiled at her. "Nothing serious."

"You did some of the interviews, didn't you?"

"Yeah." He wet a finger and rubbed at a spot on his pant leg. "I thought we'd pretty well covered everybody she knew."

"Well, it seems she left a lot of people out last time we asked."

"Hmm. I'm gonna be among the newcomers, I guess. I mean, if she hasn't put me there, you might as well."

"Uh huh." Eddie's phone buzzed.

He got to his feet. "Okay. Good," he said. "Thanks, Sarge."

"No problem."

He went to the door, and Eddie picked up her phone.

"Okay, it's all arranged," said Marjorie. "You come to my place Thursday evening, the dog'll be here."

"Marjorie, what if he doesn't like me?"

"He'll like you."

"How can you be sure?"

"Easy. He likes everybody."

"Great. Wonderful."

"Hey, one meeting and you decided he was going be yours. You've got to trust that, go with it."

"Yeah. You're right. Okay. I'll get the five-thirty ferry. I can be at your apartment around seven."

"See you then."

Eddie, putting down the phone, found that her gaze was drawn to the clouded glass pane in her office door: she imagined Glen Hammond's outline there. And staring at this imagined profile of a man she barely knew, she felt a jolt of dismay.

———

He went directly home from work, changed his clothes, and washed the Lexus. Vacuumed the interior. Burnished the dashboard. Polished the windows, inside and out.

He stood back and scrutinized his vehicle, taking pleasure in its gleam and comfort in its spotlessness. It was immaculate. He got into the driver's seat and turned the key in the ignition, listening intently; the motor sprang instantly to life, sounding healthy and cosseted.

It was almost dark by now. He sat in the dark with the motor running, imagining her house, on the other side of the marina. He wondered if the cat had ever come back.

He'd been thinking a lot about his mother again. He had loved her, of course. Never really tried to deny it. She was his mother. Round and soft and spirited. Quick to laugh, quick to anger. His dominant memory of her was sublimely sensual — like hot sunshine, or a roasted marshmallow, or sailing high on a backyard swing.

It was summer. His mother was sitting on a blanket she had spread beneath the chestnut tree. She had a glass of something — probably lemonade — and some spears of newly cut grass were sticking to the beads of water that had formed on the outside of the glass. She was wearing a sundress and sandals, and she sat with her back against the tree trunk, reading a paperback book. He saw all this as he approached her, running, to tell her something. It must have been something very exciting, because he ran to her without a wisp of uncertainty, dropped unafraid next to her on the blanket, and just blurted it out, whatever it was he had to tell her. She threw back her head and laughed, and he flushed with joy. Then she looked at him, smiling, put her book aside, and hugged him.

Her plump arms embraced him, drawing him close to her pillowy breasts, and she pressed her damp, fleshy cheek against his. Tendrils of her hair, which was honey-coloured with streaks of caramel, fell around her face, and one of them tickled his nose but he didn't move, didn't try to blow it away. He was transfixed, transported by the hugeness and the power of her love for him. He thought he felt it surging into his body and his brain, where, he later decided, it was converted into a kind of energy that he would never lose. It was like being forever accompanied — even occupied — by his mother, by her compelling regard for him in the one single unsullied moment that he could remember.

He retrieved this memory again and again, so often that eventually it came to him of its own accord, at moments that were not always comfortable.

The Lexus purred. He stroked the steering wheel. After a while he drove smoothly out of his neighbour's driveway.

He parked several blocks from her house, not in the same vicinity as the last time, or the time before that. He locked up the Lexus and started walking.

A fine mist was in the air, not quite a drizzle. He was wearing his navy blue water-resistant jacket with the hood, over a navy sweatshirt and jeans, and he had dark blue socks and sneakers on his feet.

He didn't know what he was doing, coming back here again, except that he was so bloody pissed off about being on her fucking list. He didn't know what he could do about it — what was he going to do, trash her fucking house again? He knew what he'd *like* to do, he'd like to —

He stopped, suddenly, and put his hand on top of a low stone wall that he remembered from the last time he'd been on this street. Its surface was bumpy and rough, and he concentrated on that, on pressing the palm of his hand against the grainy roughness of the stone. He looked up at the house that sat behind the wall. There

was a large window on either side of the front door, four
small ones on the second storey. Nostalgia swept through
him, making him feel physically ill. He'd never lived in a
house that looked like this one. What was it, then, that
was reminding him of his childhood?

Perhaps he was only trying to distract himself, with
powerful memories, from the vivid image that had
entered his head. He flattened his other hand upon the
stone. In this fantasy he had felt his hands around her
fucking neck. . . .

He shook his head slowly from side to side. His
insides were crumpling. There was a sound in his head,
a sweet keening.

He pushed away from the stone wall and continued
up the block, walking uncertainly, as if he were drunk.
And he rubbed his palms hard against his thighs, trying
to eradicate the sensations that lingered there.

Across the street, a young woman strode along,
accompanied by a large black dog on a leash. He thought
it was the same dog he'd seen lying on a sofa, its head
hanging over the back, looking out at him through the
window. The woman glanced in his direction without
slowing. She might have seen him before. It was possible, it was more than possible, the way he'd been swinging through this neighbourhood over the last few
months — it was likely, even probable that if this woman
and her dog hadn't noticed him before today, somebody
else had.

His heart sat high and light in his chest, beating fast
in the top part of his throat and getting in the way of his
breathing.

He hadn't had what could be called a distinguished
career but his record was at least respectable. Was this
important? How important was it?

A moment later a car approached from behind, passed
him, and disappeared around the bend in the road.

He moved beneath a large cedar growing in the front yard of the house across the street from Rebecca's. This was where he'd waited for her to come home with her goddamn "date," more than three months ago. The lowest branches of the tree fell almost to the ground. He had to reach out and part them with his hands in order to see her house. He stared at the house until his arms ached and he had to drop them.

It wasn't late. The people who lived in the house behind him might decide to go out, and as they passed the cedar tree they might see him. Or he might be seen by someone walking by. He knew this, but he didn't care.

He squatted at the base of the tree. From this position he could see her house below the drooping branches.

There were two cars in her driveway. A 1999 Ford Escort was parked behind her filthy Accord. Didn't she ever wash that damn car?

She'd go to the door with whoever was visiting her, when they went home, and he'd be able to get a look at her. That was all he wanted, just to get a good look at her.

It occurred to him of course that her visitor might be planning to spend the night, like her goddamn "date" had done. The thought of it made him sick to his stomach, but he knew it was possible, she was capable of anything, so how long was he going to wait, then? He bounced up and down on his haunches, lightly, restlessly, flexing his hands, feeling the power in them.

Fifteen minutes later, her front door opened and she emerged, wearing a raincoat, talking over her shoulder to someone behind her; he followed her out the door, a short, fat old guy hunching himself into a quilted jacket.

Crouched by the tree trunk across the street, he watched them approach the Ford and heard their voices clearly in the cool, misty evening.

"I do know how to cook, you know. We don't have to eat out every single night," said Rebecca crossly, opening the passenger door.

"I like that place. The Chinaman's place. Damn good food."

"Please, Dad, for god's sake," she hissed.

The old guy stood by the driver's door, digging in his pocket for the keys. "What's the matter?"

"You don't use words like that. 'Chinaman.' For heaven's sake." She got in the car, and so did her father.

Two doors slammed and the engine started. The Ford had a muffler problem — it sounded like a fucking tractor. As it backed out of the driveway he saw the rental company sticker on the bumper.

He watched it drive away, then stood up and leaned against the trunk of the cedar tree. The air was moist and fragrant. He reflected idly that spring had come while he wasn't looking. He squinted up into the tree branches. They swept softly toward the ground, embracing the terrain he had temporarily claimed, enfolding and concealing him.

He returned to the Lexus and drove out of the village. Half an hour later, he turned off the highway and followed one of the several roads that led to the sea. He parked in a small gravel clearing, turned off the motor, and looked out across the changeable sea, which was several shades of silvery grey in the fading light of day. He didn't like it that her goddamn father had shown up. He felt — forestalled. Checkmated.

But prevented from doing what? It wasn't as if he wanted to keep prowling her neighbourhood, sniffing around her house like a randy hound pursuing a bitch in heat. Jesus.

The twilight had deepened, and darkness had fallen. The sky and the sea had become one, in darkness and in the falling rain.

He got out of the Lexus, locked it up, and made his way over the rocks to a log. House lights were scattered along the edge of the bay. The sea swelled toward the shore and exploded upon the rocks. From one sea to another, across the width of a continent he'd come. Thousands of miles from the beaches that were home.

Thousands of miles from . . .

The ironic thing was that his dad had asked him to do it, sick with the flu, aching and feverish. "Go get your mother, will you son? I'm lonely in here," he'd said.

And of course, he'd volunteered to keep his dad company, but an eleven-year-old kid wasn't what his dad needed — not what he wanted, anyway.

He'd said in what he knew to be his whiny little-boy voice, Why couldn't his sister do it? But his sister was having her piano lesson.

He didn't know where his mother was, didn't know where she'd gone, and neither did his dad. So finally he just went out onto the front porch and sat on the step with his chin in his hands. He'd wait for her to come home and as soon as he saw her, he'd tell her his dad wanted her.

But he got bored after a while and ended up wandering off to the beach.

They lived on the outskirts of the city and the beach wasn't a long way away, not when it was Saturday and you were an easily bored kid with plenty of time and energy. He had put on his winter jacket because although it wasn't quite winter yet, it was cold and would be even colder by the sea. When he got there, the beach was empty except for some people a long way away who looked like they were collecting shells.

But in the parking lot was a familiar car — he'd had a thing about cars even then. This one was a '64 Pontiac Parisienne convertible, blue with a white top. The top was up, of course. He didn't know who owned this car, but he'd sure like to. He'd seen it driving past the house, maybe dropping off his mom from some meeting or other. He glanced up the beach. The owner could be one of the people looking for shells. But they were moving in the opposite direction. It would be ages before they returned to the Parisienne.

He started toward it. He was pretty sure it was an automatic, and for sure it'd have a blue interior.

He saw before he got within ten feet of the vehicle that it was moving — not going anywhere, just ... moving. And he stopped and peered at it more closely, but it still looked empty. He crept closer, and closer, until he was near enough to look inside.

He stared, blinking.

His mother was in the back seat, on her back. Her eyes were scrunched closed, but her mouth was open and she was breathing so hard that her face was red. Her legs were lifted high and wrapped around the waist of a naked guy. As he watched, they lurched into a rhythmic pattern: the man's butt rose and fell; when it fell, his mother gave a little cry; when it rose, he saw his mother's coiled pubic hair and the man's cock joined in what appeared to be battle, but he knew it wasn't. He had watched, fascinated, for the several seconds required for the scene to imprint itself into his brain. Then he had clapped his hands over his mouth and run, and fallen upon his hands and knees and vomited in the sand. . . .

He stood up and stumbled over the rocks to his car and drove back to Gibsons, because he had nowhere else to go.

He hadn't told his dad what he'd seen.

He hadn't told his mother, either. But she'd known. Somehow, she'd known.

He'd never felt the same way about either of his parents, ever again. The most important relationships in a person's entire fucking *life*, screwed up, screwed up *forever*, because of that bitch-in-heat his fucking *mother*. From then on, he had felt like some big, brightly-coloured bird, a parrot or something, kept in a huge gold cage, and she — his mother — would fuss over him and hang his cage in the window and feed him special stuff day after day . . . until she got another interest, and then she'd forget all about him. He wondered why he hadn't fucking died, of neglect, long before she did.

He was coming into town now, slowing because the traffic had gotten heavier.

And of course, he was checking out the other vehicles as he drove, looking now for the old guy's rented Ford as well as for Rebecca Wilson's grungy Accord. It was instinctive. He was always automatically aware of the people and the vehicles around him, his brain clicking away like a computer, making connections, filing information away. Typical cop behaviour.

Rebecca. What *was* it about her?

Oh, he knew all about faithless women alright, but he'd never encountered one so *blatant*, so *cruel* as Rebecca fucking Wilson.

And now her father was sitting on her tail, keeping an eye cocked, on the lookout for the big bad cop who had scared the living shit right out of her.

Except, of course, the old guy didn't know it was a cop he was on the lookout for.

Olive Parfit had spent the afternoon with the senior citizens, helping make crêpe paper wedding decorations, which was a source of income for the group. She left the hall in somewhat of a stupor, with the texture of the crêpe paper embedded in her fingertips. The other women — no men had joined their small circle — had been polite but not really very friendly, and she was beginning to fear that small-town warmth and congeniality was only a myth.

The rain was falling again as she made her way through the dusk from the hall to the street where her car was parked, her handbag tucked under one arm, clutching her hooded raincoat around her. She was slightly stooped, straining in the poor light from the streetlamp to locate the keyhole, poking around with the key and probably gouging new scratches in the paint, when suddenly a car roared around the corner and headed rapidly toward her.

Olive knew next to nothing about cars. She could have lived in Gibsons alongside the Lexus for the rest of her life and never recognized it. Except that at this moment it inserted itself into her vision at precisely the same angle and with the motor howling precisely the same terrifying threat as when it had attacked her. Olive sprang to the sidewalk and watched it race past, and this time she memorized the licence plate.

By the time she got home, the rain was falling harder and the wind had come up. It shook the trees around her house as she hurried from the car to her front door, and she thought she saw the lights in her neighbours' houses flicker.

She went inside with trepidation, as usual. She carefully unlocked the door, which was, in fact, locked. She had taken the sergeant's advice and affixed to it a neat little sign — LOCK ME — that she couldn't help but see whenever she went out.

Once inside, she went immediately into the kitchen and wrote the killer car's licence plate number on the memo pad. This time she would report him. First thing in the morning. This time she had something to offer the police.

Upstairs, she turned on all the lights and checked each room. Then she did the same thing downstairs. And then she re-locked the door. She no longer locked it when she first entered the house in case she discovered something that frightened her and had to get out in a hurry.

As she followed this procedure, she muttered irritably to herself. She deeply resented having to do this. This — this mudsucker, whoever he was, had robbed her of security, made her feel lonely and vulnerable in her own home, and she hated him for it.

She sat down on the stairs, suddenly exhausted. She removed her glasses and rubbed the grooves the side pieces had etched behind her ears. A month from now, Danny would be gone, moved to Toronto. But soon afterwards she would be gone, too, launched on a tour of Italy and the south of France. And then it would be Christmas. Danny was going to fly home and spend Christmas with her. So life was good, really, Olive told herself. She had her health, she had a comfortable income, she was about to start travelling.

The lights guttered, and went out.

Olive sat in the dark, blinking hard, terrified for a moment that it might be her eyes that had stopped working. But soon shapes thrust themselves out of the darkness: the square of glass in the top of the front door, the arched entrance into the living room across the hall, and at the other end of the hall, the kitchen window, still bare because Olive had decided she preferred it without curtains.

"Damn," said Olive, pushing herself to her feet. With one hand stretched in front of her and the other off to the side, she made her way down the hall and into the kitchen, giving the light switch there a futile flick as she passed it. In the dim light coming through the window she ran her hand over the countertop, feeling for the portable telephone.

The counter was bare. The phone was gone.

Olive turned and leaned against the counter. Her palms tingled and her throat was tight. She strained to listen, over the drumming of her suddenly anxious heart, for unfamiliar sounds, for clues.

She backed toward the door that led out into her garden, her hand outstretched behind her, seeking the knob, finding it, turning it. The door opened a crack. She pushed, putting her full body weight into it, but the door refused to open farther, and through the crack she saw that something — she couldn't make out what — had been solidly wedged against it. Olive whimpered, and stifled the sound with her hand.

She heard something in the living room fall to the floor.

She remained at the back door, unable to move, shuddering in terror. "Okay," she whispered. "Okay. Oh please god. Okay."

She would have to go back down the hall to the front door. She would have to pass the living room. He would hear her coming, he would see her through the living-room doorway. Was he armed?

"Oh please god don't let him have a knife," she whispered, "let him shoot me oh please I don't — oh please — I can't be — please. . . ."

She was shaking so hard she could hardly move. He would certainly hear her coming. Her bones were clanking, her teeth were clattering, and little moans kept issuing from her lips, small panicked utterances that she simply couldn't restrain.

She tiptoed down the hall, her eyes fixed on the front door, getting nearer and nearer to the door, which was not only darkened, but blurry: she wasn't wearing her glasses. They were still on the stair. Carefully, she held this thought in her mind, side by side with the shadowy image of the intruder, once concept, now flesh and blood; once an abstract force, now here, present in her living room. As she approached the archway, the left side of her body shriveled, and she cried out — and in that moment, she heard the crunch of her eyeglasses, demolished by a heavy foot.

Olive leapt, shrieking, for the front door, burst through it, and stumbled down the walk. She floundered and fell and scrabbled upright and finally broke into a lurching run that took her to her neighbours' front door.

TWENTY

In the patrol car, driving back to the detachment, he took deep breaths and tried to remember that practice he'd read about, or heard about — you breathe in to a count of three, hold your breath for a count of three, and breathe out to a count of four. Or was it four, four and four? Shit, he couldn't remember.

Just breathe deep and slow, he told himself. Keep your fucking foot light on the accelerator. . . .

He wanted to turn on the lights and the siren and slam his foot to the floor. He imagined a long, straight, silver highway, and himself in the Lexus skimming it like a waterbug until he came to the end, where there was a cliff. And when he saw the cliff, the pressure of his foot on the pedal would increase, his grip on the wheel would tighten, his body would bend forward in anticipation — and he'd sail right off the edge, right off the goddamn edge.

He pulled off the highway and got out of the car. It was raining, which he hadn't noticed until now. He leaned heavily on the hood and tried it again, the deep breathing. His hands were flat against the hood, and he was staring down at the gravel shoulder. Breathe in, hold, breathe out. . . .

And just like that, he knew the ending of it.

Just like that.

———

"So who are you *really*, Harry my boy?"

He laughed. Then he wrote, "Not allowed."

"Humour me."

"You're taking the fun out of it." Why was it, he wondered, that he never entered the chat room without a beer in his hand? He set the bottle down on the blistered, whitened spot on the coffee table that had been created by its predecessors.

"I'll tell you, if you'll tell me."

"You sound like a six-year-old, offering to show me her private parts."

"Them too, if you like."

"Come on, Jemima. Lighten up."

"It's just that you're sounding different tonight, Harry."

"Different how?" He had a smile on his face. He could feel it there, stretching his skin, pushing at his cheeks.

"Wait while I think."

He drank, emptying the bottle.

"Don't know. Sorry. Just — different."

"How about 'Resolute.' How about 'Empowered.'"

"Hmmm."

"I'm out of beer," he wrote. "Gotta go."

He switched off the laptop and put it on the coffee table. Got himself another bottle of beer. Settled in the leather chair, which welcomed him with a sigh, like the driver's seat of the Lexus every time he slid behind the wheel.

He went through it in his mind again. A very simple plan, like all good and beautiful things.

It all came down to not minding. Like they say, if you can't do the time, don't do the crime.

The door opened a crack, and Olive Parfit's right eye peered out at them.

"Good evening, Ms. Parfit," said Eddie.

The door opened wider. Now all of Olive's face was visible. Her eyes were huge behind her glasses, the pupils dilated. She was huddled close to the door, her hand tightly clutching its edge.

"This is Corporal Sheffield," Eddie went on. "He's going to look around outside a bit, while you tell me what happened."

Olive nodded. She moved away from the door, and the ice in the glass she was holding rattled. Eddie followed her inside. "My neighbours wanted me to stay over there," Olive said. "They seem like very nice people." She led the way into the living room, where the TV was tuned to "Seinfeld." "Sit down, Sergeant, please." Olive sat in a wingback chair by the fireplace, setting her glass down on a small end table.

Eddie took the sofa and flipped her notebook open.

"I'm going to leave this on, if you don't mind," said Olive, indicating the television. "I need the company. Not that you aren't company, but I feel that I know these people, ridiculous as it sounds, and I hardly know you at all."

"Of course," said Eddie. "But could you turn down the volume just a bit?"

Olive did so.

"Thank you," said Eddie.

"The lights came back on," Olive said, watching intently as Kramer made an explosive entrance into Jerry's apartment. "I went to the neighbours' house to call you, and I was holding the phone and looking out the window to see if I could spot anyone lurking around, and suddenly all the lights were on again. They wanted me to stay with them until you got here. The neighbours, I mean. They seem like very nice people. But I couldn't. I can't let that damn man scare me out of my own home. My god, I am so angry." She picked up the glass and lifted it to her lips with a hand that shook. Her hair was disheveled and her face was pale, but she did look to Eddie more angry than frightened.

"What's going on around here?" Eddie had said to Buster, after she'd told him about Olive Parfit's frantic call. "What the hell's going on in this town?"

"Don't let's jump to conclusions," Buster had replied. "Let's just get over there. See what we can find out."

"Can I offer you something?" Olive asked distractedly. "Tea? Coffee?" She lifted her glass. "Vodka?"

Eddie smiled. "No thank you. Tell me what happened, Ms. Parfit."

"I did lock the door this time, Sergeant."

"I'm sure you did," said Eddie. "I saw the note."

"So then — how did he get in?"

They heard a knock on the front door. Buster Sheffield called out, "It's me, Ms. Parfit. Corporal Sheffield." He appeared in the living-room doorway. "I'll poke around inside the house now, if you don't mind."

"Of course I don't mind," said Olive sharply. "That's why I called you."

Buster backed away and they heard him mounting the stairs.

"Give me every detail," said Eddie. "Start from the beginning."

"Which would be when?" said Olive.

On the television screen, Elaine was gyrating clownishly around a dance floor, watched by an astonished crowd.

"Let's say, from when you pulled off the highway."

"I drove down the hill, turned up my street, and parked next to my front gate, in my usual spot."

"Did you notice anybody? Anyone at all."

Olive took another swig of vodka. Eddie hoped this was her first drink and that she wouldn't want a second, at least not until the interview was over.

Olive squeezed her eyes closed in an apparent attempt to encourage recall. "The boy who lives up the street was skateboarding. I remember thinking that wasn't too bright, in the rain, in the dark — there was a car behind me, driving up the street, and I thought he might not see him in time — but the boy was wearing something that glowed white and there were sparkly luminous stickers on his board. And besides, the other car stopped, two houses along. And the man who lives there got out and walked to his front door. And went inside, I suppose. That's all."

"Did you see any unfamiliar vehicles parked in the street?"

"Oh, I don't know who belongs to what vehicle, they all look the same to me. Except. . . ." She had placed the glass of vodka on a small end table, and her hands were clutching the arms of the wingback chair. "This is going to sound so odd. Irresponsible." She swung her gaze directly at Eddie. "Several months ago, a person in a car almost ran me down. I didn't report it at the time. My brother had just died — anyway . . . anyway, I didn't. Yesterday, I saw that car again. And this time, I got the licence plate number. Wait a minute." She got up and hurried from the room, returning with a piece of paper torn from a memo pad. "Here," she said, handing it to Eddie. "The man is a menace. He can't be allowed to drive any more."

Eddie studied the slip of paper. It was a vanity plate: RAPTOR. "Ms. Parfit, are you making a connection between the driver of this car and what happened here tonight?"

Upstairs, Buster Sheffield stepped on a squeaky board, and Olive shot a fearful look up at the ceiling. "My god, my nerves are in tatters. I don't know, Sergeant. I don't know what to think. Has anybody else in town report-ed something like this? I mean, is this man torturing a whole bunch of people, or is it just me?"

"Do you know a woman called Rebecca Wilson?" said Eddie. "She's a social worker."

"No. Has he done this to her, too?"

"Ms. Parfit, I'm going to ask you to make a list for me of every man you know in Gibsons."

Abruptly, Olive stood up. Her arms were straight at her sides, her fists clenched. "I'm sorry. I cannot do this any more." She walked swiftly from the room.

Eddie got to her feet and followed her into the hallway, where Olive had opened the door.

"I'm sorry."

"Please do the list for us," said Eddie.

"I will," said Olive stiffly.

"I'll give you a call tomorrow and come round to pick it up."

"Fine."

Buster came down from upstairs and joined Eddie as she stepped out onto the porch. "Are you going to be alright, Ms. Parfit? Shouldn't you perhaps stay with someone tonight?"

"I believe I'll spend the night in a motel," said Olive.

"Good. That's a good idea."

"I'll phone you when I've done the list."

"Thank you. Good night, Ms. Parfit."

"Good night."

The door closed, and Eddie heard it lock. She and Buster went down the walk to the gate. "Let's wait here," she said, "keep an eye on things, until she leaves."

They got into the patrol car, which was parked across from Olive's house, and waited.

They were silent for a few minutes, looking out into the rainy night, occasionally glancing at their notebooks.

"So the phone, it was on the floor in the dining area," said Eddie finally.

"Yeah. And the back door was blocked by this wheelbarrow-type thing. It only had a few empty little plant pot things in it, nothing heavy, but the wheel had gotten caught in a crack in the concrete." Buster sighed, and closed his notebook, gazing at Olive Parfit's front door.

"And the glasses," said Eddie. "She now figures that instead of putting them down on the stair, she actually dropped them on the hall floor when she stood up after the lights went out."

"Yeah. And smashed them to smithereens herself, making a run for it. So what do you think?" He glanced at Eddie, then back at Olive's house. "Have we got some nut running around harassing more than one woman?"

Eddie shook her head. "Hers wasn't the only house where the lights went out. Still, I think something funny's going on here alright. But it definitely isn't the same thing as over at Rebecca's."

"No violence. No destruction."

"No anger. Look. Here she comes."

The lights were extinguished, except for the porch light, and Olive Parfit emerged, carrying a small bag. As she hurried to her car, Eddie flicked the lights on the patrol car and gave her a wave. An expression of enormous gratitude blossomed on Olive's face. Eddie rolled down her window.

"We'll follow you," she said. "Okay?"

"Okay," said Olive. "Thank you. Very much."

Buster started the motor and they set off after Olive, keeping a respectful distance behind.

"She says somebody tried to run her down," said Eddie. "Several months ago, she says."

Buster glanced at her. "And?" he said, turning onto the highway.

"She had no information about the car until she saw it again yesterday."

"Uh huh."

"She got the plate number. It's Glen Hammond's Lexus."

They travelled slowly through the village, up the hill, and along the highway toward Sechelt.

"And you're thinking, what?" said Buster.

"He's also on the list, isn't he? Rebecca Wilson's list."

"Yeah. They're on a Neighbourhood Watch thing. Is this significant? Are you trying to suggest something?"

"Jesus. I don't know." Eddie looked out the window. "Is it raining? Can you tell?"

"Drizzling, maybe."

"I'm gonna talk to him," said Eddie, as Buster signalled to pull off the road. The patrol car crunched onto a gravel forecourt and stopped behind Olive Parfit's Chevy Malibu. "First thing tomorrow."

Olive emerged from her vehicle, clutching her handbag, and gave them a wave.

TWENTY-ONE

Saturday morning was overcast. Although Eddie preferred sunshine to cloud any day, she had learned to find variety in the often sunless, misty sky of southwestern British Columbia. It wasn't a smooth, colourless blank canvas at all but a shifting kaleidoscope ranging from alabaster to silver, from ash to champagne; the clouds were a swirl of cream and ivory, they were opalescent, they gleamed like pewter and shone like ivory. And always, somewhere beneath or far above, there was the shifting shadow of blueness, cold and crystalline in winter, warm and sensual in summer and fall, delicate like birdsong in spring; at any moment in the year, a breeze, a wind, could spring up and wipe the sky wholly or partially clear, revealing patches of its true self, the blueness that dwelt behind the clouds.

It was spring, and already the world had begun to blossom. Eddie noted this as she drove to Gibsons on her day off. This unwelcome chore might well have kept until Monday, and yet she felt an inexplicable urgency, as if she had an opportunity to head off some kind of disaster. If it *was* Glen Hammond who'd — but she didn't believe this was possible, not really.

The car business, that was something else again. Eddie was perfectly prepared to believe that he drove that damn Lexus recklessly. Though she certainly would have heard, if there'd been any complaints about him.

She mulled these things over as she sailed along the highway, aware of the restless, ever-moving clouds and the pink and white billowings of the early flowering trees and the stands of daffodils that fluttered in spring gardens.

It was mid-morning when she arrived in Gibsons. She parked on the street by his house, tramped down the ramp and across the sand, through a gate that dangled from a broken hinge, up some steps, and onto the porch.

He opened the door before she had a chance to knock. "Gotta get that gate fixed," he said with a smile. "Very bad impression, that gate."

"Hi, Glen. Got a minute?"

"Sure, Sarge. For you, any time." He stood back and, with a flourish, held the door open wide, then closed it behind her.

Eddie found herself standing in a cramped square of a hallway. There was a closet, the door standing half-open, and on the floor lay a pair of sneakers, one fallen on its side; they looked somehow innocent and cheerful, like they'd been kicked off by a very large child.

"You want some coffee?" said Glen, and she followed him out of the hall and into the living room. In one corner stood a desk with a p.c. monitor, a printer, a pair of oversized speakers, and a joystick; the hard drive sat on the floor.

"Wow," said Eddie, pointing.

He laughed and touched the back of the desk chair. "Yeah."

"So what is it?"

"It's a car-chase video game." He kicked one of the chair legs, gently. "I'm a sucker for all sorts of techno-crap, Sarge."

"How does it work?"

"You sit in the chair — here, you want to try it?"

"No thanks."

"You sit in the chair, and there's speakers here, see? And you get the sound of the chase coming up through here, and the vibration, too, just like you were actually on the road."

Eddie shook her head, grinning.

"You really ought to try it."

She laughed. "No thanks. Another time, maybe."

"So how about it? Coffee?"

"Yeah. Sure."

In another corner of the room sat a twenty-six-inch television, and opposite, a worn leather chair with an end table next to it and a floor lamp in behind. Against one wall, a long sofa. On the coffee table there was a laptop computer, a pile of newspapers, and a beer can.

"Cream? Sugar?" he called from the kitchen.

"Neither."

He returned to the living room with two mugs of coffee.

"Thanks," said Eddie. She took the mug from him and sat down on the sofa. "Is this place yours? I mean, do you own or rent?"

"Rent." He was looking at her speculatively. "What brings you here, Sergeant?"

He was perched on the edge of the leather chair, sitting forward and holding the coffee in both hands. Eddie tried to keep her contemplation of him relaxed and casual. She wasn't able to decide if there was truly something just a little bit different about him today or if she was making it up. He was scrubbed and shiny, his hair still wet from the shower; it kept falling across his forehead and he kept brushing it aside. His eyes gleamed and sparkled — with humour? With secrets?

"I got a complaint about your car yesterday," said Eddie. "I wanted to talk to you about it, off the record, at least at first."

"What kind of a complaint?"

"A woman — a pedestrian — says you almost ran her down."

The look of surprise that spread across his face certainly appeared genuine. His forehead scrunched in thought. He looked through the window in the wall above the sofa. He gave his head a definitive shake. "Nope. Never happened."

"This was several months ago," she said.

"Really," said Glen. "And she waited until now because . . . ?"

"She saw your car again. Recognized it. And this time, got the plate."

"Where was this supposed to have happened?"

Eddie described the incident, as told to her by Olive, watching his face impassively.

"It'd never happen," he said with conviction when she'd finished. "No way I'd risk putting a single scratch on that vehicle. Is this an older lady, by any chance?"

"Why?" said Eddie.

"Sometimes older people, they get a bit confused."

He drank, looking at her over the top of the coffee mug.

"I'll talk to her again on Monday," said Eddie. "But if she sticks to her story, I'm gonna have to let her lay an official complaint."

"Sure. Of course."

Eddie put the mug down on the coffee table, next to the beer can. "I'd better be going. Sorry to stick my nose in on your day off."

"No, not at all, I'm glad you told me."

She was halfway to the front door when she turned to him. "I never asked you why you decided to join the Force."

He'd shoved his hands in the back pockets of his jeans. "I guess you didn't."

"So? Why?"

He opened his mouth to speak automatically and obediently, but as he looked at her, studying her face, he changed his mind about whatever he had been going to say.

"I was in my third year at Dalhousie," he told her. "A student got murdered. The police descended on the campus, interviewed pretty well everybody there, including me. Then there was another killing — another student. And then a third. And you can imagine the chaos." He turned to look out the window again, as if waiting for sunlight to break through the cloud cover. "I got to know one of the officers covering the case. He was a young guy, not much older than I was. It fascinated me. And so I decided to become a cop." He looked back at Eddie. "I chose the RCMP because I wanted to get out of Halifax, out of Nova Scotia."

"Well, you've certainly done that," said Eddie. "You've seen a lot of the country."

He was looking at her quizzically. "It's funny, though. I've never had a file like that, like the one at Dalhousie."

"You sound disappointed."

"Well, I am. The job's turned out to be . . . not what I expected."

"No serial killers," said Eddie.

"No serial killers."

"Why not try the suits?"

He shrugged. "I don't know. Maybe I like the uniform too much," he said with a grin.

"What *has* the job turned out to be, for you?"

He looked at her as if he had asked the question, and was waiting for her to answer. He seemed less scrubbed and shiny all of a sudden. Something had been bleached from his blue eyes, which now looked cold to Eddie, like marbles. "It's dealing with — with an endless parade of losers," he said distantly. "It doesn't matter where you're doing it. The parade's always the same."

Eddie continued to look at him, their eyes level.

He saw that her head was filled with questions. He smiled, feeling almost sorry for her, knowing that she wouldn't ask any of them.

He saw her to the door and watched her leave, easing through the broken gate and striding up the ramp to the green Mercedes parked by the curb. Jesus. An RCMP sergeant, driving a bloody diesel.

When she'd driven away, he walked onto the beach and looked out at the ocean, thinking about the Nova Scotia coastline, imagining himself there, wishing he could be transported home.

She'd never be able to make it stick. He'd never had so much as a parking ticket, he was too damn smart for that. He hadn't wanted the Lexus flagged up and down the coast for chrissake. He always drove conservatively, except when he was absolutely sure he could get away with a little bit of speed.

She'd never be able to make it stick. All he had to do was deny it, calmly, consistently.

But he knew this would have been the last straw, if he'd needed one.

He squatted on the beach and let sand filter through his fingers. The grey sea rippled toward him, and away . . . toward him, and away. . . .

Eddie went directly back to her office and looked up Glen Hammond's file. Her palms were damp and cold as she dialed the number for his last detachment.

She'd been going over it in her head in the car. There was no bloody point in holding back, in trying to be diplomatic. She did wonder what might end up in her own file as a result, but she couldn't help that; alarm bells were chiming, and Eddie was afraid.

She pulled his file up on her computer screen and dialed Glen Hammond's last detachment. The receptionist

was young and cheerful and Eddie had a spasm in her chest
— she didn't think she'd ever heard Beatrice on the phone
and resolved to listen in on her, and soon.

"Staff Sergeant Wolensky, please," said Eddie, and
introduced herself.

"I'm sorry, the staff sergeant is on leave, can the
sergeant help you?"

"How long has the sergeant been with you?"

"Oh, gee, longer than me. Which would be six years."

"What's his name, please? Or hers," she added quickly.
The receptionist laughed. "Ruth Lumbers."

"Yeah," said Eddie, "okay. I'll talk to her."

There were more and more women among the ranks
of the RCMP, too many for Eddie to know them all, but
she had a friendly, though not close, relationship with
Ruth Lumbers. More important, she knew her not to
gossip or to bad-mouth her colleagues.

"Ruth," she said, when they had exchanged greetings,
"I'm in a somewhat delicate position here. I need to
know what you can tell me about Glen Hammond."

"Why?" said Ruth, who had a low, even, dispassionate voice Eddie thought would be useful in volatile situations but might be unhelpful in this particular conversation. She wished they could meet face to face, and
tried to conjure Ruth Lumbers up there in the air in
front of her: brown hair cut straight across right under
her ears, bangs, slightly pudgy cheeks, and eyes that were
deep brown, long-lashed and gorgeous.

"Why," Eddie repeated glumly, her forehead in her
hand. "Well, I've got this perp. I think he might be him."
She almost whispered it, with a glance at her closed
office door.

She told Ruth about the break-ins, and confided her
suspicions about Glen.

"Is there anything in his file?" said Ruth, who was
also keeping her voice down.

"That's why I wanted to talk to Wolensky," said Eddie. "I can't tell what's between the lines, you know? If there *is* anything between the lines." She heard Ruth sigh.

"I can only talk to you from my own personal perspective," said Ruth. "And that's not going to help you. It wouldn't surprise me if he turned out to be the guy you're looking for. And yet — I wouldn't have thought he'd be stupid enough to get caught. I'm not going to say anything else. And I wouldn't say any of it officially."

"Yeah," said Eddie. "Okay, well, I appreciate your talking to me, Ruth." She hung up and sank back in her chair. Good. Fine. She'd done what she could do. Now she had to think of what *more* she could do. She hadn't got firm corroboration from Ruth Lumbers, but she'd got something; enough to be going on with.

She figured her next step was to work on Buster Sheffield.

Late that afternoon, Rebecca lowered the kitchen window blind against the encroaching evening, hungering for summer, for daylight saving time, for long, languid, sunlit days and the briefest of nights.

"Can I help?" asked her father from the living room.

"In a few minutes you can set the table," she called back.

She turned the steaks, which were marinating in a glass dish, took a head of broccoli from the fridge, and started preparing it for the steamer. Tom the cat padded into the room and rubbed absently against her ankles on his way to his water dish.

"Any word from the police today?" William called.

"No, Dad," said Rebecca irritably. "If I'd had any word from the police, don't you think I would have told you?"

They'd be going through her list name by name, moving through it with ponderous, stubborn, bureaucratic formality. God only knew how the damn cops

ever got anything done, they were *so* by-the-book. Such
a bunch of droners, she told herself furiously, hacking up
the broccoli. Always seeing only the trees, slowly, deliberately, one by one, every single damn tree — and never
taking a look at the forest.

Rebecca knew she was being unreasonable.
Illogical. It was her way of fighting back. She experienced life these days as one long screech of chalk on a
blackboard. Yes, she felt safer with her father there; her
fear had definitely diminished. But the *stress* was the
same. She was so damn *nervous*. The smallest thing
made her jump — and then she was immediately
angry with herself for jumping. And so she found herself carping. Complaining. Bitching. Anything could
set her off.

She couldn't help but think about the people on the
list, imagining their reactions when the cops came calling. "Excuse me, sir," he'd say. . . . She could just see it,
the cop on the porch, knocking on the poor guy's door.
They didn't give a damn, really, any of them. He'd have
all kinds of other stuff on his mind, the cop would —
they all did.

And he'd say, "Can you tell me where you were, sir,
and what you were doing on the following dates?" And
this poor schmuck, whoever he was — the guy who
worked in her bank, or the wizened-up fellow who
looked after her car when she remembered to take it in
for servicing, or Damon who'd fixed her leaky kitchen
faucet. . . .

"Oh, hell," Rebecca groaned, leaning heavily on the
edge of the kitchen counter, the paring knife clutched in
her fist. Damon. A black-haired twenty-something
Italian kid who thought he was god's gift to women. She
had been stern and matronly with him, in a futile
attempt to chill him out. He'd probably take this as some
kind of half-assed flirtation, her setting the cops on him.

Oh god, he'd probably be on the phone to her as soon as they were out the door.

And then there was the pharmacist. . . . She set the steamer into a pot with an inch of cold water and dumped in the broccoli. She could just see him at the door, listening to the cop, exchanging astonished glances with his wife (she was sure he'd have a wife). He'd frown and flip willingly through his Daytimer, the quintessential cooperative citizen. "Well, now, let me see, on New Year's Eve the wife and I. . . . And on that other date, now let me see — oh, yes, we went bowling." Or whatever. And he'd say — they'd *all* say, curiously — "What's this about, Officer?" And the cops would say, "Well it's about this female who's got someone stalking her, don't you know. . . ."

"Reporting for kitchen detail," said her father, materializing next to her.

Rebecca shrieked and clapped her hands over her mouth.

"Sweetie, I'm sorry," said William. He wrapped his arms firmly around her.

"No, my god, *I'm* sorry," said Rebecca into his shoulder. Gently, she pulled away and patted his back. "It's a good thing I wasn't still holding the knife. I would've probably flung it at you."

The portable telephone rang. "I'll get it," said William.

"Or let the machine," said Rebecca, but her father had already picked it up.

"Hello?"

Rebecca hauled a grill pan out of the drawer below the oven and placed it on the stove top.

"Who is this?"

Rebecca glanced at him. His frown vanished, and he looked at her excitedly, holding up a finger. But as she watched him, he moved away, toward the living room.

"Why?" she heard him say.

She turned on the burner under the grill pan and, with a pair of tongs removed the steaks from the marinade, letting them drip into the sink for a moment before putting them down on a platter.

"Well, can't you tell me what it is? I don't understand this, why —" said her father.

Rebecca took a bottle of olive oil from the cupboard. She held her hand over the grill pan and decided it wasn't hot enough yet.

"Yeah. Okay. Alright. Ten minutes." Her father turned off the phone and put it back in its cradle.

"What was that all about?" said Rebecca.

"Better turn off the fire. I'm wanted down at the police station."

"Why? What for?"

He shrugged. "Don't know. They've got some new evidence, he said."

Rebecca, suddenly boneless, slumped against the counter. "My god. Dad. Do you — do they know who it is, then? I can't believe it. I can't believe it."

"No — I don't know, I don't know, Rebecca."

She hurled herself at the stove and began turning off burners. "Wait a minute, wait a minute, I'll just be a minute," she said, "and the oven, right, there. Oh god I'm shaking, I'm so excited I'm shaking."

"Rebecca," said her father loudly, "he said not you, he said only I'm to go."

She whirled around. "That's ridiculous," she said.

"Honey, I'm sorry."

"It's my damn case, damn it. Of course I'm going too."

"Rebecca." He put firm hands on her shoulders. "I think they know best. I think it's something that might upset you."

"Like what?" She felt the blood rushing close to her skin, very close. She thought she could hear it, a collective of streams and brooks and rivulets gathering speed, flowing fast, just below the surface of her.

"I don't know. But I promise you, anything I find out, anything at all, I'll tell you what it is." He was searching her eyes, her face, worriedly, looking at her like a dad.

"Okay."

"I won't be long," he said, releasing her. He grabbed his jacket from the back of the sofa. Rebecca followed him to the door. "Lock up after me," he said, and kissed her cheek. "I'll be back soon."

He turned off his cell phone and tossed it into the glove compartment.

He'd parked the Lexus on the opposite side of the street and up a block, facing away from her house. It was nudged under some kind of big bush, and he would've fretted about this once. He would have worried about bugs, and twigs, and sap damaging the paint.

He could see her front door in his rearview mirror. A moment later, the old guy hurried outside and climbed into the rental car and drove away.

He figured he had ten minutes.

When he looked back now, he saw that the end of it had been coming up on him for days, for weeks, maybe even for months. He had only *felt* his life to be confused and aimless. In reality, events had been proceeding according to plan, arranging themselves in a sequence that had always been intended. Things had been decreed. *This* had been decreed. Getting out of the Lexus. Crossing the street. Tapping on her door. Doing what he had to do. It was the perfect resolution to the puzzle that was his whole entire goddamn life. There was beauty in it, stunning and bleak. And knowing this made him calm. It gave him serenity, and it made him merciless.

He got out of his vehicle. The door closed with a

comforting *chunk*. He waited for a yellow Volkswagen bug to pass, then crossed the street.

Rebecca sat in front of the television with Tom curled up on the sofa next to her. She couldn't figure out what they had to say to her father, or show him, that they couldn't say or show to her. And who had called, anyway? Her father had said "he," so it hadn't been Sergeant Henderson. Of course, the sergeant couldn't be expected to be there all the time. It was Saturday evening; she was probably off for the weekend.

Rebecca got up to adjust the thermostat. It was hard to keep her house warm. Cold air sneaked in under the doors and around the windows and through invisible cracks and crevices. Her dad had been scolding her about the ineffectual insulation and the lack of double-glazed windows.

It would take him less than ten minutes to get to the detachment, five more to hear whatever they had to say, another five to discuss it. Maybe they'd call her, whoever was in charge over there tonight, or her dad. What on earth kind of evidence could they have found that would upset her, for godsake? Tom-Tom was here, safe and sound, and only the dead body of her cat could qualify as something likely to upset her.

"For godsake," said Rebecca indignantly. "This is ridiculous. I'm not having it."

She was on her way to the kitchen, to the telephone, when someone knocked on her door. This is more like it, she was thinking when she turned and hurried to answer it. She had it in her mind that her father had convinced the cops to give the information, whatever it was, directly to her. And when she unlocked the door and opened it, for a moment this was confirmed: he wasn't in uniform, but he was certainly a police officer.

"Hi," she said. He stepped behind her into the house

and she peeked down the driveway, her fingers resting lightly on the edge of the open door. "Where's Dad?"

He took her firmly by the wrist and pulled her inside, closed the door, and locked it.

Rebecca looked at him in astonishment. "What's going on?"

She was close enough to smell his aftershave.

She was embarrassed, because they were too close to each other and because his hand was still tight around her wrist.

She watched the rise and fall of his chest as he breathed. This is silly, she thought. She pulled free and lifted her gaze to his face.

There was a moment in which Rebecca's spirit faltered and her strength abandoned her: it was the moment when she knew this man would kill her. But it was only a moment, and then she was herself again, brave and curious and combative until death.

When William arrived at the detachment, he found the door locked. He rattled the knob furiously and ineffectually, then finally noticed the sign that told him to ring the buzzer. He did so, and eventually a disembodied voice issued from the grill covering the intercom.

"Can I help you?"

"It's William Wilson here. Are you the person who called me?"

There was a pause. "Beg pardon, sir?"

"I said I'm William Wilson, Rebecca Wilson's father. Somebody just called me from here — one of your officers — he told me to get down here, said you had new evidence. About the — the person who's been hassling her. My daughter." Another silence. "Hello? Hello?"

"Sorry, sir. Just a minute. I'll be right with you."

William waited. Watched traffic pass. Watched a rollerblader swoop by. He imagined he could hear halyards chiming on the boats in the marina. But this couldn't be true; it was too far away, way down at the bottom of the hill.

The door opened. "Come in, Mr. Wilson. I'm Matt Tomlinson."

"I remember you, yes." William sat down on the bench that was just inside the door. He would have preferred to remain standing, but he was feeling sick. His stomach churned; alarm had curdled his juices. He had to stay strong. But he needed to sit down. And he badly needed Jane, his wife, too.

"Nobody phoned you, Mr. Wilson. I've been alone here all evening. Tell me about the call."

"So it wasn't you? You're telling me it wasn't you who phoned?"

Matt Tomlinson nodded. "Tell me about the call." He sat down next to William, who had spread his open hands upon his thighs, pressing.

"He said, 'Mr. Wilson. I'm glad it's you.' I think he meant he was glad it was me answering the phone. Then he said, 'Can you get down here to the detachment?' He said, 'We've got a lead — but don't let your daughter come with you.' He said it was something you needed to talk to me about first. Because it might be distressing, I think he said, for Rebecca."

"He didn't tell you his name?"

William shook his head.

Matt reached through the opening in the glass panel above the receptionist's desk and picked up the phone. "What's your daughter's number, Mr. Wilson?"

TWENTY-TWO

Forty-five minutes later Eddie pulled up across the street from Rebecca Wilson's house. Once again it was surrounded by police crime-scene tape.

She saw Rebecca's father sitting next to Marlise Beyer in the back of a patrol car that was parked in front of the house, flanked by two more. A van had been backed into the driveway, behind Rebecca's Honda.

The front door of the house was open. The drapes at the living-room windows were closed, but there was a gap between them, and Eddie could see a white-clad figure moving around.

She switched off the Mercedes and crossed over to the house, wearing the workout clothes she'd changed into before climbing onto the treadmill an hour earlier: sneakers and socks, sweatpants, sweatshirt, her hair tucked into a Montreal Expos cap.

Matt Tomlinson had been watching for her. He emerged onto the porch. "There's a suit and some shoe things in my trunk, Sarge."

Eddie went to the middle patrol car and looked through the car window at William Wilson, who stared into her face as if he'd never seen her before, as if she wasn't even there.

She opened the driver's door and popped the trunk lever. Closed the door. Took from the trunk the plastic suit and the shoe covers and put them on, and joined

Matt on the porch. "Where's Sheffield?"

"In the hospital," said Matt. "Getting stitches. Some kind of accident at home. So I called Nick, and he's in there now, with Johnny Greig. And the doctor."

Eddie moved into the living room. The coffee table lay on its side. She had to resist picking it up — it was the only visible evidence of disorder. Maybe if she picked it up all this nightmare shit would go away.

A bouquet of red tulips trembled in a glass vase on top of the piano.

"She put up a fight," said Matt. "We've bagged her hands."

Now, through the doorway, Eddie saw Rebecca Wilson's legs, sprawled on the kitchen floor. And slow-moving shadows in the kitchen that could be anything or anybody.

"Nick called Dr. Evans," said Matt. "He's in there with her."

Eddie heard the clicks and whirs of cameras, still and video.

"She's been strangled," said Matt.

Eddie squinted at Rebecca's legs. She'd been wearing jeans when she died. And thick white socks. She had on one moccasin. Eddie's eyes travelled over the floor and located the other one, lying on its side near the overturned coffee table. "Where was William?" she asked. "Her father?"

"At the detachment," said Matt. "The guy lured him away. Told him he was a cop, said there was new evidence."

The whole of Eddie's scalp moved, all at once, a hideous crawling sensation as if skin and hair were separating from her head. "Nick," she called out.

Nick Orsato emerged from the kitchen.

"You're in charge here. Don't miss a single goddamn thing. Matt, come with me."

Outside, she stripped off the crime-scene suit and boots and stuffed them back into the trunk of Matt's patrol car, and Matt did the same. "Where are we going?" he wanted to know.

Eddie rapped at the window and Marlise Beyer, with a glance at William, who didn't appear to have moved, opened the door and slipped out.

"You're going to have to move him into one of the other cars. We need this one."

"Okay."

"Wait. You're working on the list she made, right?"

Marlise nodded.

"And Glen Hammond's on it."

"Yes — why?"

"Have you talked to him yet?"

"No. Haven't got to him."

"Come on," said Eddie to Matt. "I'll explain on the way." And while she did, she got the shotgun out from under the seat. She also called the dispatcher and told him to get out descriptions of Glen Hammond and his vehicle to the ferries and the airstrips. "Just do it," she shouted, over his stuttered protests.

"He keeps that car of his in a rented garage," said Matt, rounding the corner at the bottom of the hill.

"Where?"

"Don't know. It's got to be nearby, though. It's a neighbour's garage."

"We'll check out the house first," said Eddie.

Matt parked on the street two blocks away from Glen Hammond's house. They agreed that he would proceed along the walk while Eddie dropped down to the beach. She hoped like hell nobody was watching from the restaurant above as she hurried toward Glen's house, or at least that if they saw her, they weren't noticing the shotgun under her arm. Soon she could see his front door, and at almost the same moment she saw Matt coming down the ramp from the street, on her left. She remembered that he thought he was fearless. "Jesus," said Eddie under her breath.

"I don't have a hell of a lot of time Jemima. I wish you were here. I want to say goodbye. I wish we'd met. Though no I guess I really don't. It's always better not to know stuff about people. Better to take what they want to show you and make up the rest."

He dug his fingertips into his temples and squeezed his eyes shut.

"No regrets, you know? I've got no regrets. Too young to die, yeah sure. But too stupid to live.

"Ah it kills me it kills me to think about it. Big mistakes. Big mistakes. But I don't know what I would have done different — don't know what I *could* have done different. They're all the way they are, you can't do anything about that, you can't make people change. And after a while you can't even pretend anymore, can't pretend they're not like they are, can't pretend they feel something they don't, can't pretend that life's gonna be fucking different. Because it isn't."

He was going to take the Lexus out into the woods and set it on fire, that was the plan. And before it got too ugly, before it got too painful, before the agonizing swish and the fiery roar that would devour his car alive, he'd sit down on the ground near it, lean against a tree, and eat his gun. But he had to wait until he knew it was too late for the Lexus.

He switched off the computer and picked up his weapon from the desktop.

The gate in the picket fence surrounding Glen Hammond's house hung open, as it had that morning. The porch was flanked by four-foot high evergreen bushes Eddie thought might be laurel. Patches of grass struggled to grow in the small yard, which was mostly sand. Behind the house stood an enormous tree, dwarfing the building, its bare branches thrust gracelessly skyward like a collection of exclamation marks.

Eddie gestured to Matt to go around back. She held up her hand, fingers spread, three times.

He passed through the gate ... *one, two* ... and slipped around the house to the left, where it nestled against the incline that sloped generously from the beach up to the main road ... *six, seven* ... Eddie knew that blackberry bushes grew there, almost completely filling the space between the hillside and the house. She imagined him squeezing through, imagined the thorns snatching at his uniform; she could almost hear the rasp of the brambles catching at the fabric. She kept her eyes glued to Glen Hammond's front door while she shadowed Matt ... *ten, eleven* ... He ought to be rounding the corner now. Eddie edged through the open gate and sped up the walk and onto the porch. She held the shotgun high, her left hand on the door knob. Had he heard anything? Had he seen Matt? Was he in the back of the house, waiting for Matt? Or just inside the front door, waiting for her ... *fourteen, fifteen*. ...

Eddie turned the knob and pushed.

In the tiny hall she flattened herself against the front of the closet. Her mouth was dry and her heart was hammering. She peered cautiously around the corner into the living room.

Glen Hammond was looking straight at her. He was sitting in his leather chair, his weapon in his hands, pointed at the floor.

"It's been a long day," he said.

"Put your piece on the floor, Glen. Kick it toward me."

From the back of the house they heard the clink of breaking glass.

"Shit," he said. He shook his head. "Not giving this up. Not doing it, Sarge."

"Come on, Glen. On the floor. Now." Through the kitchen doorway, she saw the back door opening.

He got to his feet, slowly, as if he were very tired, or in pain.

"Constable," said Eddie sharply. "Put the fucking weapon on the floor."

He was holding it between his legs, in both hands. "You don't want to blow me away, do you Sarge? So let me do this."

Eddie was crouched like a spring, every muscle drawn tight like a stressed-out rubber band.

"Who's with you, coming in the back?"

"You're pretty well cornered, Glen. Think about it," said Eddie, as Matt advanced across the kitchen floor.

"Oh, I know I'm *cornered*, for fuck's sake. Do you think I give a fuck? That's the whole point here, Sarge, I do not *give* a fuck."

"Then put down your weapon. Let's talk."

"Talk." He laughed. "Forget it. Nothing works out the way I fucking plan it. At least I'm gonna get this right."

"Hold it, Glen," said Matt Tomlinson.

Glen Hammond stared incredulously from one of them to the other. They had both assumed the classic shooting stance. He looked as if he might burst into laughter.

Then suddenly, swiftly, his profile to Eddie, he raised his weapon.

Eddie let go of the shotgun and sprang at him, smashing into his torso. His weapon discharged and for a moment Eddie thought she'd been shot in the head — but it was only noise throbbing and stabbing there. She scrambled to her feet.

They had fallen across the arm of the leather chair, knocked over the end table, and set the floor lamp rocking on its base. Matt had possession of Glen Hammond's weapon.

Glen sat on the floor with his back against the front of the leather chair, hands cuffed behind him.

Eddie touched her head and looked at her fingers, which were covered with blood.

"You okay?" said Matt.

"It's nothing. I must have hit the table."

Glen Hammond laughed.

Eddie remembered his profile, just before he'd tried to blow himself away. It was a silhouette she had seen before. She thought it was probably indelibly etched into the pane of clouded glass in her office door.

TWENTY-THREE

"I should have seen it," said Eddie dully to the floor.

"Sure you should've," said Buster.

"I *did* see it."

"Sure you did."

They were in Eddie's office. Glen Hammond was in the cells, under a suicide watch.

The vinyl chair squealed as Buster shifted position, moving to rest his right ankle, which was in a cast thanks to a fall from the roof of his shed earlier that day, on his left knee. "You gotta be clear-headed here, Eddie. You got no room in you for lamentations."

"Sure I do." She sat up straight behind her desk, crossed her arms and stared at the window. "I got plenty of room in me for lamentations."

Corinne and her husband took William Wilson into their home and fixed up the guestroom for him. He lay on their spare bed in the dark with his eyes wide open, listening to the sounds of a family preparing for night. He had talked briefly to Jane, and she would be arriving the next day.

"It was a cop, Mother," he'd kept saying to her. He'd made sure their neighbour was there with her before he'd given her the news — but it wasn't right that they should be so far apart at such a time, that he should have to tell her this terrible thing on the telephone.

"I left her alone, Mother." That was the other thing he'd kept saying.

The only thing he remembered Jane saying was, "It's alright, William, we're going to be alright." And, "I love you, William. We'll survive this."

But they couldn't start trying to survive it until they were together again. And so William lay awake, his dry eyes scratching at the insides of their lids every time he blinked, waiting through an endless night, waiting for his wife, who would come to him, and for exoneration, which wouldn't.

"We don't think he's been bothering you, Ms. Parfit," said Eddie on Monday morning. "Except yeah, he does admit, now, to operating a motor vehicle without due care and attention in your vicinity."

"You mean, he admits trying to run me down," said Olive dryly.

Eddie nodded. "He says, if it's any consolation, that it was nothing personal. You just reminded him of his mother." She shrugged apologetically.

"But isn't it too much to believe, that there'd be *two* of them?" said Olive, who was sitting on the other side of Eddie's desk.

Eddie took a deep breath. "Your box of books was stolen," she said. "That's been established. But the rest of it . . ." She got up and went around to the vinyl chair and hunkered down next to Olive. "Do you think it's possible that you imagined the rest of it?" she asked softly. "Believe me, I do not want to offend you, but — what do you think? Is it possible?"

Olive lifted a shaking hand to her grey curls. She pursed her lips and thought about the trip she was going to take in the fall. "If I say no, will you continue to investigate?"

"We will," said Eddie, "but I have to tell you, it won't be a high priority."

"Because you've already made up your minds," said Olive bitterly.

Slowly, Eddie stood, and returned to the chair behind her desk. "Tell you what," she said, standing, her fingertips resting on the desktop. "How about we call it quits for now. But if anything else happens — anything at all — you report it immediately, and I'll re-open the file."

Olive nodded. "That sounds fair. Alright." She picked up her handbag from the floor and stood up. "Thank you for your courtesy, Sergeant," she said.

Eddie never heard from her again.

The night after the news broke, the young woman named Rhoda lay sleepless in the bed where she had made love with Glen Hammond. Her eyes were wide open in the darkness, but she saw nothing that was there, not the light leaking through the bedroom curtain, not the shapes of dresser and chest of drawers and night table, not the duvet that covered her or the ceiling that sheltered her.

She knew he was in the slammer; she'd read it in the paper and seen it on TV. But she kept thinking she heard him, outside in the hallway, breaking into her apartment with a credit card or however they did it.

He'd have no reason to hurt her, even if he did break out of jail, or get out on bail, which he probably would, wouldn't he? Because of how he was a cop. No, he had no reason to hurt her.

But he'd had no reason to hurt that other girl, either, probably.

And so Rhoda lay sleepless, afraid for her heart, labouring in her chest; afraid for her throat, in case instead of his gun, he brought a knife. She had always been afraid of knives.

The following Thursday, Eddie took the five o'clock ferry to Horseshoe Bay, drove to Marjorie's apartment in

Burnaby, and picked up Andrew and a manila envelope containing his papers and his vaccination record. She and Marjorie loaded his bed, a box of tinned food, a bag of dry food, matching food and water dishes, and several toys into the back seat of the Mercedes. Marjorie showed Eddie how to put a special harness on him so he could be seatbelted into the passenger seat of the car. And they drove off.

The dog panted, softly, regarding the world calmly through the windshield.

On the ferry Eddie decided to stay in the vehicle with him. She unhooked the harness and let him climb into the backseat, where he delicately sniffed at his belongings, nudging them with his long elegant nose as if making sure nothing had been left behind.

Eddie hadn't known that poodles came in a large size. She also hadn't known they were German dogs, not French. Nor that they were, according to the books provided by the previous owner (which she was now paging through), among the smartest of dogs, and athletic, and good-tempered, et cetera, et cetera, et cetera. They didn't shed, but on the other hand you had to get them clipped every six weeks or so because their hair kept on growing. So she wouldn't have to make him look like an idiot, with ruffles and naked-ness, she could get him an all-over trim. He would be — well — dog-shaped.

Eddie was worried that he'd be homesick, that he would wonder where his owner had gone, that he would feel he'd been abandoned. She sat behind the wheel and watched him in the rearview mirror and the magnitude of the responsibility she had assumed suddenly became tangible. She looked at the dog with something approaching panic.

Andrew eventually leapt back into the passenger seat and she hooked up his harness again.

He was polite, but aloof. Was he waiting for his owner to show up? Eddie felt incredibly guilty, as if she were kidnapping him.

People were beginning to return to the car deck now. Eddie spotted someone who looked familiar emerging from the door that led to the elevator. My god it was Nick Orsato, with an affectionate arm around one of the tellers from the bank across the street from Earl's café. She watched as they sauntered away from her, Nick's arm tightening around the teller's waist, his lips murmuring into her temple.

Eddie wanted to laugh. She was sure glad she hadn't asked anybody else if they thought Nick was gay. How the hell did you ever know you were right about anything? Was she really in the right fucking job? She shivered, and felt a cold nose exploring the region just behind her right ear. "Oh, hi," said Eddie. "Good boy," she said, reaching clumsily to rub his neck.

It was about nine-thirty when they got home. Eddie set the dog's bed on the floor in the laundry room, loaded his food into cupboards, put his toys on the floor and filled his water dish. Then she took him outside and they toured the backyard, which was fully fenced so she didn't have to worry about him running away. Which he'd probably want to do, she thought, watching him roam the yard, paying particular interest to its perimeter. Just like in *Lassie, Come Home,* the damn dog would probably take off at the first opportunity, find his way onto the ferry and along the highway and across the bridge and into Burnaby.

"They're gone though, Andrew," she called out to him. "Moved away." He stopped where he was, a pale woolly form in the corner of her yard, one paw lifted, his nose raised in her direction. Then he continued about his business, snuffling at the base of the laurel hedge that grew in front of the fence.

Finally, he peed, and ambled toward her and past her into the house.

When she was ready for bed she went looking for him. He was lying by the front door, with his head on his paws.

"Come on, Andrew," she said. He looked at her, got up and followed her into the laundry room. "There's your bed. This is where you sleep."

He looked at it for a moment, then climbed inside and curled up.

Eddie turned off the light. "Good-night, Andrew." He didn't move, and made no sound, but his eyes glowed in the light from the kitchen.

Eddie read for a while.

Then she lay on her back in the darkness with her hands behind her head as usual, going over it again and again — what she should have done to prevent Rebecca Wilson's death.

Why hadn't she insisted on somehow tracking down Staff-Sergeant Wolensky, wherever the hell he'd gone on leave? Why had she been content with Ruth Lumber's equivocal assessment?

Why hadn't she confronted him? Of course he would have denied it — but he would have been warned then, and surely then, he would have backed off, changed his mind, let Rebecca live.

Was it because he was a cop? Was that it? If he hadn't been a cop, would she have acted differently? Quickly? Decisively? And saved somebody's fucking life?

She heard an unfamiliar sound and turned her head to see Andrew in the doorway.

"Andrew?" She sat up and looked at him. She'd read a lot of dog obedience books, recently. She had decided that Andrew belonged in his bed, and Andrew's bed belonged in the laundry room. And all the books told her that on this issue, as on many others, it was imperative that she remain firm.

Andrew's head dropped, then lifted.

Eddie patted the edge of her bed.

The dog advanced. He stood next to her, looking into her face.

Eddie stroked the top of his head. "Okay," she said resignedly.

Andrew leapt up onto the bed.

Eddie lay down, pulling the covers up to her chin. Andrew lay down too, with a sigh, and put his head in her lap.

Eventually Eddie fell asleep, with an ache in her heart and her hand resting on her dog's woolly head.

Note to Reader

I write these words with a lot of sadness and a lot of pride. L.R. Wright completed this novel in the last months of her battle with breast cancer, finishing the final draft in late November 2000. She went into palliative care in late January 2001, where, from her hospital bed she began, in spite of rapidly increasing frailty, to lead her family through the final copyedits. By mid-February she seemed confident that we had the hang of it and let us continue on our own. She died February 25, and I finished the copyedits in the week that followed. It is not an overstatement to say that *Menace* kept L.R. Wright alive for a good while after her body was ready to quit. But we never doubted that she'd hang on long enough to see it finished — and finished well.

The Wright family extends heartfelt gratitude to Drs. Shenkier, McKillop and Grantham, and to Anne, Carol, Pat, and the rest of the staff at the Palliative Care Unit of Vancouver Hospital, all of whom saw *Menace* as a big stack of paper in Mom's lap. This is what it looks like in the end, folks. Thank you.

Mom was vigorously enjoying the process of getting to know Eddie Henderson. We hope you like her too. No doubt Eddie had many other adventures waiting for her.

Katey Wright
Vancouver, B.C.

About the Author

L.R. Wright is the author of fifteen novels. She is the two-time winner of the Arthur Ellis Award for crime fiction, first for *A Chill Rain in January*, and then for *Mother Love*, which also won the Canadian Authors Association Award for literary fiction. She received the coveted Edgar Allan Poe Best Novel Award for *The Suspect*. L. R. Wright died in February 2001. In Spring 2001 the Crime Writers of Canada honoured L.R. Wright with the Derrick Murdoch Award for lifetime achievement and outstanding contribution to crime fiction.